THE PENGUIN CLASSICS

FOUNDER EDITOR (1944–64): E. V. RIEU

EDITORS:
Robert Baldick (1964–72), *Betty Radice, C. A. Jones*

IVAN TURGENEV, Russian novelist, was born in Oryol in 1818, and was the first Russian writer to enjoy an international reputation. Born into the gentry himself, and dominated in his boyhood by a tyrannical mother, he swore a 'Hannibal's oath' against serfdom. After studying in Moscow, St Petersburg, and Berlin (1838–41), where he was influenced by German Idealism, he returned to Russia an ardent liberal and Westernist. He gained fame as an author with a series of brilliant, sensitive pictures of peasant life. Although he had also written poetry, plays, and short stories, it was as a novelist that his greatest work was to be done. His novels are noted for the poetic 'atmosphere' of their country settings, the contrast between hero and heroine, and for the objective portrayal of heroes representative of stages in the development of the Russian intelligentsia during the period 1840–70. Exiled to his estate of Spasskoye in 1852 for an obituary on Gogol, he wrote *Rudin* (1856), *Home of the Gentry* (1859), *On the Eve* (1860), *Fathers and Sons* (1862), but was so disillusioned by the obtuse criticism which greeted this last work that he spent most of the rest of his life at Baden-Baden (1862–70), and Paris (1871–83). His last novels *Smoke* (1867), and *Virgin Soil* (1877), lacked the balance and topicality of his earlier work. He died in Bougival, near Paris, in 1883.

RICHARD FREEBORN is at present Professor of Russian Literature at the School of Slavonic and East European Studies, University of London. He was previously Professor of Russian at Manchester University, a visiting Professor at the University of California at Los Angeles, and for ten years he was Hulme Lecturer in Russian at Brasenose College, Oxford, where he graduated. His publications include *Turgenev, A Study* (1960), *A Short History of Modern Russia* (1966; 1967), a translation of *Sketches from a Hunter's Album* (Penguin Classics, 1967), and a couple of novels.

Ivan Turgenev

HOME OF THE GENTRY

TRANSLATED BY
RICHARD FREEBORN

PENGUIN BOOKS

Penguin Books Ltd, Harmondsworth, Middlesex, England
Penguin Books Inc., 7110 Ambassador Road, Baltimore, Maryland 21207, U.S.A.
Penguin Books Australia Ltd, Ringwood, Victoria, Australia

—

This translation first published 1970
Reprinted 1971, 1974

—

Copyright © Richard Freeborn, 1970

—

Made and printed in Great Britain
by Hazell Watson & Viney Ltd
Aylesbury, Bucks
Set in Monotype Bembo

To Ros and Liz

Introduction

Home of the Gentry (*Dvoryanskoye gnezdo*) is Turgenev's second novel, conceived in 1856 shortly after the completion of his first novel *Rudin*, and written for the greater part at Spasskoye during the summer of 1858. It was completed on the eve of Turgenev's fortieth birthday (27 October 1858), revised in December of the same year and published in the *Contemporary* at the beginning of 1859.

This work has received many titles in English translation (*Liza, or a Nest of Nobles, A House of Gentlefolk, A Nest of Gentlefolk, A Nest of the Gentry, A Nest of Nobles, A Nest of Hereditary Legislators, A Noble Nest, A Nobleman's Nest*), all of which testify to the inherent difficulty of combining in English the twin concepts of which the Russian title is composed. The word 'nest' in association with 'nobility' has its Victorian charm, or it may seem faintly Wodehouse-ish (the Hereditary Legislators are bound to have kept some sort of Jeeves in their Nest), or it may sound like Maudie Littlehampton trying to be chummy. Turgenev himself alleged (probably untruthfully) in a letter to W. R. S. Ralston, his English translator, that the title was chosen by his publisher, not by him. He approved of Ralston's proposal to use the heroine's name in the title of the first authorized English translation (of 1869) and this much licence has clearly done nothing to inhibit the extraordinary variety of subsequent titles. The grounds for clarifying the title still further by substituting 'home' for 'nest' are to be found in the novel itself: it is a novel about the home of Turgenev's class, the gentry (or nobility), and about the problems of Turgenev's generation in readjusting to their homeland after experiencing the profound but fickle influence of European ideas.

7

Ivan Sergeyevich Turgenev (1818–83) had his own Russian home on the large estate of Spasskoye-Lutovinovo in the province of Oryol. Here, as a boy, he experienced something of the harshness from his mother that he describes in the strange education which his hero, Fyodor Lavretsky, received from his father (chapter XI). Like Lavretsky, though at a much earlier age than his hero, he escaped from his mother's tutelage, attended the universities of Moscow and St Petersburg and in 1838 travelled to Berlin, where his university education was to be completed. He emerged from what he called his plunge into 'the German sea' with a clear conviction of the need for Russia to follow Europe. After returning to his own country in 1842, he soon made a reputation for himself as a leading writer of the period known as 'the forties'. He began publishing his famous *Sketches** of peasant life in the *Contemporary* in 1847 and the first separate edition of this work appeared in 1852. He wrote about rural Russia, about his own 'home', meaning the province of Oryol, with the mastery of one who was both a landowner, a member of the gentry class, and an intellectual, a member of the newly-emerged Russian intelligentsia. He combined the urbanity of the intellectual with the mildly laconic manner of the sporting country gentleman, the compassion of the educated reformer with the sensitive eye of the poetic observer, the artist's fine sense of balance with the poignancy of the tragic philosopher. But his *Sketches*, even if they acquired fame as pictures drawn from the life of the peasantry, were concerned quite as much with the life of the landowning class, the gentry; and their effectiveness as propaganda against serfdom was due less perhaps to their sympathetic and humane portrayal of peasant types than to their exceedingly clearly observed, laconic, wryly satirical and unsentimental portraits of the gentry. Of all the *Sketches* concerned with the gentry the most satirical

* *Sketches from a Hunter's Album*, selected and translated by Richard Freeborn, Penguin Classics, 1967.

and the most compassionate is *Hamlet of the Shchigrovsky District*, for in it Turgenev deals not only with the gentry class at its most fatuous and repellent, but also with the type of introspective, Hamlet-like intellectual who was, despite his manifest inadequacies, the conscience and saving grace of his class and his generation.

Turgenev became the chronicler of this type of 'super-fluous man' intellectual. His studies, moving gradually from censure of the type towards a more balanced and sympathetic treatment of his problems, culminated in his first novel, *Rudin*, which portrayed probably the most typical example of such a 'superfluous man' – an intellectual, educated abroad, who can find no place for himself in semi-feudal Russian society and whose primary function becomes that of an eloquent, but ineffectual, disseminator of ideas. When the heroine of the novel, Natalya, inspired by his high-minded talk of service and sacrifice, challenges him to act upon his words, he fails her. All he can offer her is the advice to submit – to submit to their inevitable parting, to circumstances, to Fate – and his own life, after his parting from Natalya, becomes an inglorious saga of lost opportunities and failed hopes until he sacrifices himself on the Paris barricades of 1848.

Rudin was written during the final stages of the Crimean War (1854–5) but was concerned with the Western-orientated intelligentsia of a decade earlier. *Home of the Gentry*, though ostensibly concerned with the 1840s (it opens in 1842), reflects in many ways the new upsurge of nationalist and Slavophil feeling experienced by the intelligentsia in the years immediately following the Crimean War. Turgenev was himself unsympathetic to Slavophilism, which united a Romantic belief in Russia's superiority to Europe with an ultra-conservative admiration for the Orthodox Church, but he was dispassionate enough as a writer to recognize its appeal. This was a period, moreover, when the authority of

Turgenev's generation of the intelligentsia (the so-called 'men of the forties') was first seriously challenged by the new, radical, nihilist generation of the 1860s, whom Turgenev was to depict obliquely in *On the Eve* (1860) and directly in the figure of Bazarov in *Fathers and Children* (1862). *Home of the Gentry* is thus the last of Turgenev's major works to be concerned exclusively with his own generation. It is both valedictory in its elegiac treatment of Lavretsky's failure to achieve happiness and optimistic, if cautiously so, in its twin assumptions that Lavretsky's unspectacular determination 'to plough the land' is a worthy task and that another, younger, generation is likely to revitalize the 'home' of the gentry when Lavretsky has gone. Lavretsky's biography (chapters VIII to XVI) can be criticized for obtruding into and delaying the action of the novel, but it has an essential function despite this: it relates the novel to its time, recapitulating in miniature the experience of Turgenev's own generation of the intelligentsia by showing how its Western education served to uproot it from Russia, to divorce it from its 'home' and to make it ultimately superfluous. Two characters in the fiction serve to highlight the ideological aspect of Lavretsky as a representative of his generation: Mikhalevich, his impoverished university friend, and Woldemar (or Vladimir) Panshin, his rival for Liza's hand.

Mikhalevich's arrival at Vasilyevskoye (chapter XXV) may seem gratuitous, just an interpolation, but Mikhalevich himself is not an interpolation in Lavretsky's life. He is a ghost of Hamlet's father come to remind him of the idealism ('Religion, progress, humanity!' he shouts as he leaves, almost falling out of the tarantass) to which he, Lavretsky, had aspired before his wife's betrayal and four years of solitary reflection had nurtured such scepticism in his soul. Mikhalevich has the enthusiasm and idealism of a previous epoch and he indicts Lavretsky, notwithstanding the latter's emotional state, for taking refuge in the self-pitying apathy of the well-read gentry, who excuse their inaction by assuming that 'everything's nonsense'. Man of words though he may be, Mikhalevich insists that 'each individual has a duty, a great responsibility before God, before the people and before himself!' – the duty, in other words, of the intelligentsia to work for Russia. It may be noticed that Lavretsky does not defend himself, for he does not conceive his duty in quite such grandiose terms. The curious and unbalanced education which he received from his father has taught him the danger of trying to implant ideas by force, of implementing changes from above without due regard for those who are to be changed. If it is the intelligentsia's duty to act, what form should the action take? Lavretsky's answer becomes clear in chapter XXXIII during the controversy with Panshin. Here he forthrightly opposes Panshin's view that changes must be introduced from above by speaking out in favour of Russia's youth and independence and by demanding above all a recognition of Russia's own 'truth' and reconciliation with it. But, though Turgenev ascribes these vague Slavophil senti- ments to his hero, Lavretsky's only statement of purposeful action is expressed in the words 'To plough the land' – to cultivate his garden, one supposes, in Voltairean fashion or to do his duty as a landowner in his own 'home of the gentry'. In the Epilogue, which carries us eight years forward, we learn that 'Lavretsky had a right to be satisfied: he had really made himself into a good proprietor, he had really learned how to plough the land, and he laboured not for himself alone; so far as was in his power, he tried to ensure and stabilize the livelihood of his peasants'. This, then, is the single positive achievement in Lavretsky's life; in this way, and in this way only, Lavretsky readjusted to his home, became reconciled to its 'truth' and found his own 'nest'.

All Turgenev's novels have a topical reference. They are works which chronicle the 'body and pressure of time', meaning chiefly the evolution of Russian society and the Russian intelligentsia in its several epochs of the 1830s, 1840s and 1860s. Yet, though topical, they entirely lack that rumbustiousness, that sense of being written out of the noise and activity of their time, which is the pervasive sea-shell whisper in the novels of Charles Dickens; or in George Eliot's *Middlemarch*, where her hortatory sermonizing, conjuring with manifold themes, presumptuousness towards her characters leave the impression that, through the window of the room where she writes and intermingling with her fiction, come the bustle and roar of a Victorian England which is for her more important than her representation of it; or in the work of Henry James, ever conscious of the noise outside, whose eloquence is of the slightly defensive kind which recognizes that an author's voice must be tempered to the four walls of his novel's setting. But the greatest of the nineteenth-century Russian novelists wrote out of the profundities of a silent country. In a real and literal sense Dostoyevsky wrote out of the nocturnal silence of St Petersburg, Tolstoy from the rural silence of Yasnaya Polyana and Turgenev from the summer quiet of Spasskoye. Their novels have the special, spell-binding absorption of voices speaking out of a natural stillness. None of Turgenev's novels is more eloquent of such stillness than *Home of the Gentry*.

It is precisely such stillness that Lavretsky discovers when he returns finally to his 'home', the Vasilyevskoye that he preferred to the Lavriki of his boyhood (chapter XX):

And once again he began to listen to the silence, awaiting nothing – and yet at the same time endlessly expectant: the silence engulfed him on every side; the sun ran its course across the tranquil blue of the sky, and the clouds floated silently upon it; it seemed as if they knew why and where they were going. At that very time, in other places on the earth, life was seething, hurrying, roaring on its way; here the same life flowed by inaudibly, like water through marshy grass; and until evening Lavretsky could not tear himself away from contemplation of this receding, outflowing life; anguish for the past was melting in his soul like spring snow and – strangest of all! – never before had he felt so deep and strong a feeling for his country.

The boredom of such stillness will, he hopes, bring him to his senses and prepare him to 'take up his task without hurry'. What awaits him, though, in his homeland is not such leisurely recovery but the exultation and heartbreak of his love for Liza. This experience is suggested to us as much in terms of sound as explicitly in terms of Lavretsky's emotions. The novel is a Prospero's isle in which the silence of Lavretsky's homecoming is broken by the music of Liza's presence. Lemm's music, in which he invokes the stars (chapter XXII), is the accompaniment to the first stage in this process, interwoven as it is with Mikhalevich's visit; but Lemm's romance, like his cantata, 'had striven to express something passionate and profound, but nothing had come of it' and it is only through a vicarious sense of the passion and profundity of Lavretsky's feeling that he is able to achieve his masterpiece and thereby orchestrate Lavretsky's exultant love at the end of chapter XXXIV. This is the moment of climax in the novel when Lavretsky triumphs both ideologically and personally in his defeat of Panshin and his winning of Liza's heart. The practically immediate reappearance of his wife (chapter XXXVI) is accompanied not only by the repugnant smell of patchouli, but also by her fondness for showy music. Her playing and singing, in dilettante partnership with Panshin, nicely offset and enhance, by their artificiality, the heartbreak of Lavretsky's parting from Liza. When, after eight years, he returns to the Kalitins' house, it is the single reverberant note played on the piano that summarizes for him the extent of his loss.

The impossibility of happiness is the novel's underlying theme. Turgenev tended to believe that man is never destined to experience happiness save as something ephemeral and inevitably foredoomed. In *Home of the Gentry* Lavretsky

13

tries initially to assume that happiness is dependent upon the truth of the heart, as he tells Liza in chapter XXIX, but eventually he is obliged to accept Liza's view that 'happiness on earth does not depend on us'. But the pessimism implicit in this Turgenevan view of life is relieved throughout the novel by the affirmation of nature's power to redeem, by the summer atmosphere in which the brief and poignant story is clothed and by the poetry with which Turgenev has invested the portrait of Liza, the heroine.

Naturally this portrait, so central to the novel, caused Turgenev more difficulty than any other. When the novel was given its first reading in draft form to an 'areopagus' (Turgenev's term) of advisers in St Petersburg in late November or early December 1858, the chief criticism, it seems, was concerned with the religious background of Liza. Turgenev took particular care to amplify the portrait after this criticism by stressing aspects of her religious nature and by adding chapter XXXV which describes her religious upbringing. The uniqueness of Liza's portrait is due chiefly to the fact that no other Turgenevan heroine has her specifically religious character, and commentators have consequently been tempted to seek for living prototypes, of whom the most frequently quoted is Countess E. E. Lambert who was Turgenev's correspondent during the years when he was meditating his novel. His letters to her mirror the elegiac feeling which pervades his novel, but her claims as a prototype for Liza seem slender. Ivan Goncharov, the novelist, suspected that Turgenev had plagiarized the figure of Liza from his own heroine, Vera, of *The Precipice* (*Obryv*), claiming that he had told Turgenev the plan of his novel in 1855. *The Precipice*, however, was not published until 1869, which means that the plagiarization, even allowing for the possibility, could not have been based on anything more substantial than Goncharov's initial sketches of his heroine's character. Goncharov nursed his suspicions of Turgenev's perfidy for the rest of his

life. It is no more absurd to point to the faint similarity between Turgenev's heroine and Tolstoy's Liza of *Two Hussars*
(1856), a work conceived and written at a time when both
writers were living in close proximity and on fairly amicable
terms.

The genesis of Turgenev's heroine may be in doubt; there
is no doubt that Turgenev's hero is based to a great extent on
autobiographical experience. Lavretsky's portrait is the fullest
of any hero in Turgenev's novels. His life is traced to its
source in the mixed blood of his birthright and the vivid
record of his boyhood, adolescence and early adulthood.
With this burden of experience, mature and vulnerable, he
appears at the fiction's beginning. His emotional and psychological state is explored carefully and charted with a subtle
exactitude through the various stages of the novel. His is
obviously the dominant portrait. But Turgenev devoted great
care also to the characterization of Panshin, second only
(among the minor figures) to the care which he lavished on
the wickedly convincing portrait of Lavretsky's wife, Varvara
Pavlovna. Convincing and detailed observation of character
traits, rather than a plumbing of psychological states, is the
principle governing Turgenev's portrayal of such minor
figures. They have the veracity of roles well acted upon a
stage. There is a theatrical principle also about the way in
which Turgenev offers his fiction to us. Despite the freedoms
permitted by the novel, he restricts the action of his work to a
particular time and place, and supplies his characters with
biographies and characteristics in order to 'place' them in a
particular setting and then permit them to enact their separate
roles within those confines. It is not difficult to see how the
novel is composed of different worlds which are contiguous
but alien: Marfa Timofeyevna's world upstairs, Marya
Dmitrievna's downstairs, the world of the Kalitins' home
and the external official or social world represented by
Panshin and Varvara Pavlovna, Lavretsky's world of Vasilyev-

skoye and the modest, cell-like world of Liza's room. The destinies of the characters appear to be dictated by the worlds to which they belong and are ultimately as separate and irreconcilable as are the two figures of Lavretsky and Liza in our final glimpse of them.

No other work by Turgenev is quite so 'Turgenevan' as this novel. At its first appearance in 1859 it received abundant critical praise. In the West, particularly in England, it suited Victorian tastes and appealed to many writers, some of whom, like Galsworthy, show signs in their work of having imitated its quietly elegiac tone. It is a novel without stridency, true to life in the subtlety of its detail, well-wrought in the care and delicacy of its dialogue and descriptive writing, touched by a wry humorousness and the lustre of a warm, civilized intelligence. To present-day tastes its treatment of love may seem low-toned, even a trifle mawkish; perhaps the nightingales have a way of singing a little too appropriately and the stars shine just a little too sweetly for our neon-dazzled eyes. If time has taken its toll in this respect, in all other respects it is a novel that beautifully evokes an age and has the magical property of a fiction that gives a lucid being to its characters which time has not obscured. This translation has striven, by attempting to represent the original Russian as faithfully as possible, neither to increase nor to lessen that obscurity.

I

A BRIGHT spring day was drawing towards evening; small
pink clouds stood high in a clear sky and seemed not so much
to float past as to recede into the very depths of the blue.

Before the opened window of a handsome house, in one of
the streets on the outskirts of the provincial town of O . . . (it
was 1842), sat two ladies, one of fifty and the other an old
lady of seventy.

The first was called Marya Dmitrievna Kalitin. Her
husband, formerly a provincial procurator and well known in
his time as a businessman – a lively and decisive chap, conten-
tious and stubborn – had died ten years before. He had
received an unusually good education and had been to a
university, but, being born in poor circumstances, he had
early understood the need to make his own way in the world
and accumulate money. Marya Dmitrievna had married him
for love: he had been handsome, clever and, when he wished,
very courteous. Marya Dmitrievna (whose maiden name was
Pestov) had lost her parents when she was still a child and had
spent several years in an institution in Moscow; and when she
returned from there she lived about thirty miles from O . . .,
in her native village of Pokrovskoye, with her aunt and elder
brother. This brother soon moved to St Petersburg on
government service and kept his sister and aunt in virtual
bondage to him until his death put an end to his career. Marya
Dmitrievna inherited Pokrovskoye, but did not live there
long; in the second year of her marriage to Kalitin, who had
succeeded in capturing her heart after only a few days'
courtship, Pokrovskoye was exchanged for another estate
that was much more profitable, but inelegant and lacking a

manorial house. At the same time Kalitin acquired a house in the town of O ... as a permanent residence for his wife and himself. The house had a large garden and on one side it faced open country beyond the town. 'So,' decided Kalitin, who was no lover of rural quiet, 'there'll be no need to go traipsing off into the country.' More than once Marya Dmitrievna pined for her pretty Pokrovskoye with its gay little stream, broad meadows and green woods, but she did not gainsay her husband in anything and stood in awe of his intellect and knowledge of the world. When, after fifteen years of marriage, he died, leaving her a son and two daughters, Marya Dmitrievna had become so accustomed to her house and to town life that she had no wish to leave O ...

In her youth Marya Dmitrievna had enjoyed a reputation as a very pretty blonde, and at fifty her features were not devoid of pleasantness, although they had become a little puffy and fat. She was more emotional than kind-hearted and had retained the ways of a schoolgirl even into her maturity, indulging herself, being easily irritated and even becoming tearful when her routine was disturbed; on the other hand, she was very charming and courteous when all her wishes were fulfilled and no one contradicted her. Her house belonged among the pleasantest in the town. She was extremely well-off, due not so much to what she had inherited as to what her husband had acquired. Both her daughters lived with her; her son was being educated at one of the best official schools in St Petersburg.

The old lady sitting with Marya Dmitrievna by the window was that very same aunt, her father's sister, with whom she had once spent several solitary years in Pokrovskoye. She was called Marfa Timofeyevna Pestov. She passed for an eccentric, was of independent character, spoke the truth to people's faces and acquitted herself on the most modest means as if she were worth thousands. She could not tolerate Kalitin, and as soon as her niece married him she retired to her own village, where she spent ten whole years living in a peasant's hut that did not even have the amenity of a chimney. Marya Dmitrievna was always apprehensive of her. With black hair and rapidly darting eyes even in her old age, small and sharp-nosed, Marfa Timofcycvna walked about with a lively step, held herself very straight and spoke quickly and distinctly in a delicate, resonant little voice. She invariably wore a white cap and a white blouse.

'What is it?' she suddenly asked Marya Dmitrievna. 'What are you sighing for, my dear?'

'Just sighing,' the other murmured. 'What marvellous clouds!'

'Sighing because you're sorry for them, is that it?'

Marya Dmitrievna did not answer.

'Why doesn't that Gedeonovsky come?' asked Marfa Timofeyevna, briskly plying her needles (she was knitting a large woollen scarf). 'He'd be able to keep you company in your sighs – or tell some tall story or other.'

'You're always so severe about him! Sergey Petrovich is an eminently respectable man.'

'Eminently respectable!' the old lady repeated sarcastically.

'And how devoted he was to my late husband!' declared Marya Dmitrievna. 'He cannot be indifferent to his memory even now.'

'Of course he can't! It was your husband who dragged him out of the mud by the ears,' Marfa Timofeyevna muttered, and the needles worked even quicker in her hands.

'He looks so inoffensive,' she began again, 'with all his grey hair, but as soon as he opens his mouth he either tells lies or spreads scandal – and he's a councillor, mind you! Well, it's only to be expected; after all, he's the son of a priest!'

'Who is faultless, aunt dear? Of course he has this weakness. Sergey Petrovich hasn't, of course, received a proper education and cannot speak French. But no matter what you say, he is an agreeable man.'

'Agreeable, yes, because he's always kissing your hands. So he doesn't speak French – a great pity that is! I'm not very strong myself in the French "dialect". It'd be better if he didn't speak any language at all, then he wouldn't tell lies. But there he is, speak of the devil,' added Marfa Timofeyevna, glancing at the street. 'Striding along, he is, your agreeable man. What a long, thin fellow, just like a stork!'

Marya Dmitrievna patted her curls. Marfa Timofeyevna looked at her with a wry smile.

'What's that, my dear, surely it's not a grey hair? You must give your Palashka a talking-to. What's she got eyes for?'

'Oh, auntie dear, you're always ...' muttered Marya Dmitrievna in vexation and began tapping her fingers on the arm of her chair.

'Sergey Petrovich Gedeonovsky!' squeaked a rosy-cheeked servant-boy, jumping in from behind the door.

II

A TALL man entered in a smart frock-coat, rather short tight trousers, grey chamois gloves and two cravats – a black one on top and a white one below. Everything about him exuded propriety and respectability, beginning with his noble-looking face and smoothly combed temples right down to his shoes that were heel-less and squeakless. He bowed first to the mistress of the house, then to Marfa Timofeyevna and, slowly drawing off his gloves, approached Marya Dmitrievna's hand. Having kissed it respectfully twice in succession, he sat down unhurriedly in an armchair and inquired with a smile, rubbing the tips of his fingers together:

'And is Elizaveta Mikhaylovna well?'

'Yes,' answered Marya Dmitrievna, 'she is in the garden.'

'And Elena Mikhaylovna?'

'Lenochka is also in the garden. Haven't you any news for us?'

'Haven't I indeed,' the guest responded, giving slow winks and protruding his lips. 'Hm! . . . mark you, there is something very surprising about this piece of news: Fyodor Ivanych Lavretsky has come back.'

'Fedya!' exclaimed Marfa Timofeyevna. 'Are you sure you're not making this up, my good man?'

'Not in the least. I saw him with my own eyes.'

'Well, that's hardly any proof.'

'He looks very well,' Gedeonovsky continued, pretending not to have heard Marfa Timofeyevna's remark, 'broader in the shoulders than he ever was and a good colour in his cheeks.'

'So he looks very well,' said Marya Dmitrievna, pausing between the words. 'What, I wonder, is there to make him look so well?'

'Yes, indeed,' responded Gedeonovsky, 'another man in his place would have thought twice about appearing in society.'

'Why so?' interrupted Marfa Timofeyevna. 'What sort of nonsense is that? A man has returned to his birthplace – where else do you want him to go? And anyhow he wasn't to blame!'

'A husband is always to blame, I beg to inform you, my good lady, when a wife behaves herself badly.'

'You say that, my good sir, because you've never been married.'

Gedeonovsky gave a forced smile.

'Permit me to be so curious as to inquire', he asked after a short silence, 'for whom that charming scarf is intended?'

Marfa Timofeyevna directed a quick glance at him.

'It is intended for someone', she replied, 'who never gossips, is never underhand and never makes up stories, if there is such a person in the world. I know Fedya well. All he can be blamed for is spoiling his wife. Well, yes, of course, he also married for love, and nothing worth while ever comes of love matches,' the old woman added, glancing sideways at Marya Dmitrievna and rising to her feet. 'And now you, my good sir, can sharpen your teeth on anyone you like, even on me; I'm going, I won't be any more bother to you.'

And Marfa Timofeyevna went out.

'That's how she always is,' said Marya Dmitrievna, following her aunt with her eyes, 'always!'

'Ah well, at her age! There's nothing to be done about it!' remarked Gedeonovsky. 'Mark you, her ladyship was kind enough to mention "someone who is never underhand". But who is never underhand nowadays? It's a sign of the times. A friend of mine, highly respectable and, I assure you, a man of no mean rank, has made a habit of saying that nowadays even a chicken – to give you one instance – can't approach a grain without being underhand, darting up to it, you know, and pecking it sideways. But now that I look at you, my dear lady, I see you have a truly angelic temperament. Permit me to kiss your snowy white hand.'

Marya Dmitrievna smiled faintly and extended to Gedeonovsky her plump hand with the little finger raised. He pressed his lips to it while she moved her chair towards him and, bending slightly forwards, asked in a low voice:

'So you've seen him? Is he really all right, you know – healthy, happy?'

'Indeed he's well and happy,' answered Gedeonovsky in a whisper.

'And have you heard by any chance where his wife is now?'

'She was lately in Paris; now it's said she's settled in Italy.'

'Fedya's position is certainly horrible; I don't know how he endures it. Misfortunes can happen to anyone, of course, but his, one might say, have been broadcast all over Europe.'

Gedeonovsky gave a sigh.

'Yes, indeed, indeed. They say, you know, that she's keeping company with artists and with pianists, and with lions, as they call them over there, and wild beasts of every sort. She has completely lost all shame . . .'

'I'm very, very sorry,' declared Marya Dmitrievna. 'I speak as a relative: you must know, Sergey Petrovich, that he's a second cousin of mine.'

'Of course, of course. How could I not know everything that concerns your family? Indeed I do know it.'

'Do you think he'll come to see us?'

'It must be supposed he will; yet it's said he's intending to go to his own house in the country.'

Marya Dmitrievna raised her eyes heavenwards.

'Ah, Sergey Petrovich, Sergey Petrovich, when I consider how careful we women must be in how we behave!'

'Not all women are the same, Marya Dmitrievna. There are unfortunately those of inconstant temperament ... and of course those of a certain age. And again there are those who have not been taught the rules when they were little.' (Sergey Petrovich drew a blue check handkerchief out of his pocket and began to unfold it.) 'Such women do exist, of course.' (Sergey Petrovich raised a corner of the handkerchief to each eye in turn.) 'But generally speaking, if one considers, that is ... There's an extraordinary amount of dust in town today,' he concluded.

'Maman, maman,' cried a pretty little girl of eleven, running into the room, 'Vladimir Nikolaich is coming to visit us on horseback!'

Marya Dmitrievna rose. Sergey Petrovich rose also, bowed, said: 'Our most humble respects to Elena Mikhaylovna,' and, withdrawing into a corner out of politeness, proceeded to blow his long straight nose.

'What a wonderful horse he has!' the little girl continued. 'He was by the gate a moment ago and told Liza and me he'd ride right up to the porch.'

A clatter of hooves was heard outside, and the well-knit figure of a rider on a beautiful bay horse appeared in the street and stopped before the open window.

III

'GOOD DAY, Marya Dmitrievna!' exclaimed the rider in a resonant and pleasant voice. 'How do you like my new purchase?'

Marya Dmitrievna approached the window.

'How do you do, Woldemar! Oh, what a splendid horse! Who did you buy it from?'

'From the remount man. He charged me dearly for it, the thief.'

'What do you call it?'

'Orlando. . . . But it's a stupid name; I want to change it. . . . *Eh bien, eh bien, mon garçon*. . . . How restless he is!'

The horse was snorting, prancing and tossing its foam-flecked muzzle.

'Lenochka, stroke him, don't be afraid. . .'

The little girl stretched her hand out of the window, but Orlando suddenly reared up on his hind legs and shied away. The rider did not lose control, gripped the horse with his legs, drew his whip against his neck and, despite his resistance, brought him back again in front of the window.

'*Prenez garde, prenez garde*,' Marya Dmitrievna urged repeatedly.

'Lenochka, stroke him,' said the rider. 'I won't let him get out of hand.'

The little girl again stretched out her hand and shyly touched the quivering nostrils of an Orlando who ceaselessly trembled and champed.

'Bravo!' exclaimed Marya Dmitrievna. 'Now get down and come in and see us.'

The rider swiftly turned the horse, pressed in his spurs and, after galloping a short way along the street, rode into the yard. A moment later, waving his whip, he ran through the hall door into the drawing-room; at that very instant a graceful, tall, dark-haired girl of about nineteen appeared in another doorway – Marya Dmitrievna's elder daughter, Liza.

IV

THE young man, with whom we have just acquainted our readers, was called Vladimir Nikolaich Panshin. He was serving in St Petersburg as an official in the special duties department of the Ministry of Internal Affairs. He had come to the town of O . . . on a temporary official assignment and was at the disposal of the Governor, General Sonnenberg, to whom he was distantly related. Panshin's father, a retired cavalry captain and notorious gambler, a man with sugary eyes, wrinkled face and nervously twitching lips, had spent all his life among the aristocracy, frequenting the English Clubs of both capitals and having a reputation as a clever, not very reliable, but nice and jovial fellow. Despite his cleverness he was practically always on the very brink of penury and left his only son paltry and chaotic material means. On the other hand, after his own fashion he did take trouble over his son's education: Vladimir Nikolaich could speak French beautifully, English well and German badly. Which is as it should be: decent people are ashamed of speaking German well, but the art of dropping a German word into one's conversation at certain, usually humorous, moments – *c'est même très chic*, as our St Petersburg Parisians express it. From fifteen years of age Vladimir Nikolaich knew how to enter any drawing-room without embarrassment, engage in pleasant chit-chat and withdraw at the right moment. Panshin's father had gained his son many connexions. Shuffling cards between rubbers or after a winning grand slam, he never let pass the opportunity of dropping in a word about his 'little Volodya' to one or another of those important people who liked to play cards for financial gain. For his own part, Vladimir Nikolaich during his university years (he graduated without distinction) became acquainted with several aristocratic young men and began to be received in the best houses. He was always treated as a welcome guest; he was not at all bad-looking, gay, entertaining, always in good health and ready for anything; respectful whenever necessary, scathing whenever possible, an excellent comrade, *un charmant garçon*. The promised land of high society spread out before him. Panshin soon learned the secret of such a life; he learned how to imbue himself with real respect for its rules, how to talk nonsense with quasi-facetious importance and give the impression of considering everything important to be nonsense, how to dance to perfection and dress in the English style. In a short time he passed as one of the most delightful and clever young men in St Petersburg. Panshin was indeed very clever, no less than his father; but he was also very gifted. Everything came to him easily: he could sing nicely, make lively sketches, write verse and act a part far from badly on the stage. He was only in his twenty-eighth year and already the holder of a post at court with an exceptionally high rank in the civil service. Panshin believed firmly in his own powers, in his intelligence and his perception; he went ahead boldly and joyously, at full speed, and his life was all plain sailing. He was used to being liked by everyone, old and young, and he imagined that he understood human nature, particularly women: he knew well enough their common weaknesses. As a man not entirely alien to things artistic, he sensed in himself a certain fire, a certain enthusiasm, even a high-flown zeal and as a consequence permitted himself to deviate in various ways from the rules by making merry and associating with those who did not belong to high society and generally by being free and easy. But basically he was cold and devious, and even during the wildest of debauches his clever brown eyes were ever watchful and on guard; this bold, this free-and-easy young man could never forget himself and abandon himself completely. In fairness to him it must be said that he never boasted of his conquests. He made his appearance in Marya Dmitrievna's house immediately upon arrival in O... and was soon quite at home there. Marya Dmitrievna doted on him.

Panshin bowed graciously to everyone in the room, shook hands with Marya Dmitrievna and Lizaveta Mikhaylovna, tapped Gedeonovsky lightly on the shoulder and, turning on his heels, caught Lenochka by the head and kissed her on the temples.

'Aren't you afraid of riding such a frisky horse?' Marya Dmitrievna asked him.

'Oh, he's actually quite quiet. But I'll tell you what I am afraid of – I'm afraid of playing preference[1] with Sergey Petrovich. Yesterday at the Belenitsyns' he cleaned me out.'

Gedeonovsky broke into thin, sycophantic laughter: he sought to ingratiate himself with the brilliant young official from St Petersburg, the Governor's favourite. In his conversations with Marya Dmitrievna he often referred to Panshin's remarkable capabilities. Mark you, he would deliberate, how can one fail to sing his praises? The young man shone in the highest spheres of life and was also an exemplary civil servant, and there wasn't a trace of arrogance in him. As a matter of fact, even in St Petersburg Panshin was regarded as a business-like official: his hands were always busy, although he talked slightingly of his work as befitted a man of the world who ascribes little significance to his labours; yet he was an 'executive type'. Heads of departments like that kind of subordinate; he himself never doubted that, if he wished, he would in time become a minister.

'You are good enough to say that I cleaned you out,' said Gedeonovsky, 'but who was it last week that won twelve roubles off me? What's more ...'

'Naughty, naughty,' Panshin interrupted with agreeable but ever so slightly disdainful negligence and, turning away, approached Liza.

'I haven't been able to find the overture to *Oberon*[2] here,' he began. 'Mrs Belenitsyn was only boasting when she said she had all the classics – in fact she has nothing except polkas and waltzes. But I've already written off to Moscow and in a week you'll get the overture. By the way,' he continued, 'yesterday I wrote a new romance to my own words. Would you like me to sing it? I don't know how it's turned out. Mrs Belenitsyn found it very charming, but what she says means nothing at all. I'd like to know your opinion. Though I think it would perhaps be better later on.'

'Why later on?' interposed Marya Dmitrievna. 'Why not now?'

'Certainly,' said Panshin, with a kind of bright and sugary smile which would appear on his face and vanish all in a flash, and nudged a chair forward with his knee, seated himself at the piano and then, having struck a few chords, began to sing the following romance with clear articulation of each word:

> The moon sails high above in majesty
>   Amid the paling clouds;
> But from on high it moves the billowy sea
>   With its enchanting powers.
>
> My own heart's sea does surely know
>   You are its moon,
> So it is moved – in joy and woe –
>   By you alone.
>
> My heart is full of love's regret,
>   Of love's dumb pain;
> I pine. . . . But you are free of pain as yet,
>   Like that disdainful moon.[3]

The second verse was sung with particular expressiveness and force; the stormy accompaniment suggested the sound of billowing waves. After the words: 'I pine . . .' he gave a faint sigh, lowered his eyes and dropped his voice in a dying *morendo*. When he finished, Liza praised the *motif*, Marya Dmitrievna said: 'Charming,' and Gedeonovsky even exclaimed: 'Entrancing! The words and the music – both equally entrancing!' And Lenochka gazed at the singer with childish awe. In a word, everyone in the room very much enjoyed the young dilettante's composition; but beyond the drawing-room door, in the hall, there stood a new arrival, an old man who, judging by the expression on his downcast face and the way he shrugged his shoulders, took no pleasure in hearing Panshin's romance, despite all its charm. After a moment's pause to flick the dust from his shoes with a thick handkerchief, this man suddenly screwed up his eyes, dolefully pursed his lips, bent his already bent back and slowly entered the drawing-room.

'Ah, good day, Christopher Fyodorych!' Panshin was the first to cry out and quickly jumped up from the chair. 'I'd no idea you were here. Had I known you were, nothing on earth would have made me sing my romance. I know you're not fond of light music.'

'I have not heart,' said the new arrival in his poor Russian accent and, bowing to everyone, stopped awkwardly in the middle of the room.

'Have you come, Monsieur Lemm,' asked Marya Dmitrievna, 'to give Liza her music lesson?'

'No, not Lisafet Mikhaylovna, but Elen Mikhaylovna.'

'Ah! Well, that's splendid. Lenochka, go upstairs with Mr Lemm.'

The old man was about to follow the little girl out of the room, but Panshin stopped him.

'Don't go away after the lesson, Christopher Fyodorych,' he said. 'Lizaveta Mikhaylovna and I will be playing Beethoven's Sonata for four hands.'

The old man muttered something under his breath, but Panshin continued in his badly pronounced German:

'Lizaveta Mikhaylovna showed me the religious cantata which you brought her – a beautiful piece! You mustn't think that I don't know how to appreciate serious music. On the contrary: it is sometimes boring, but beneficial as well.'

The old man crimsoned to the roots of his hair, threw an oblique glance at Liza and hurriedly left the room.

Marya Dmitrievna asked Panshin to repeat his romance, but he announced that he had no wish to offend the ears of the learned German and suggested to Liza that they should practise the Beethoven Sonata. Then Marya Dmitrievna sighed and suggested for her own part that Gedeonovsky should accompany her for a walk in the garden. 'I wish', she said, 'to have a few more words with you about our poor Fedya and to seek your advice.' Gedeonovsky grinned, bowed, picked up his hat with two fingers at the point where his gloves had been neatly laid on its brim and departed with Marya Dmitrievna. Panshin and Liza remained in the room; she drew out and opened the Sonata; both of them sat down silently at the piano. From above resounded the faint sounds of scales played over and over by Lenochka's unskilled fingers.

V

CHRISTOPHER THEODORE GOTTLIEB LEMM was born in 1786 into a family of penurious musicians in the town of Chemnitz in the Kingdom of Saxony. His father played the French horn, his mother played the harp; by his fifth year he was himself practising three different instruments. At eight he was orphaned and at ten he began earning his daily bread by his playing. For a long time he led a vagrant life, playing everywhere – at inns, at fairs, at peasant weddings and at balls. Finally he found a place in an orchestra and, moving ever higher and higher, eventually became conductor. He was a rather poor performer, but he had a fundamental understanding of music. In his twenty-eighth year he emigrated to Russia. He had been booked by a grandiose member of the gentry who could not endure music but maintained an orchestra for show. Lemm spent seven years as his director of music and left without a penny to show for it: the gentleman in question went bankrupt, wanted to give him an I.O.U. but later refused to give him even that – in short, did not pay him a farthing. He was advised to go abroad; but he did not wish to return home from Russia a beggar, from that great Russia, the gold mine of all artists. He decided to remain and try his luck. The poor German tried his luck for twenty years: he was employed by various gentlemen, lived both in Moscow and in provincial towns, endured and suffered much, experiencing poverty and struggling for life like a fish out of water. But the idea of returning to his homeland never left him amid all the misfortunes which beset him. That idea alone kept him going. Fate, however, did not think fit to gladden him with this first and last happiness: at fifty, sick and prematurely decrepit, he found himself in the town of O . . . and remained there forever, having finally abandoned all hope of leaving the Russia that was so hateful to him and relying somehow on his lessons to make a paltry living. Lemm's appearance was no advantage to him. He was short in stature, round-shouldered, with protuberant bent shoulder-blades and shrunken stomach, large flat feet and pale-blue nails on the stiff, inflexible fingers of his sinewy red hands. He had a wrinkled face, sunken cheeks and compressed lips which were endlessly making a chewing motion that, combined with his usual taciturnity, produced an almost menacing effect. His grey hair hung in tufts over his low forehead. His tiny motionless eyes had a dull glow like recently extinguished coals. He had a ponderous gait, swinging his cumbersome body from side to side at each step. Some of his movements were reminiscent of the preenings of an owl in a cage when it feels it is being watched and yet itself can hardly see out of its large, yellow, fearful and sleepily blinking eyes. Longstanding, implacable grief had left its ineradicable mark upon the poor musician and contorted and disfigured his already unbecoming person; but for

31

those who could see beyond first impressions there was something kindly, honourable and unusual to be discerned in this half-ruined man. A devotee of Bach and Handel, expert at his craft, gifted with a lively imagination and that boldness of thought which is uniquely characteristic of the Germans, Lemm in time – who knows? – might have taken his place among the great composers of his country if life had led him on a different course; but he was not born under an auspicious star. He had written a great deal in his time – and he had not succeeded in seeing a single one of his compositions published; he had no idea how to set about things in the right way, to whom to bow at the right moment or when was the best time to busy himself. Somehow or other, a long time ago, an admirer and friend of his, also a German and also poor, had printed at his own expense two of his sonatas – and yet these remained entirely unsold in the storerooms of music shops; they vanished without sound or trace, literally as if they had been thrown into a river overnight. Lemm finally said good-bye to his dreams; the years, what is more, had taken their toll: he had grown crusty and hard like his fingers. All by himself, save for an old cook-housekeeper he took from the poor-house (he had never married), he lived in O . . . in a little house not far from the Kalitins', passing much of his time in taking strolls and reading the Bible, a collection of Protestant psalms and the works of Shakespeare in Schlegel's translation. It was a long time since he had composed anything new; but clearly Liza, his best pupil, had stirred his creative powers and he had written for her the cantata to which Panshin referred. The words of the cantata had been taken from the collection of psalms, though he had added some verses of his own. It was to be sung by two choirs of the lucky and the luckless – and in the finale they were to be reconciled and sing together: 'Merciful Lord, forgive us, Thy sinners, and save us from all wicked thoughts and worldly hopes.' On the title page, in extremely neat lettering and even suitably embellished, was the following: 'Only the Righteous shall be Justified. A Religious Cantata. Composed and dedicated to my dear pupil, Miss Elizaveta Kalitin, by her teacher, C.T.G. Lemm.' The words: 'Only the Righteous shall be Justified' and 'Miss Elizaveta Kalitin' were surrounded by decorative rays. Below had been written: 'For you alone, für Sie allein.' This was why Lemm had reddened and looked obliquely at Liza; Panshin's mention of his cantata in his presence was very painful to him.

VI

PANSHIN struck the first chords of the Sonata loudly and resolutely (he was playing the bass part), but Liza did not begin her part. He stopped and looked at her. Liza's eyes, directed straight at him, expressed displeasure; there was no smile on her lips and her face was stern, almost sad.

'What's wrong?' he asked.

'Why didn't you keep your word?' she asked. 'I showed you Christopher Fyodorych's cantata on the condition that you did not speak to him about it.'

'I'm sorry, Lizaveta Mikhaylovna, the words just popped out.'

'You've upset him – and me, too. Now he won't trust even me any more.'

'What can I do about it, Lizaveta Mikhaylovna? Ever since I was so high I haven't been able to look at a German without wanting to tease him.'

'How can you say that, Vladimir Nikolaich! This German is a poor, lonely, crushed man – can't you feel sorry for him? Why do you want to tease him?'

Panshin became confused.

'You're right, Lizaveta Mikhaylovna,' he said. 'What's to blame is my eternal lack of forethought. No, don't contradict me – I know myself only too well. My lack of forethought

33

has done me great harm. Through it I've gained a reputation for being an egoist.'

Panshin paused. No matter how he began a conversation, he usually ended by talking about himself, and it somehow came out so nicely and unaffectedly, so warmly, as though it were quite against his will.

'Here in your house as well,' he continued, 'your mother is, of course, so gracious to me – she is such a kind person. And you ... but I'm afraid I don't know your opinion of me, whereas I know your aunt can't stand me. I must've offended her as well by something thoughtless and foolish I've said. It's true she doesn't like me, isn't it?'

'Yes,' said Liza a little uncertainly, 'she's not fond of you.'

Panshin quickly ran his fingers along the keys and a faintly perceptible grin flickered on his lips.

'Well, what about you?' he asked. 'Do I also seem to be an egoist to you?'

'I still know so little about you,' Liza replied, 'but I don't consider you an egoist. On the contrary, I must be grateful to you ...'

'I know, I know what you mean,' Panshin broke in and again ran his fingers along the keys. 'You're grateful for the music and books I bring you, for the poor drawings with which I decorate your album, and so on, and so forth. I can do all that and still be an egoist. I dare to think you're not bored in my company and you don't consider me bad, but you still imagine I'd – how's that saying go? – I'd spare neither father nor friend for a pretty phrase.'

'You're absent-minded and forgetful, like all socialites,' said Liza. 'That's all.'

Panshin frowned slightly.

'Listen,' he said, 'let's not talk about me any more. Let's start playing our sonata. I ask you to do only one thing,' he added, smoothing out the sheets of the music book on the stand, 'think what you like about me, even call me an egoist

34

– so be it! but don't call me a socialite: I can't stand that title
... *Anch'io sono pittore*, I'm also an artist, if a poor one, and
that's precisely what I'm going to prove to you now in fact.
Let's begin.'

'All right, let's begin,' said Liza.

The first *adagio* went fairly smoothly, although Panshin
made more than one mistake. He played his own compositions
and whatever he had studied very nicely, but he was bad at
reading music at first sight. Consequently the second part of
the Sonata – a fairly fast *allegro* – was a disaster: at the twentieth
bar Panshin, already two bars behind, gave up and pushed his
chair back with a laugh.

'No, I can't play today!' he exclaimed. 'It's a good thing
Lemm didn't hear us – he'd've had a fit.'

Liza stood up, closed the piano and turned to Panshin.

'What shall we do now?' she asked.

'I knew you'd ask that! You can never sit about with your
arms folded. Well, if you like, let's do some drawing while
it's still light enough. Maybe another muse, the muse of
drawing – what was she called? I forget – will be kinder to
me. Where's your album? I remember my landscape's not
yet done.'

Liza went into the next room to find her album while
Panshin, left alone, drew a cambric handkerchief out of his
pocket, rubbed his nails and scrutinized his hands. They were
very beautiful and white; on his left thumb he wore a spiral
gold ring. Liza returned. Panshin sat down by the window
and opened the album.

'Aha!' he exclaimed. 'I see you've begun to copy my landscape – and splendidly. Very good indeed! It's just that here –
please let me have a pencil – the shadows aren't filled in
strongly enough. Look.'

And Panshin made several brisk long strokes. He always
drew one and the same landscape: in the foreground were
large dishevelled trees and in the background fields with

jagged mountains on the horizon. Liza looked over his shoulder as he worked.

'In drawing, as generally in life,' said Panshin, bending his head to right and left, 'the main thing is dexterity and daring.'

At that moment Lemm entered the room and, giving a drily formal bow, tried to withdraw, but Panshin threw the album and pencil to one side and barred his exit.

'Where are you off to, my dear Christopher Fyodorych? Aren't you going to stay for tea?'

'I am going home,' said Lemm in a gloomy voice. 'My head aches.'

'Well, that's nothing. You stay here. We'll discuss Shakespeare.'

'My head aches,' the old man repeated.

'In your absence we tried the Beethoven Sonata,' Panshin went on, amiably taking him by the waist and smiling brightly, 'but the whole thing was hopeless. Just imagine it, I couldn't play two notes in a row correctly.'

'You would besser your romance haf played again,' Lemm retorted, removing Panshin's hands, and went out of the room.

Liza ran after him. She caught up with him at the porch.

'Christopher Fyodorych, please listen,' she said in German, accompanying him to the gate across the short green grass of the yard, 'I'm to blame for hurting you. Forgive me.'

Lemm did not answer.

'I showed Vladimir Nikolaich your cantata because I was sure he would appreciate it – and he did really like it very much.'

'It doesn't matter,' he said in Russian, and then added in his own language: 'But he cannot understand anything; can't you see that? He's a dilettante – that's all there is to it!'

'You're being unfair to him,' Liza replied. 'He understands everything, and he can do almost everything.'

'Yes, if it's second-rate, lightweight stuff, all done in a hurry. What he does is liked and he's liked and he's pleased

36

with himself – well, good luck to him! But I'm not annoyed; this cantata and I are both old fools. I'm a little ashamed, but it doesn't matter.'

'Forgive me, Christopher Fyodorych,' Liza repeated.

'It doesn't matter, it doesn't matter,' he repeated, again in Russian. 'You're a kind girl. . . . But here's someone coming to see you. Good-bye. You're a very kind girl.'

And Lemm set off with hurried step towards the gate, through which there had just entered a gentleman who was unknown to him dressed in a grey overcoat and wide straw hat. Bowing courteously to him (he bowed to all the new faces he saw in the town of O . . ., but made it a rule of his to turn his back on those he knew), Lemm walked past and disappeared beyond the fence. The newcomer stared after him in astonishment and then, glancing in Liza's direction, went straight up to her.

VII

'YOU won't recognize me,' he said, taking off his hat, 'but I've recognized you even though ten years have passed since I last saw you. You were a child then. I'm Lavretsky. Is your mother at home? May I see her?'

'Mother will be very glad,' Liza replied. 'She's heard about your arrival.'

'It seems to me you're called Elizaveta, aren't you?' Lavretsky asked, climbing the porch steps.

'Yes.'

'I remember you well. Even then you had a face one does not easily forget. In those days I used to bring you sweets.'

Liza blushed and thought what a strange person he was. Lavretsky stopped for a moment in the hall. Liza went into the drawing-room, where Panshin's voice and laugh resounded as he related some town gossip to Marya Dmitrievna and Gedeonovsky who had just returned from their walk in the garden, and Panshin himself laughed loudly at what he was telling. At Lavretsky's name Marya Dmitrievna became quite flustered, grew pale and walked across to meet him.

'Hello, hello, my dear cousin!' she exclaimed in a traily and almost tearful voice. 'How glad I am to see you!'

'How do you do, my kind cousin,' Lavretsky responded and affectionately pressed her outstretched hand. 'Is the good Lord treating you kindly?'

'Sit down, do sit down, my dear Fyodor Ivanych. Ah, how glad I am! Let me first of all introduce you to my daughter Liza . . .'

'I have already introduced myself to Lizaveta Mikhaylovna,' Lavretsky interrupted her.

'Monsieur Panshin . . . Sergey Petrovich Gedeonovsky. . . . Do please sit down. I look at you and, you know, I can hardly believe my eyes! How are you keeping?'

'As you can see, I am flourishing. And you, cousin, I would say – at the risk of offending you – have looked after yourself in the last eight years.'

'To think we haven't seen each other for such a time,' Marya Dmitrievna mused. 'Where have you just come from? Where have you left . . . That's to say, I mean,' she hurriedly corrected herself, 'I mean, will you be staying with us long?'

'I've just come from Berlin,' Lavretsky replied, 'and tomorrow I'll be going off to the country – probably for a long time.'

'You will be living in Lavriki, of course?'

'No, not in Lavriki. I have a little village about fifteen miles from here; that's where I'll be going.'

'Is that the village you received from Glafira Petrovna?'

'It is.'

'Forgive me, Fyodor Ivanych, but at Lavriki you have such a delightful house!'

Lavretsky's brows knit very slightly.

'True. . . . But there's a small place in that village, and I

38

don't need anything more at present. That'll be the most suitable place for me now.'

Marya Dmitrievna was again so put out that she straightened herself in her chair and spread her hands wide. Panshin came to her aid and engaged Lavretsky in conversation. Marya Dmitrievna grew calmer, sank back into her armchair and only made occasional contributions to the conversation; but all the while she looked so pityingly at her guest, sighed so meaningfully and gave such despondent shakes of the head that he could finally stand it no longer and asked her fairly sharply whether she was all right.

'Yes, thank God,' Marya Dmitrievna answered. 'Why do you ask?'

'It seemed to me you were not yourself, that's all.'

Marya Dmitrievna assumed a dignified and slightly injured look. 'If that's how things are,' she thought, 'then I'm past caring. To you, my good man, it's obviously just like water off a duck's back; some other person would have wasted away with grief, but you're plumper than ever.' When she talked to herself, Marya Dmitrievna did not stand on ceremony; aloud she was more refined.

In fact, Lavretsky bore no resemblance to a victim of fate. His red-cheeked, very Russian face, with the large white forehead, slightly thick nose and broad regular lips, literally exuded the healthy life of the steppes and a powerful, durable strength. He had a magnificent build, and his fair hair curled on his head like a boy's. Only in his blue, protruding and rather immobile eyes could be discerned a cross between pensiveness and tiredness, and his voice somehow sounded a little too smooth.

Panshin meanwhile continued to keep the conversation going. He raised the topic of sugar refining, about which he had recently read a couple of French pamphlets, and with quiet modesty he undertook to expound their contents without, however, mentioning a single word about them.

'It must be Fedya!' Marfa Timofeyevna's voice was suddenly heard to exclaim beyond the half-open door of the next room. 'It is Fedya!' And the old woman rushed into the drawing-room. Lavretsky did not succeed in rising from his chair before she had embraced him. 'Let me see how you look, let me see,' she said, drawing back from his face. 'Ah, splendid! A little older but not a whit less handsome. Now don't you go kissing my hands – you give me a real kiss, if my wrinkled old cheeks don't repel you! I don't suppose you asked whether your old aunt was alive or not, did you? But you were a new-born baby in my very arms, you rascal! Still, that doesn't matter: you've no reason to remember me all that well! Only you've done the right thing in coming back. Well, mother,' she added, turning to Marya Dmitrievna, 'have you offered him anything?'

'I don't need a thing,' Lavretsky hastened to answer.

'Well, at least have some tea, my dear. Good heavens, he's come from God knows where and they won't even give him a cup of tea! Liza, go and see about it, quick as you can. I remember that when he was little he had a voracious appetite, and I don't doubt he still likes his food even now.'

'My respects to you, Marfa Timofeyevna,' said Panshin, approaching the agitated old lady from one side and bowing low to her.

'Forgive me, my good sir,' responded Marfa Timofeyevna, 'I didn't notice you in my state of elation. You've begun to look like your mother, the darling child,' she continued, addressing herself again to Lavretsky, 'only your nose was your father's and your father's it's remained. Well now, have you come to visit us for long?'

'I am leaving tomorrow, auntie.'

'Where are you going?'

'To my own estate, to Vasilyevskoye.'

'Tomorrow?'

'Tomorrow.'

'Very well, if it's to be tomorrow, tomorrow it is. God be with you – you know best. Only you make sure to come and say good-bye.' The old lady tapped him on the cheek. 'I didn't think I'd live to see you back here. And that doesn't mean I was getting ready to die – oh, no, I've got a good ten years to go yet: all we Pestovs are long-livers; your late grandfather used to call us double-lifers. But God alone knew how long you'd go on wasting your time abroad. Well, anyhow, you're looking fine, really fine. I suppose you can still lift ten stone with one hand as you used to? Your late father, foolish though he was – you must forgive me for saying so – did well to engage that Swiss for you. Do you remember how you used to have fist fights with him? It's called gymnastics, isn't it? But I mustn't go on chattering so; all I'm doing is preventing Mr Panshín' (she never called him Pánshin, as she should have done) 'from continuing what he was saying. Besides, it would be better if we had some tea. Let's go out on the terrace to have it, my dear. We have wonderful cream, not the sort of stuff in your Londons and Parises. Let's go, let's go, and you, my dear Fedya, give me your hand. Oh, such a big one. No one'll fall down with you holding them!'

They all rose and withdrew to the terrace with the exception of Gedeonovsky, who made his way out of the house on the quiet. During the whole of the conversation between Lavretsky and the mistress of the house, Panshin and Marfa Timofeyevna, he had sat in his corner blinking attentively and pouting his lips in childish amazement: now he hurried off to spread news of it all about the town.

On that day, at eleven o'clock in the evening, this is what was happening in Mrs Kalitin's house. Downstairs, on the threshold of the drawing-room, having seized a suitable moment, Vladimir Nikolaich was saying good-bye to Liza and telling her as he held her by the hand: 'You know what makes me come here; you know why I am always coming to your house; there's no point in putting it into words when it's all so clear.' Liza said nothing in reply and unsmilingly stared at the floor, slightly raising her eyebrows and blushing, but without withdrawing her hand; meanwhile upstairs, in Marfa Timofeyevna's room, by the light of a lamp hanging in front of the ancient lacklustre icons, Lavretsky was sitting in an armchair with his elbows on his knees and his face in his hands; the old lady, standing in front of him, from time to time silently stroked his hair. He had spent more than an hour with her, after saying good-bye to the mistress of the house; he had said practically nothing to his kind old friend and she had not asked him anything. . . . For what was there to say, what was there to ask? She literally understood everything, literally felt all the things with which his heart was over-flowing.

VIII

FYODOR IVANOVICH LAVRETSKY (we must ask the reader's permission to break the thread of our story for a while) came of ancient gentry stock. The founder of the Lavretsky line came from Prussia during the reign of Basil the Blind and was granted eight hundred acres of land in the Upper Bezhetsk region. Many of his descendants were numbered among those who served in various posts under princes and men of title in remote provinces, but not one of them rose above chancery rank or amassed a significant fortune. The richest and most remarkable of all the Lavretskys was Fyodor Ivanovich's great-grandfather Andrey, a cruel, bold, intelligent and crafty man. To this day there is still talk of his arbitrariness, his fiery disposition, his wild generosity and insatiable greed. He was very corpulent and tall in stature, beardless and swarthy of face, spoke with a drawl and seemed half-asleep; but the more quietly he spoke, the more those around him trembled. He took as his wife a woman to match him. With protruding eyes, a hawk's nose, round yellowish face, of gipsy origin, quick-tempered and vindictive, she never for a moment gave in to her husband, who was darned near the death of her and whom she did not survive even though she was incessantly badgering him. Andrey's son Pyotr, Fyodor's grandfather, did not take after his father: he was a simple country squire, fairly devil-may-care, loud-mouthed and slow-witted, rude but not malicious, fond of entertaining and following the hounds. He was over thirty when he inherited from his father two thousand souls in perfect condition, but he soon dispersed them, sold part of the estate and over-indulged his house-serfs. Like cockroaches, various nonentities, both friends and strangers, crawled from all sides into his spacious, warm and dowdy manor house; the whole lot of them ate their fill of whatever came their way, drank themselves tipsy and pilfered what they could, praising and glorifying their gracious host as they did so; and the host, when he was in low spirits, also glorified his guests with such titles as spongers and scoundrels, but grew bored without them. Pyotr Andreyich's wife was a mild creature; he had taken her from a neighbouring family by his father's choice and ordinance; she was called Anna Pavlovna. She never interfered in anything, received guests affably and gladly made calls of her own, although to be powdered, she would say, was death to her. In her old age she used to describe how they would put a felt head-band on you, comb all the hair upwards, smear it with grease, sprinkle flour on it and insert iron pins – and you couldn't wash it out afterwards! But people would take offence if you paid visits without being powdered: it was sheer murder! She loved to go out driving with fast horses, was ready to play cards from morning to night and would always conceal with her hand the place where she had noted down her tiny winnings whenever her husband approached the card table; but she handed over all her dowry and money into his undisputed keeping. She bore

43

him two children: a son Ivan, Fyodor's father, and a daughter Glafira. Ivan was not educated at home, but in the house of a rich old aunt, Princess Kubenskaya, who had made him her heir (without this his father would not have let him go). She dressed him up like a doll, hired every kind of teacher for him and placed him in the charge of a tutor, a certain M. Courtin de Vaucelles, a Frenchman, former abbé and disciple of Jean-Jacques Rousseau, a sly, refined smoothy – the very, as she used to express it, *fine fleur* of the emigration – and ended, when she was almost seventy, by marrying this very same *fine fleur*. She transferred to his name all her wealth and possessions and soon afterwards, made up to the eyebrows and perfumed with scent *à la Richelieu*, surrounded by little Negro pages, short-legged dogs and shrieking parrots, died on a bent little Louis XV silk divan, with an enamelled snuff-box by Petitot in her hand – died, what is more, abandoned by her husband; the ingratiating M. Courtin had preferred to withdraw to Paris along with her money. Ivan was only just twenty when this unexpected blow (we refer to the Princess's marriage, not her death) broke over him; he had no further desire to remain in his aunt's house, where he had suddenly been transformed from a rich heir into a hanger-on; in St Petersburg the society in which he had grown up closed its doors to him; he felt an aversion to working his way up the difficult and obscure rungs of the civil service (all this occurred at the very beginning of Alexander I's reign)[1]; despite himself, he was obliged to return to the country, to his father. His 'nest of the gentry' appeared dirty, impoverished and unkempt to him; the stagnation and squalor of provincial life insulted him at every turn; he fell prey to a gnawing boredom; and, to crown it all, everyone in the house except his mother gave him unfriendly looks. His father took a dislike to his city ways, his frock-coats, ruffles, his books, his flute and his punctilious neatness, in which he sensed blatant disgust; and every so often he complained and railed at his son. 'Nothing's

44

to his taste here,' he would say. 'He picks at his food at table, doesn't eat, can't stand honest human smells or a bit of stuffiness, gets upset by the sight of drunkenness, won't have me knocking the servants about and yet he won't do any work of his own because – would you believe it? – his health's not strong enough! You're a mother's darling, that's what you are! And all because you've got your head crammed full of Voltaire!'[2] The old man was particularly scathing about Voltaire and that 'barbarous' Diderot, although he had never read a line of their works: reading was not his speciality. Pyotr Andreyich was not mistaken: it was precisely Diderot and Voltaire who were crammed into his son's head, and not only them – Rousseau and Raynal and Helvétius, and many others like them, were also there. But they were only in his head. Ivan Petrovich's former instructor, the retired abbé and encyclopaedist, had contented himself with pouring the undiluted wisdom of the eighteenth century into his pupil, and the pupil went about filled to the brim with it; but it dwelt in him without mixing with his blood, without penetrating his soul, without assuming the form of strong convictions. . . . Indeed, how could one demand convictions of a young man fifty years ago when we haven't grown up sufficiently to have them even today? Ivan Petrovich was also an embarrassment to his father's guests; he found them repugnant and they feared him, while with his sister Glafira, who was twelve years his senior, he did not get on at all. This Glafira was a strange creature: unbeautiful, round-shouldered, thin as a stick, with severe, wide-open eyes and a delicate, pinched mouth, she took after her grandmother, the gipsy, Andrey's wife, in her looks, her voice and her brisk angular movements. Insisting on having things her own way, loving her own authority, she would not hear of marriage. Ivan Petrovich's return did not appeal to her one little bit. So long as Princess Kubenskaya had kept him with her, she had hoped to receive at least half her father's estate: she took after her

45

grandmother in her miserliness as well. What is more, Glafira envied her brother for his education and for being able to speak French so well, with a Parisian accent, while she could scarcely say '*bonjour*' or '*comment vous portez-vous?*' True, her parents had no knowledge of French, but that was little comfort to her. Ivan Petrovich was bored stiff and did not know where to turn; he had hardly spent a year in the country, but that one year seemed to him like ten. He opened his heart only to his mother and would sit with her for hours at a time in her low-ceilinged rooms, listening to her inconsequent, kind-hearted chatter and eating his fill of jam preserves. It so happened that among Anna Pavlovna's maid-servants there was one very pretty girl with lucid, gentle eyes and delicate features, by name Malanya, of intelligent and modest character. From the very beginning she had caught Ivan Petrovich's eye, and he fell in love with her: he fell in love with her shy movements, her bashful answers, her quiet little voice and placid smile; she seemed to grow nicer and nicer with each day. And she was attracted to Ivan Petrovich with all the strength of her soul, as only Russian girls know how to be attracted – and she gave herself to him. In a country house of the gentry no secret can be kept for long: soon everyone knew about the young master's affair with Malanya; finally news of the affair reached Pyotr Andreyich. At another time he would probably have paid no attention to such an unimportant matter; but he had long had a bone to pick with his son and was overjoyed at the opportunity of putting the St Petersburg wiseacre and dandy to shame. All hell broke loose: Malanya was locked in a store-room and Ivan Petrovich was ordered to see his father. Anna Pavlovna also rushed in to see what the noise was all about. She was on the point of trying to soothe her husband's feelings, but he was already beyond listening to reason. He swooped on his son like a hawk and heaped imprecations on him for his immorality, atheism and hypocrisy; he also took the opportunity of wreaking upon him all his accumulated anger at Princess Kubenskaya and showered him with insults. To start with Ivan Petrovich braced himself and kept silent, but when his father took it into his head to threaten him with a shameful punishment he could stand it no longer. 'That barbarous Diderot's going to put in an appearance again,' he thought. 'Very well, then, I'll well and truly make use of him – I'll surprise the lot of you.' And there and then in a calm, level voice, although shivering inwardly in every limb, Ivan Petrovich declared to his father that he was mistaken in blaming him for immorality, that although he did not intend to justify his guilt he was ready to put things right, and all the more willingly since he felt himself to be above all prejudices – he was ready, in fact, to marry Malanya. In uttering these words Ivan Petrovich had indisputably achieved his object: he so startled Pyotr Andreyich that the latter stared goggle-eyed and was momentarily rendered speechless; but he instantly recovered himself and, dressed just as he was, in his jacket lined with squirrel fur and with no more than slippers on his bare feet, literally flung himself, fists flying, at his son who had that day, as if by intention, given himself a hair-do *à la Titus*[3] and decked himself in a new English blue frock-coat, boots with little tassels on them and fancy buckskin breeches of skin-tight fit. Anna Pavlovna emitted a mighty wail and covered her face with her hands, while her son ran right through the house, jumped out into the yard, dashed into the kitchen garden and through the garden proper and took flight towards the road and went on running without a backward glance until he finally ceased to hear the heavy tramp of his father's footsteps and his strenuous, intermittent shouts – 'Stop, you scoundrel! Stop! I'll put a curse on you!' Ivan Petrovich took refuge at the house of a neighbouring smallholder and Pyotr Andreyich returned home utterly worn-out and pouring with sweat to declare, scarcely able to draw breath as he did so, that he was depriving his son of his blessing and his inheritance, that all his idiotic books were to be burnt and the girl Malanya was to be packed off to a distant village without delay. Kind people were found who sought out Ivan Petrovich and told him of all this. Humiliated and infuriated, he swore to avenge himself on his father and that very same night, having waylaid the peasant cart in which Malanya was being carried off, forcibly abducted her, galloped with her into the nearest town and married her. Money had been supplied him by a neighbour, an eternally drunk but most kind-hearted retired sailor who took a huge delight in any, as he expressed it, 'noble exploit'. The next day Ivan Petrovich wrote a caustically chilly and polite letter to his father and then set off for the village where his cousin Dmitri Pestov lived with his sister Marfa Timofeyevna, who is already familiar to the reader. He told them everything, declared that he intended to go to St Petersburg to seek a place for himself and begged them to look after his wife, at least for a time. At the word 'wife' he burst into bitter tears and, despite all his city upbringing and philosophy, humbly prostrated himself at his relatives' feet like any wretched peasant supplicant and even struck his forehead against the floor. The Pestovs, commiserative and tender-hearted people, gladly agreed to his request; he spent three weeks or so with them in secret expectation of an answer from his father; but no answer came, nor could one come. Pyotr Andreyich, having learned of his son's marriage, took to his bed and forbade anyone to mention the name of Ivan Petrovich in his presence; save that his mother, without her husband's knowledge, borrowed five hundred roubles in notes from the archdeacon and sent them to his wife, together with a little icon; she feared to write, but ordered that Ivan Petrovich be told by the spare little muzhik sent as messenger, who could walk as much as fifty miles a day, that he must not be too downcast, that, God grant it so, everything would turn out all right and his father would put aside his anger in favour of forgiveness; that she would have preferred another daughter-in-law, but it was evident that God was pleased to arrange things as they were and so she would send Malanya Sergeyevna her parental blessing. The spare little muzhik received a rouble, asked permission to see the new mistress (he happened to be her godfather), kissed her little hand and dashed off home.

And Ivan Petrovich set off for St Petersburg with a light heart. An unknown future awaited him; poverty might threaten, but he had said good-bye to hateful country life and – most important of all – he had not betrayed his teachers, had in fact 'put them to good use' and vindicated Rousseau, Diderot and *la déclaration des droits de l'homme*. A feeling of duty accomplished, of triumph, a feeling of pride filled his soul; separation from his wife, what is more, did not dismay him unduly; rather, he would have been annoyed by the necessity of having to live constantly with her. That matter was now done with; the time had come to do other things. In St Petersburg, contrary to his expectations, luck smiled on him; Princess Kubenskaya, whom M. Courtin had already succeeded in abandoning, but who had not yet succeeded in dying, by way of atonement to her nephew, recommended him to all her friends and made him a gift of five thousand roubles (almost the last of her money) and a watch by Lepic inscribed with his monogram in a garland of cupids. Before three months were up he had received a post with the Russian mission in London and on the first outward-bound English sailing ship (there were no steamships in those days) voyaged away across the sea. A few months later he received a letter from Pestov. The kind-hearted landowner congratulated Ivan Petrovich on the birth of a son, who had seen the light of day in the village of Pokrovskoye on 20 August 1807 and had been named Fyodor in honour of the holy martyr Theodore Stratelates.[4] On account of her weak condition Malanya Sergeyevna had added only a few lines; but even

49

these few lines astonished Ivan Petrovich, for he did not know that Marfa Timofeyevna had taught his wife to read and write. Still, Ivan Petrovich did not succumb for long to the sweet thrill of parental pride: he was busy paying court to one of the famous beauties of the time, some Phryne or Laïs (classical names were much in vogue); the Tilsit⁵ peace had just been concluded and everyone was in a hurry to enjoy himself, all went spinning in a frenzied whirlwind of pleasure, just as the black eyes of his vivacious beauty sent his head spinning. He had very little money; but he was lucky at cards, struck up many acquaintanceships, took part in every conceivable kind of entertainment – in short, sped along under full sail.

IX

FOR a long while old Lavretsky was unable to forgive his son for having got married; if, after six months, say, Ivan Petrovich had appeared before him with his head hung in shame and thrown himself down at his feet, he would most likely have pardoned him, having first given him a good talking-to and a tap or two with his stick so as to instil the requisite respect; but Ivan was living abroad and, by all accounts, didn't give a tinker's cuss. 'Hold your tongue! Don't you dare!' Pyotr Andreyich would insist to his wife every time she tried to incline him towards thoughts of forgiveness. 'That puppy-dog, he ought to thank God eternally that I didn't lay my curse on him; my late lamented father would've killed him with his own bare hands, the good-for-nothing, and it'd have been a good thing if he had.' In face of such terrible speeches Anna Pavlovna could do no more than cross herself in secret. So far as Ivan Petrovich's wife was concerned, Pyotr Andreyich at first would not even hear of her and in answer to a letter from Pestov, in which his daughter-in-law was mentioned, even ordered him to be informed that he had no knowledge of any such daughter-in-law and that it was forbidden by law to harbour runaway serf-girls, about which he considered it his duty to give him due warning; but later, having learned of the birth of his grandson, he softened and gave orders that he should be made privy to any news about the mother's health and also, as if it were not from him, sent her a little money. Fedya was not yet a year old when Anna Pavlovna contracted a fatal illness. A few days before her death, when she was already confined to her bed, with reticent tears brimming in her fading eyes she announced to her husband in the presence of the priest that she wished to see and say good-bye to her daughter-in-law and pronounce her blessing upon her grandson. The old man, in great distress, comforted her and at once sent his own carriage to fetch his daughter-in-law, calling her for the first time Malanya Sergeyevna. She came with her son and with Marfa Timofeyevna, who would on no account have let her come alone and be slighted. Half-dead with fright, Malanya Sergeyevna entered Pyotr Andreyich's study. Behind her came a nurse carrying Fedya. Pyotr Andreyich looked at her in silence; she approached his hand; her trembling lips were scarcely able to form themselves into a soundless kiss.

'Well, my fine backstairs young lady,' he said eventually, 'how do you do? Let us go to the mistress.'

He rose and bent towards Fedya; the baby smiled and stretched out its pale little hands to him. The old man was overcome.

'Oh,' he cried, 'my poor orphaned child! You were imploring me for your father; I'm not one to forsake you, poor mite.'

Malanya Sergeyevna no sooner entered Anna Pavlovna's bedroom than she dropped on her knees by the door. Anna Pavlovna signalled for her to come to the bed, embraced her and blessed her son; then, turning a face utterly wasted by her cruel disease towards her husband, showed that she wished to speak . . .

'I know, I know what it is you want to ask,' said Pyotr Andreyich. 'Don't be sad: she will stay here with us, and for her sake I'll forgive Vanka.'

With an effort Anna Pavlovna took her husband's hand and pressed her lips to it. That same evening she died.

Pyotr Andreyich kept his word. He informed his son that for the sake of his mother's dying wish and for the sake of the infant Fyodor he was returning to him his blessing and allowing Malanya Sergeyevna to remain with him in his house. She was given two rooms in the attic, and he introduced her to his two most honoured guests, the one-eyed brigadier Skurekhin and his wife. He also gave her two maids and a boy to run her errands. Marfa Timofeyevna said good-bye to her: she could not stand the sight of Glafira and in the course of one day quarrelled with her three times.

It was hard and uncomfortable for the poor woman at first, but later she learned to put up with things and became accustomed to her father-in-law. He also grew used to her and even became fond of her, although he hardly ever spoke to her and such endearments as he offered her were notable for a kind of involuntary deprecation. Malanya Sergeyevna had most of all to put up with from her sister-in-law. While her mother was still alive Glafira had succeeded in gradually taking over the running of the whole house: everyone, beginning with her father, submitted to her authority; a lump of sugar could not be handed out without her permission; she would rather have died than allow her authority to be shared with another mistress – and what a mistress! Her brother's marriage had incensed her even more than it had Pyotr Andreyich: she took it upon herself to teach the upstart a lesson, and from the very start Malanya Sergeyevna became her slave. For how could she stand up against the wilful, arrogant Glafira, she who was so docile, so constantly fearful, afraid and in poor health? A day did not pass without Glafira reminding her of her former position and commending her for not having forgotten. Malanya Sergeyevna would gladly have reconciled herself to these reminders and commendations, no matter how bitter . . . but Fedya was taken away from her, that was what crushed her. On the pretext that she was in no condition to see to his upbringing, she was hardly allowed to see him at all; Glafira undertook to do this; the child passed entirely into her keeping. In her grief Malanya Sergeyevna began to implore Ivan Petrovich in her letters to return as soon as possible; Pyotr Andreyich himself wished to see his son; but all he did was to write back thanking his father for looking after his wife and for sending money and promising to come soon – and he did not come. The year 1812 brought him back finally from abroad. When they met for the first time after the six-year separation, father and son embraced and did not mention a word about their former discord; that was not the time for it: all Russia was up in arms against the enemy, and both felt that there was Russian blood flowing in their veins. Pyotr Andreyich fitted out a whole regiment of militia at his own expense. But the war ended and the danger passed; Ivan Petrovich again grew bored, once again felt drawn to distant parts, to the world with which he had grown familiar and where he felt himself at home. Malanya Sergeyevna could not prevent him; she meant too little to him. Even her hopes had not materialized: her husband also found that it was much more suitable for Glafira to take charge of Fedya's upbringing. Ivan Petrovich's poor wife did not survive this blow and their second parting: uncomplainingly, in a matter of a few days, her life was snuffed out. Throughout her whole life she had never known how to gainsay anything, and she did not struggle with her illness. She was already unable to speak, already the shadows of the grave were lying across her face, but her features expressed as ever a patient bewilderment and a perpetual meek resignation; with the same dumb submissiveness she looked at Glafira, and as Anna Pavlovna on her deathbed had kissed Pyotr Andreyich's hand so she pressed her lips to Glafira's hand, entrusting to her, Glafira, her one and only son. So ended the earthly existence of this quiet and kindly soul who had been torn, for God knows what reason, from her native soil and cast aside at once like an uprooted sapling with its roots in the sun; it had withered and gone without trace, this poor soul, and no one grieved for it. Malanya Sergeyevna's passing was regretted by her servants and by Pyotr Andreyich. The old man missed her silent presence. 'Forgive me – farewell, my docile one!' he whispered, making a final obeisance to her, in the church. He wept as he threw a handful of earth into her grave.

He had not long to outlive her, not more than five years. In the winter of 1819 he died quietly in Moscow, where he had gone with Glafira and his grandson, and requested in his will that he be buried alongside Anna Pavlovna and 'Malasha'. Ivan Petrovich was then in Paris, enjoying himself; he had gone into retirement soon after 1815. When he learned of the death of his father, he decided to return to Russia. It was essential to give some thought to the management of the estate and what is more, according to a letter from Glafira, Fedya was already twelve and the time had come to be seriously concerned about his education.

X

IVAN PETROVICH returned to Russia an Anglomaniac. With his hair cut short, the starched frill on his shirt-front, the long pea-green frock-coat with its multitude of collars, a sour expression on his face, something both brusque and negligent in his manner, the pronunciation of words through his teeth, a sudden wooden laugh, lack of smiles, exclusively political and politico-economic talk, a passion for underdone roast-beef and port wine – everything about him literally reeked of

Great Britain; he seemed to be entirely saturated in its spirit. But – wonders will never cease! – having turned himself into an Anglomaniac, Ivan Petrovich at the same time became a patriot, or at least he called himself a patriot, although he did not know Russia well, did not uphold a single Russian custom and had a strange way of expressing himself in Russian: in ordinary conversation his speech, cumbersome and flaccid, was profusely dotted with Gallicisms; but as soon as a conversation turned on important matters, there at once appeared on Ivan Petrovich's lips expressions such as: 'occasion new lessons in self-endeavour', 'that does not accord, egad, with the very nature of the circumstances' and so on. Ivan Petrovich brought with him several draft plans which were concerned with the arrangement and improvement of the estate; he was very dissatisfied with everything he saw – the absence of system particularly aroused his bitter animosity. Upon seeing his sister his very first words to her were a declaration that he intended to introduce radical changes and that from henceforth in his house everything would be run on a new system. Glafira Petrovna made no answer to Ivan Petrovich apart from gritting her teeth and mentally asking herself: 'I wonder where I'll fit into all this?' However, having arrived at the country estate along with her brother and nephew, she was soon consoled. Certain changes were certainly made in the house: the spongers and parasites underwent immediate expulsion; among those who suffered were two old women, one blind, the other afflicted by paralysis, and a decrepit major of Ochakov days who, by virtue of his truly remarkable greediness, had been fed exclusively on black bread and lentils. An order was also issued not to receive former guests: they were all superseded by a distant neighbour, some fair-haired scrofulous baron, who was a very well-educated and very stupid fellow. New furniture appeared from Moscow; spittoons, hand-bells for the table and wash-hand-stands were introduced; lunch was served in a new way; foreign wines ousted vodka and native spirits; the servants had new liveries made for them; the family crest had the words *In recto virtus* ... added to it. In essence Glafira's authority was in no way reduced: the responsibility for all outgoings and purchases still rested with her; the valet from Alsace, who had been brought from abroad, attempted to cross swords with her – and lost his post despite the fact that the master of the house was his patron. So far as the economics and management of the estate were concerned (Glafira Petrovna went into all these matters), despite Ivan Petrovich's repeatedly expressed intention to breathe new life into this chaos, everything remained as before, save that quit-rent payments were increased here and there and the compulsory work on the master's land was made more onerous, and the peasants were forbidden to approach Ivan Petrovich directly. The patriot had a very low opinion of his fellow citizens. Ivan Petrovich's system was applied in full force only to Fedya; his education really underwent 'radical transformation': his father concerned himself with it to the exclusion of all else.

XI

UNTIL Ivan Petrovich's return from abroad Fedya, as has already been said, was in the hands of Glafira Petrovna. He was not yet eight years old when his mother died; he saw her infrequently and he loved her passionately: his recollection of her calm white face, her despondent eyes and timorous displays of fondness remained imprinted in his heart forever; but he had a vague awareness of her position in the house; he sensed that between him and her there existed a barrier which she neither dared to, nor could, break down. He avoided his father, and Ivan Petrovich for his part never showed him any affection; his grandfather occasionally stroked his head and allowed him to kiss his hand, but used to call him surly and considered him a fool. After Malanya Sergeyevna's death his aunt finally got him into her hands. Fedya was frightened of her, frightened of her penetrating bright eyes and her sharp voice; he dared not open his mouth in her presence; if he so much as began to stir on his chair, she would hiss out: 'Where are you off to? Sit still.' On Sundays after dinner he was allowed to play, that is to say he was given a mysterious stout book, the work of a certain Maximovich-Ambodik, entitled *Symbols and Emblems*[1]. This book contained about a thousand partly very enigmatic drawings, with as many equally enigmatic descriptions in five languages. Cupid, with a naked, chubby body, played a great part in these drawings. To one of them, with the title 'The Saffron Flower and the Rainbow', was given the explanation: 'The Effect of Ye Flower is Greater'; opposite another depicting 'A Heron flying with a Violet in its Beak' stood the inscription: 'To Thee All Things Are Known'. 'Cupid and a Bear licking her Young One' signified: 'Little by Little'. Fedya used to study these drawings; they were all known to him down to the smallest details; some, always the same ones, made him stop to think and aroused his imagination; he knew no other pastimes. When the time came for him to be taught languages and music, Glafira Petrovna engaged for a pittance an elderly maiden lady, a Swede with darting eyes, who could just manage to speak French and German and played the piano so-so, but was above all excellent at pickling cucumbers. In the company of this instructress, his aunt and an old maid-servant, Vasilyevna, Fedya spent four whole years. There were times when he used to sit in a corner with his *Emblems* – and go on sitting there for hours at a time; the low-ceilinged room had a smell of geraniums, a single tallow candle burned faintly, a cricket sang monotonously, literally as if it were bored, a little clock ticked briskly on the wall, a mouse furtively scratched and gnawed behind the wallpaper, and the three old women, like the Parcae, would rapidly and soundlessly ply their needles, and the shadows from their hands would run up the walls or quiver strangely in the half-light of the room, and strange, similarly half-dark thoughts would swarm in the boy's head. No one would have called Fedya an interesting child: he was fairly pale, but fat and of awkward and ungainly build – a real muzhik, in Glafira Petrovna's words; the pallor would soon have vanished from his face if he had been sent out in the open air more often. He did his lessons well enough, although he was frequently lazy; he never cried; yet at times he would be possessed by a savage obstinacy and then no one could do anything with him. Fedya loved none of those around him. . . . Woe to the heart that has not loved in youth!

This is how Ivan Petrovich found him and, wasting no time, he set about applying his system to him. 'Above all I want to make a man of him, *un homme*,' he told Glafira Petrovna, 'and not only a man, but a Spartan.' Ivan Petrovich began putting his intention into effect by dressing his son in a Scottish outfit: the twelve-year-old lad began to go about with bare legs and a cock's feather in his bonnet; the Swedish lady was replaced by a young Swiss who had studied gymnastics to perfection; music, as an occupation unworthy of a man, was banished altogether; the natural sciences, international law, mathematics, carpentry, as Jean-Jacques Rousseau had advised, and heraldry for the cultivation of chivalrous feelings – these were what the 'man-to-be' had to concern himself with; he was woken at four o'clock in the morning, at once doused with cold water and made to run round a high pole on a string; he ate one meal a day consisting of one dish, rode on horseback and shot from a cross-bow; at every suitable opportunity he would give himself lessons in strength of will, on the example of his parent, and each evening he would enter in a special book an account of the past day and his impressions; while Ivan Petrovich, for his part, would write him edifying dithyrambs in French in which he called him *mon fils* and addressed him as *vous*. Fedya addressed his father in Russian with the familiar 'thou', but never dared to sit down in his presence. The 'system' bemused the boy, sowed confusion in his head and cramped his mind; but, despite this, the new way of life had a beneficial effect on his health: at first he caught a fever, but he quickly recovered and became a sturdy youngster. His father was proud of him and described him in his strange manner of speaking as 'a son of nature, all my own work'. When Fedya was sixteen, Ivan Petrovich considered it his duty, in good time, to instil in him a contempt for the female sex – and the young Spartan, timid at heart, with the first down on his cheeks, full of sap, strength and new blood, made an attempt to appear indifferent, cold and rude.

Meanwhile, time was relentlessly passing. Ivan Petrovich was used to spending a great part of each year in Lavriki (such was the name of his main estate), but in the winters he went off alone to Moscow, put up in an inn, assiduously visited his club, dilated oratorically on his plans in drawing-rooms and behaved more than ever like an Anglomaniac and querulous elder statesman. Then came the year 1825[2] and brought much grief with it. Close acquaintances and friends of Ivan Petrovich underwent painful ordeals. Ivan Petrovich hurriedly withdrew to the country and locked himself in his house. Another year passed and Ivan Petrovich suddenly went into a decline, grew weak and poorly; his health played traitor to him. The freethinker began to go to church and order prayers to be said; the European began taking steam baths, dining at two o'clock, going to bed at nine and falling asleep to the old steward's chatter; the elder statesman burned all his plans and correspondence, trembled before the governor and fawned before the district police officer; the man of tempered will whimpered and groaned when a boil erupted on his skin or he was served a bowl of cold soup. Glafira Petrovna once again took charge of everything in the house; once again stewards, bailiffs and simple peasants began to frequent the back door to see 'the browbeating old bitch', as the house-serfs called her. The change in Ivan Petrovich had a powerful effect on his son; he was already nineteen and beginning to think for himself and break free of the oppressive authority wielded by his father's hand. He had previously noticed the discrepancy between his father's words and his deeds, between his broad liberal theories and crusty, petty despotism; but he had not expected such a sharp about-turn. The chronic egoist now revealed himself in his true colours. The young Lavretsky was about to go off to Moscow to prepare for the university when a new and unexpected misfortune broke over Ivan Petrovich's head: he went blind, hopelessly blind, in the course of a single day.

Mistrusting the expertise of Russian doctors, he began to petition to be allowed to go abroad. He was refused. Then he took his son with him and for three whole years wandered about Russia from one doctor to another, ceaselessly travelling from town to town and driving the doctors, his son and his servants to despair through his cowardice and impatience. He was an utterly wet rag, like a snivelling and capricious child, when he returned to Lavriki. Bitter, miserable days ensued, in which everyone had to put up with a great deal from him. Ivan Petrovich ceased his tantrums only at mealtimes; he had never eaten so greedily or so much; the rest of the time he gave no peace to himself or others. He prayed, fretted at his fate, scolded himself, scolded his politics and his system, blasphemed against all the things of which he had previously boasted and been proud, against everything which he had once extolled as an example to his son; he repeatedly asserted that he had no faith, and repeatedly started praying again; he could not stand being left alone for an instant and insisted that his servants should sit constantly beside his armchair, both day and night, and entertain him with stories which he would interrupt from time to time by exclaiming: 'You're telling a pack of lies! What bloody nonsense!'

Glafira Petrovna found it especially unbearable; he simply could not get on without her, and to the end she executed all the sick man's whims, although there were times when she could not bring herself to answer him at once for fear that her voice might betray the wrath which choked her. In this way he scraped along for another two years and died early one May, out on the balcony, in the sun. 'Glashka, Glashka! My beef-tea, my beef-tea, you old hag . . .' he mumbled with his stiffening tongue and, without finishing the final word, fell silent forever. Glafira Petrovna, who had only just taken the cup of beef-tea from the steward's hands, stopped, looked into her brother's face, slowly, with a broad flourish, made the sign of the cross and withdrew in silence; and his son, who was also present, said nothing, but leaned on the handrail of the balcony and gazed long and hard into the garden that was all perfumed and green and glistening in the rays of a golden springtime sun. He was twenty-three years old; how terribly, how insensibly swift had been the passing of those twenty-three years! . . . Life was opening its arms before him.

XII

HAVING buried his father and entrusted the running of the estate and supervision of the bailiffs to the immutable Glafira Petrovna, the young Lavretsky set off for Moscow, whither he was drawn by an obscure but strong feeling. He was conscious of deficiencies in his education and vowed to make good these deficiencies as far as possible. In the last five years he had read much and seen this and that; many ideas were fermenting in his brain; any professor would have envied him some of the things he knew, but at the same time he was ignorant of many things which every schoolboy had known for years. Lavretsky was conscious that he was not free; he secretly felt himself to be a curiosity. The Anglomaniac had played an unkind joke on his son; the capricious education brought forth its fruit. For many long years he had unaccountably humbled himself before his father and when he finally saw through him the deed was already done, the habits of his education had taken root. He had no idea how to get on with people; at twenty-three years of age, with an uncontrollable thirst for love welling up in his shame-stricken heart, he could still not bring himself to look a woman in the eyes. With his mind, so lucid and healthy, if a little pedestrian, with his tendency to stubbornness, introspection and indolence, he should have been cast into the whirlpool of life at an early age, but instead he had been kept in artificial isolation. . . . And yet now that the enchanted ring was broken he continued to stand in the same place, locked up and compressed within himself. At his age it was laughable to put on a student's uniform, but he was not frightened of sniggers: his Spartan education at least had the merit of having bred in him an indifference to others' opinions – and, without batting an eyelid, he dressed up in a student's uniform. He entered the department of mathematics and physics. Healthy, ruddy-cheeked, with an already copious beard, taciturn in his ways, he produced a strange impression on his fellow-students, and they did not even suspect that in this stern-faced grown man, who arrived punctually at lectures in a broad country-style sledge drawn by a pair of horses, there lurked scarcely more than a child. He seemed to them to be some sort of screwball pedant; they had no need of him, sought nothing from him and he avoided them. During the course of his first two years at university he made friends with only one student, from whom he took Latin lessons. This student, by name Mikhale-vich, endowed with enthusiasm and a talent for writing verses, grew sincerely fond of Lavretsky and quite by accident became guilty of causing an important change in his life.

On one occasion in the theatre (Mochalov[1] was then at the height of his fame and Lavretsky did not miss a single one of his appearances) he caught sight of a girl in a box in the dress circle – and although no woman could pass by his outwardly sombre figure without causing his heart to quiver, it had never begun beating as hard as it did now. Leaning on the velvet of the box's balustrade, the girl was utterly still; a sensitive, youthful vivacity played in every feature of her dark, round, pleasant face; a tastefully refined mind was reflected in the beautiful eyes gazing softly and attentively from beneath delicate brows, in the swift smiles of her expressive lips, in the very pose of her head and arms and neck; she was delightfully dressed. Next to her there sat a sallow, wrinkled woman of about forty-five in a low-cut dress and black toque, with a toothless smile on her intently preoccupied and empty face, while in the depths of the box could be seen an elderly man in a broad frock-coat and high cravat, with an expression of mindless stateliness and a kind of fawning suspiciousness in his tiny eyes, with dyed moustache and side-whiskers, massive but unremarkable temples and deeply creased cheeks, who gave every indication of being a retired general. Lavretsky could not take his eyes off the stunning girl. Suddenly the door of the box opened and Mikhalevich entered. The appearance of this man, almost his sole acquaintance in the whole of Moscow, in the company of the one girl who had absorbed all his attention, struck Lavretsky as ominous and strange. As he continued to watch the box he noticed that everyone in it treated Mikhalevich as an old friend. The performance on the stage ceased to concern Lavretsky; Mochalov himself, although he was that evening 'on his best form', did not make his usual impression on him. In one very moving scene Lavretsky glanced involuntarily at his beauty: she was leaning right forward and her cheeks glowed with excitement; under the influence of his steady gaze her eyes, directed though they were at the stage, slowly turned and rested on him. . . . All night he could not get them out of his thoughts. The artificially constructed dam had finally been breached; he throbbed and burned with love, and the next day set off to find Mikhalevich. From him he learned that the beauty was called Varvara Pavlovna Korobyn, that the elderly man and woman sitting with her in the box were her father and mother and that he, Mikhalevich, had got to know them a year ago during the time he had spent 'tutoring' at Count N's house near Moscow. The enthusiastic Mikhalevich expressed himself in terms of the greatest praise about Varvara Pavlovna. 'My dear fellow, that,' he exclaimed with the characteristically impetuous lilt in his voice, 'that girl's a – an astonishing, a – a creature of genius, an artiste in the true sense of the word and kindness itself as well.' Noting from Lavretsky's persistent questions the kind of impression Varvara Pavlovna had made on him, he offered to introduce him to her, adding that he was treated like one of them at their house, that the general was not at all arrogant and the mother was so silly that about all she didn't do was suck eggs. Lavretsky went red, mumbled something unintelligible and fled. For five whole days he struggled with his shyness; on the sixth the young Spartan dressed himself up in a new uniform and placed himself at Mikhalevich's disposal, who, being a friend of the family, did no more than comb his hair – and both of them set off for the Korobyns'.

XIII

VARVARA PAVLOVNA'S father, Pavel Petrovich Korobyn, a retired major-general, had spent his entire lifetime in St Petersburg on government service, had passed in his youth for a skilful dancer and parade-ground soldier, had served, through lack of means, as adjutant to two or three indifferent generals, had married the daughter of one of them, taking along with her a dowry of about twenty-five thousand, and had attained great finesse in the art of parade-ground drills and inspections; he had plodded on and on in his career and finally, after about twenty odd years, he attained the rank of general and was given a regiment. At this point he should have taken things easy and unhurriedly feathered his nest; he had reckoned on doing this, but he conducted his affairs rather incautiously; he thought up a new means of putting official funds to good use – the means proved excellent, save that he was mean with the money at the wrong moment and some-one informed against him; the whole thing emerged as a more than unpleasant, in fact a nasty story. The general somehow or other twisted his way out of it, but his career had blown up in his face: he was advised to retire. For a couple of years he hung about in St Petersburg hoping that a cosy civilian job would pop up for him, but nothing popped up for him, and his daughter left school, his expenses increased with every day that passed. . . . Reluctantly he decided to move to Mos-cow where things were cheaper, rented in Staro-Konyushenny Street a tiny, low-fronted house with a huge coat of arms fixed to the roof and set himself up as a retired Moscow general with an annual expenditure of 2,750 roubles. Moscow is a hospitable city, glad to welcome all Toms, Dicks and Harries, and generals into the bargain; the stolid, but not unsoldierly figure of Pavel Petrovich soon began to appear in the best Moscow drawing-rooms. The bare nape of his neck, with its wisps of dyed hair and greasy ribbon of the Order of St Anne worn over a cravat the colour of a raven's wing, became well known to all the blasé and pale-faced youths who used to wander morosely among the card tables during the dances. Pavel Petrovich knew how to set himself up in society; he spoke little, but nasally, as was the old-style custom – not, of course, with people of higher rank; he played a cautious game of cards, ate moderately at home, but when a guest he ate enough for six. Of his wife there was almost nothing to be said; she was called Calliope Karlovna; a perpetual tear-drop hung in her left eye, on account of which Calliope Karlovna (besides, she was of German extraction) considered herself to be a highly sensitive woman; she was in a perpetual state of nerves, looked as if she never ate enough and wore narrow velvet dresses, toques and discoloured hollow bracelets. The only daughter of Pavel Petrovich and Calliope Karlovna, Varvara Pavlovna, had only just reached seventeen when she left school, where she was considered, if not the most beautiful, then certainly the cleverest and the best musician, and where she had received the prize of the Empress's monogram as an outstanding pupil; she was not yet nineteen when Lavretsky saw her for the first time.

XIV

THE Spartan's legs were collapsing under him when Mikhalevich led him into the rather poorly furnished drawing-room of the Korobyns and introduced him. But the feeling of shyness which had possessed him earlier soon vanished: in the general the inborn kind-heartedness characteristic of all Russians was overlaid by that particular species of affability which is common to all people with a slightly tarnished reputation; his wife very soon retired into the background; so far as Varvara Pavlovna was concerned, she was so calm and endearingly self-assured that anyone would at once feel at home in her presence; moreover, her whole enchanting figure, her smiling eyes, her innocently sloping shoulders and pale-pink arms, her light-footed and, at the same time, listless walk, the very sound of her voice, so languid and sweet-toned – all rumoured of an enticing loveliness, as indefinable as a delicate perfume, of a soft, and as yet diffident, voluptuousness, of something that it is not easy to convey in words but which touched the heart and roused the feelings – and not, of course, feelings of shyness. Lavretsky turned the conversation to the theatre and the previous day's performance; she at once began talking about Mochalov and did not confine herself to exclamations and sighs, but made several sound and femininely perceptive remarks about his acting. Mikhalevich raised the subject of music; without fuss, she sat down at the piano and gave careful renditions of several Chopin mazurkas which were just then coming into fashion. The time for dinner arrived; Lavretsky wished to leave, but they restrained him; at table the general regaled him with a good Lafitte, for which the general's footman had been sent galloping off to Depré's in a cab. Late in the evening Lavretsky returned home and sat for a long while without undressing, his hand over his eyes, in an ecstasy of wonder. It seemed to him that he had only now understood why life was worth living; all his presuppositions and intentions, all that stuff and nonsense, vanished in a flash; his entire soul blended into one feeling, into one desire – a desire for happiness, for possession, for love, a woman's sweet love. From that day on he began to make frequent visits to the Korobyns'. Six months later he declared himself to Varvara Pavlovna and offered her his hand. His offer was accepted; the general had long ago, almost on the eve of Lavretsky's first visit, inquired of Mikhalevich the number of Lavretsky's serfs; and Varvara Pavlovna, moreover, who throughout the young man's courtship and even at the very moment he had declared himself to her maintained her customary serenity and lucidity of soul – even Varvara Pavlovna knew full well that her fiancé was rich; while Calliope Karlovna thought: *Meine Tochter macht eine schöne Partie*, and bought herself a new toque.

XV

So, his offer was accepted, but on certain conditions. Firstly' Lavretsky had to leave the university at once: whoever thought of marrying a student and – what a strange idea! – a landowner, who was rich and yet at twenty-six years of age was taking lessons like a schoolboy? Secondly, Varvara Pavlovna took upon herself the task of ordering and buying her dowry and even of choosing the bridegroom's gifts. She had much practical sense, much taste, a great fondness for comfort and much ability in obtaining such comfort for herself.

This ability especially amazed Lavretsky when, immediately after the wedding, the two of them set off for Lavriki in the comfortable carriage which she had bought. How well everything about him had been thought out, anticipated and cared for by Varvara Pavlovna! What charming travelling cases, what exquisite toilet boxes and coffee pots appeared in various snug corners, and how nicely Varvara Pavlovna herself made the coffee each morning! Besides, Lavretsky was in no mood to observe things carefully: he was in a state of bliss, drunk with happiness, and he surrendered himself to this emotion like a child. . . . Indeed he was as innocent as a child, was this young Alcides. The whole being of his young wife had not rumoured of delight for nothing; it was not for nothing that she had given him sensual promise of the secret luxury of hitherto unknown pleasures; she kept back for him more than she had promised. Arriving at Lavriki in the utmost heat of summer, she found the house dirty and dark, the servants ridiculous and antiquated, but she did not consider it necessary even so much as to hint of this to her husband. If it had been part of her plans to stay in Lavriki, she would have altered everything there, beginning, of course, with the house; but the idea of staying in this steppe backwater had never for a moment entered her head; she lived in the house as in a tent, meekly enduring all the inconveniences and happily making fun of them. Marfa Timofeyevna came to pay a call on her former charge; Varvara Pavlovna took a strong liking to her, but Marfa Timofeyevna did not reciprocate. The new mistress also did not get on well with Glafira Petrovna; she would have left her in peace if old man Korobyn had not wanted to get his hands on his son-in-law's affairs: the management of the estate of such a close relative, he made a point of saying, was nothing to be ashamed of, even for a general. It must be supposed that Pavel Petrovich would not have considered it beneath his dignity to manage the estate of someone entirely unknown to him. Varvara Pavlovna conducted her attack very artfully; without giving anything away, to all appearances wholly preoccupied with the bliss of her honeymoon, the quiet country life, music and reading, she gradually brought Glafira to such a pitch that, one morning, she rushed into Lavretsky's study like a mad thing and, flinging a bunch of keys on the table, announced that she hadn't the strength left to manage things any longer and didn't want to stay in the area. Suitably primed for such an eventuality, Lavretsky at once agreed to her going. Glafira Petrovna had not expected this. 'Good,' she said, and her eyes darkened, 'I see that I'm superfluous here! I know who's driving me out of here, out of my very own native home. Just you remember what I've got to say, nephew: you'll never make a home for yourself anywhere, you'll be a wanderer all your born days. That's my last word to you.' That very same day she retired to her little village, and in a week's time General Korobyn arrived and, with a pleasant melancholy in both his eyes and movements, took the management of the whole estate into his hands.

In September Varvara Pavlovna carried her husband off to St Petersburg. She spent two winters in St Petersburg (in the summer they removed to Tsarskoye Selo) in a beautiful, bright, elegantly furnished apartment; they made many acquaintances in the middle, and even higher, circles of society, went out many times and received guests by giving the most delightful musical evenings and dances. Varvara Pavlovna attracted guests like moths to a flame. Fyodor Ivanych was not quite so fond of such a disorderly life. His wife advised him to enter government service; but, in deference to his father's memory as well as to his own ideas, he had no desire to enter the service, yet in deference to Varvara Pavlovna he remained in St Petersburg. Besides, he soon found that no one prevented him from being alone, that it was not for nothing he had the quietest and most comfortable study in St Petersburg, that a solicitous wife was even ready to help him to be by himself – and from that moment on everything went beautifully. He once again devoted himself to his own – in his opinion as yet unfinished – education, again started reading, and even began studying the English language. It was a strange sight to see his powerful, broad-shouldered figure endlessly bent over his desk and his full, hairy, ruddy face half-hidden by the pages of a dictionary or notebook. He would spend each morning over his work, dine superbly (Varvara Pavlovna was a housekeeper without parallel), and in the evenings he would enter the charmed, fragrant, brilliant world wholly populated by young and joyous faces – and the pivot of this world was that very same zealous hostess, his wife. She delighted him with the birth of a son, but the poor boy did not live long; he died in the spring, and in the summer, on doctor's advice, Lavretsky took his wife abroad to a watering-place. She needed to be distracted after such a misfortune, and the state of her health demanded a warm climate. The summer and autumn they spent in Germany and Switzerland, and for the winter, as was to be expected, they went to Paris. In Paris, Varvara Pavlovna bloomed like a rose and succeeded, just as swiftly and skilfully as she had done in St Petersburg, in making a little nest for herself. She found an exceptionally pretty apartment in one of the quiet but fashionable streets of Paris, ran up a nightshirt for her husband the like of which he had never seen before; she engaged a chic maid, a superb cook and a nimble footman, and obtained an exquisite little carriage and a delightful piano. A week had not gone by before she was making her way across the street wearing a shawl, opening an umbrella or pulling on gloves no less expertly than the most pure-blooded native of Paris. And she had quickly acquired a circle of acquaintances. At first only Russians came to visit, but later came Frenchmen, extremely charming and courteous bachelors, with beautiful manners and euphonious names; all of them talked very fast and a great deal, bowed with easy familiarity and very pleasantly puckered their eyes; white teeth flashed behind their rosy lips – and how they could smile! Each of them brought his friends, and *la belle madame de Lavretzki* soon became famous from the Chaussée d'Antin to the Rue de Lille. At that time (all this occurred in 1836) the tribe of gossip-writers and reporters who now swarm everywhere like ants dug out of their heap had not yet begun to flourish; but even then there appeared in Varvara Pavlovna's salon a certain M. Jules, a man of unprepossessing appearance with a scandalous reputation, brazen and despicable, like all duellists and dead-beats. This M. Jules was very repugnant to Varvara Pavlovna, but she received him because he contributed material to several newspapers and invariably mentioned her, calling her either *Mme de L. . .tzki* or *Mme de ****, cette grande dame russe si distinguée, qui demeure rue de P. . .* and telling the whole world, or rather a few hundred subscribers who were not in the least interested in *Mme de L. . .tzki*, how agreeable and charming this lady was, a real Frenchwoman in her intelligence (*une vraie française par l'esprit*) – Frenchmen can give no higher praise – what an exceptional musician she was and how astonishingly well she waltzed (Varvara Pavlovna really could waltz so as to draw all hearts after the hems of her flying, airy skirts) . . . in a word, spread news of her throughout the world – and that, say what you will, is surely not unpleasant. At that time Mademoiselle Mars[1] had retired from the stage, Mademoiselle Rachel had not yet appeared; nevertheless, Varvara Pavlovna assiduously visited the theatre. She went into raptures over Italian music and laughed at the slapstick of Odry, yawned politely at the Comédie Française and wept at the acting of Madame Dorval in some ultra-romantic melodrama; but, most of all, Liszt himself played for her twice, and he was so nice, so simple – delightful! It was in such pleasant sensations that the winter passed, towards the end of which Varvara Pavlovna was even presented at court. Fyodor Ivanych, for his part, was not bored, although life at times weighed heavy on his shoulders

– weighed heavy because it was empty. He read the newspapers, attended lectures at the Sorbonne and the Collège de France, followed the debates in the Assembly and embarked upon a translation of a well-known academic work about irrigation. 'I am not wasting time,' he thought. 'All this is useful. But before next winter it is imperative I return to Russia and get down to work.' It is difficult to say whether he had a clear idea what this work actually consisted of, and God knows whether he would have managed to return to Russia by the winter; in the meantime he was off to Baden-Baden with his wife. . . . Then an unexpected occurrence destroyed all his plans.

XVI

ONE day, having entered Varvara Pavlovna's room in her absence, Lavretsky saw on the floor a small, carefully folded piece of paper. He automatically picked it up, automatically opened it and read the following, written in French:

Darling angel Betsy! (I cannot bring myself to call you Barbe or Varvara). I vainly waited for you on the corner of the boulevard; come tomorrow to our little apartment at half-past one. Your kind fat husband [*ton gros bonhomme de mari*] is usually burrowing around in his books at that time; we'll have another go at that song by your poet Pushkin[1] [*de votre poète Pouskine*] which you taught me: 'Old husband, threatening husband!' – A thousand kisses for your hands and feet. In anticipation.

                                                                          Ernest

Lavretsky did not immediately understand what he had read; he read it a second time – and his head began to spin, the floor began moving under his feet like the deck of a ship in a swell. He started crying out and sighing and weeping all at the same moment.

He went crazy. He had trusted his wife so blindly; the possibility of deceit and betrayal had never occurred to him.

This Ernest, this lover of his wife, was a fair-haired, good-looking boy of about twenty-three, with a turned-up nose and a delicate little moustache, almost the least noteworthy of all her acquaintances. Several minutes passed, then half an hour; Lavretsky remained standing there, squeezing the fateful note in his hand and staring senselessly at the floor; through some kind of dark whirlwind a host of pale faces flashed before him; his heart died agonizingly within him; he seemed to be falling and falling and falling, and there was no end to it. The familiar light rustle of a silk dress snapped him out of his trance; Varvara Pavlovna, in hat and shawl, was returning hurriedly from a walk. Lavretsky began trembling all over and flung himself out of the room; he felt that at that instant he was in a condition to tear her apart, beat her half to death, in peasant fashion strangle her with his own hands. The astounded Varvara Pavlovna wanted to stop him; he could only whisper: 'Betsy' – and dashed out of the house.

Lavretsky took a cab and ordered to be taken out of town. The remainder of the day and the whole night until morning he wandered about, endlessly stopping and flinging wide his arms: he was either out of his mind, or things came to seem to him somehow laughable, somehow even gay. By the morning he was thoroughly chilled and called at a miserable inn on the city's outskirts, asked for a room and sat down on a chair by the window. A compulsive yawning took possession of him. He could scarcely keep on his feet, his body was exhausted, yet he could not even feel the tiredness, though the tiredness took its toll: he went on sitting there, staring and understanding nothing; he couldn't understand what had happened to him, why he was there alone, with his limbs all numb, a bitter taste in his mouth, a dead weight on his heart, in an empty unfamiliar room; he couldn't understand what had made her, Varya, give herself to this Frenchman and how, knowing herself to be unfaithful, she could maintain her former composure, her former tenderness and trustfulness

73

towards him. 'I don't understand a thing,' his parched lips whispered. 'Who'll guarantee to me now that in St Petersburg . . .' And he could not bring himself to finish the question and yawned again, his whole body shuddering and shaking. Bright and dark memories tore with equal anguish at his heart; suddenly he recalled that a few days ago she had sat down along with him and Ernest at the piano and had sung: 'Old husband, threatening husband!' He recalled the expression on her face, the strange brilliance in her eyes and the colour in her cheeks – and he rose from the chair, wanting to go and say to them: 'You're not going to get away with making fun of me! My great-grandad used to hang his peasants up by the ribs, and my grandad was himself a peasant' – and then kill them both. Then it suddenly seemed to him that everything happening to him was a dream, and not even a dream, but just some sort of nonsense that he could get rid of by shaking himself or turning his head. . . . He turned his head and, as a hawk drives its talons into its captive prey, so the pangs of regret cut deeper and deeper into his heart. To crown it all, Lavretsky was hoping in a few months to be a father. . . . The past, the future, the whole of his life was poisoned. He returned finally to Paris, stopped in an hotel and sent Varvara Pavlovna M. Ernest's note together with the following letter:

The affixed piece of paper will explain everything to you. Incidentally, I will tell you that I found it quite unlike you – you, who are always so careful – to be dropping such important papers. [This phrase the wretched Lavretsky had pondered and pored over for several hours.] I cannot see you any more; I presume that you also have no need to see me. I assign you 15,000 francs a year; I cannot give more. Send your address to the estate office. Do what you like, live wherever you please. I wish you happiness. There is no need for an answer.

Lavretsky wrote to his wife that there was no need for an answer . . . but he waited, thirsted for an answer, for an explanation of this incomprehensible, inexplicable matter. That very same day Varvara Pavlovna sent him a long letter in French. It was the final blow; his last doubts vanished – and he felt ashamed that he had still entertained doubts. Varvara Pavlovna did not attempt to justify herself; she wished only to see him and begged him not to condemn her irrevocably. The letter was cold and strained, although in places there were traces of tears. Lavretsky gave a bitter smile and ordered the messenger to say that everything was quite all right. Three days later he had left Paris, though he travelled not to Russia but to Italy. He did not know precisely why he chose Italy; it didn't matter to him in essence where he went – so long as it wasn't home. He sent instructions to his bailiff about his wife's allowance, simultaneously ordering him immediately to take over the affairs of the estate from General Korobyn, without waiting for the accounts to be made up, and to arrange for His Excellency's departure from Lavriki; he painted a lively picture for himself of the confusion and majestic bewilderment of the expelled general and, despite all his grief, experienced a certain malicious satisfaction. Then he wrote to Glafira Petrovna asking her to return to Lavriki and sent off a power of attorney in her name; Glafira Petrovna did not return to Lavriki and herself had printed in the newspapers a statement about the annulment of the power of attorney, which was completely unnecessary. Taking refuge in a small Italian town, Lavretsky was unable to refrain for a long time from following the doings of his wife. From the papers he learned that she had left Paris, as arranged, for Baden-Baden; her name soon appeared in a little notice signed by the same M. Jules. Through the usual playfulness of this notice emerged a kind of amicable condolence; intense repugnance filled Fyodor Ivanych's soul when he read it. Later he learned that a daughter had been born; in a couple of months he received news from his bailiff that Varvara Pavlovna had asked for the first third of her allowance. Later ever-worsening rumours became current;

finally all the journals noised about a tragi-comic story in which his wife played an unenviable role. Everything was over: Varvara Pavlovna had become a 'notoriety'.

Lavretsky stopped following his wife's doings, but he could not come to terms so quickly with himself. Sometimes such nostalgia for his wife possessed him that it seemed he would give up everything, even perhaps . . . even perhaps would forgive her, if only to hear once again her caressing voice, to feel once again her hand in his. Time, however, did not pass in vain. He was not born for suffering; his healthy nature exerted its rights. Much became clear to him; the very blow that had stunned him seemed no longer unforeseen to him; he understood his wife – you only understand someone close to you fully when you've parted from that person. He could again occupy himself and work, although not with anything like the former zeal: a scepticism, nurtured by experience of life and by his education, had finally taken root in his soul. He became quite indifferent to everything. About four years passed and he felt himself strong enough to return to his native land and meet again his own people. Stopping neither in St Petersburg nor in Moscow, he arrived in the town of O . . . where we parted from him and where we now ask the benevolent reader to return with us.

XVII

The next morning, after the day previously described by us, at about ten o'clock, Lavretsky was ascending the steps to the porch of the Kalitin house. Liza met him as she came out with hat and gloves.

'Where are you off to?' he asked her.

'To Mass. Today is Sunday.'

'Do you really go to Mass?'

Liza looked at him in silence, astonished.

'Forgive me, please,' said Lavretsky, 'I . . . I didn't mean

76

that. I came to say good-bye to you because I'm leaving for the country in an hour.'

'Surely it's not far away, is it?' asked Liza.

'Fifteen odd miles.'

Lenochka appeared in the doorway in the company of a servant.

'Take care you don't forget us,' said Liza and descended the steps from the porch.

'And don't you forget me. Listen,' he added, 'since you're going to church, say a prayer for me, too.'

Liza stopped and turned to him.

'Certainly,' she said, looking him straight in the face, 'I'll say a prayer for you, too. Come on, Lenochka.'

In the drawing-room Lavretsky found Marya Dmitrievna all by herself. She smelt of eau-de-cologne and mint. She explained that she had a headache and had spent a restless night. She received him with her customary languid amiability and by degrees entered into conversation.

'Isn't it true', she asked him, 'that Vladimir Nikolaich is such a pleasant young man?'

'Who is this Vladimir Nikolaich?'

'Panshin, of course, the one who was here yesterday. He was awfully taken by you. I'll tell you in confidence, *mon cher cousin*, that he is simply out of his mind about my Liza. And what's wrong with that? He's of good family, excellent at his work, clever, with a post at court, you know, and if it's God's will . . . I, for my part, as a mother, will be very glad. It's a big responsibility, of course; of course, it's upon the parents that the children's happiness depends, and it should be said too that, whether for better or for worse, I've had to do everything, I've been the only one – bringing the children up and teaching them, I've had to do it all. . . . I've only this minute been writing to Mrs Bolyus for a French governess. . . .'

Marya Dmitrievna embarked on a recital of her worries, her endeavours and her maternal feelings. Lavretsky heard her

77

in silence and turned his hat in his hands. His cold heavy gaze embarrassed the loquacious lady.

'And how does Liza strike you?' she asked.

'Lizaveta Mikhaylovna is a very fine girl,' Lavretsky answered, rose, bowed his way out of the room and went off to Marfa Timofeyevna's. Marya Dmitrievna looked after his retreating figure with dissatisfaction and thought: 'What a fat seal the man is, a regular peasant! Now I understand why his wife couldn't remain faithful to him.'

Marfa Timofeyevna sat in her room, surrounded by her retainers. They consisted of five beings who were almost all equally close to her heart: a fat-cropped trained bullfinch, whom she loved because he had forgotten how to whistle and draw water, a small, very frightened and quiet dog named Roska, a bad-tempered tom cat named Sailor, a swarthy fidgety little girl of nine, with enormous eyes and a sharp little nose, who was called Shurochka, and an elderly lady of fifty-five dressed in a white bonnet and a short brown jacket over a dark dress, by name Nastasya Karpovna Ogarkova. Shurochka was an orphan child of lower-middle-class parentage. Marfa Timofeyevna had taken her in out of pity, as she had taken in Roska as well: she had found both the dog and the girl out on the street; both were thin and hungry, both were soaked to the skin by the autumn rain; nobody came after Roska, and Shurochka was even gladly surrendered to Marfa Timofeyevna by her uncle, a drunken shoemaker, who did not have the wherewithal to feed himself and used his last to hit his niece over the head rather than to feed her. With Nastasya Karpovna Marfa Timofeyevna struck up an acquaintance during a visit to a monastery; she had gone up to her in church (Marfa Timofeyevna took a liking to her because, in her own words, she so much enjoyed the taste of her prayers), struck up a conversation with her and invited her back to her room for a cup of tea. From that day on they had become inseparable. Nastasya Karpovna was a woman of the happiest and most modest disposition, a widow and childless, of poor noble extraction; she had a round head of grey hair, soft white hands, a soft face with large kindly features and a rather funny turned-up nose; she worshipped Marfa Timofeyevna, and the latter was very fond of her, although she used to make fun of her soft heart: she had a soft spot for all young people and couldn't stop herself from blushing like a girl at the most innocent of jokes. Her entire modest capital consisted of 1,200 roubles in notes; she lived at Marfa Timofeyevna's expense, but on an equal footing with her; Marfa Timofeyevna would not stand for any kind of subservience.

'Ah! Fedya!' she began as soon as she saw him. 'Yesterday evening you didn't see my family – take a look at them now. We're all gathered here for tea; this is our second, our Sunday tea. You can stroke all of them, except that Shurochka won't let you and the cat'll scratch. You're off today?'

'Today.' Lavretsky took a seat on a low stool. 'I've already said good-bye to Marya Dmitrievna. I've also seen Lizaveta Mikhaylovna.'

'Call her Liza, there's a good chap; since when is she Mikhaylovna to you? And do sit quietly, otherwise you'll break Shurochka's chair.'

'She was going to Mass,' Lavretsky continued. 'She isn't religious, is she?'

'Yes, Fedya, she's very religious. More than you and I are.'

'But you're religious, aren't you?' remarked Nastasya Karpovna lispingly. 'You didn't go to the early service, but you'll be going to evensong.'

'No, I shan't – you go by yourself. I'm feeling lazy, my dear,' replied Marfa Timofeyevna, 'and I've been letting myself drink too much tea.' She addressed Nastasya Karpovna with the familiar 'thou' even though she lived with her on an equal footing. She wasn't a Pestov for nothing: three of them had been put to death by Ivan the Terrible[1]; Marfa Timofeyevna knew that only too well.

'Tell me, please,' Lavretsky began again, 'Marya Dmitrievna was talking to me just now about that – what's his name? – Panshin. What sort of a man is he?'

'What a chatterbox she is, the Lord forgive her!' complained Marfa Timofeyevna. 'Probably she informed you in confidence what a fine – well – a fine suitor's turned up. She could've whispered all this to her priest's son, but no, that's evidently not enough for her. Nothing's happened for sure yet – and praise be to God for that! – but she's already gossiping.'

'Why praise be to God for it?' asked Lavretsky.

'Because I don't like the fine fellow; and what's so marvellous about it, anyhow?'

'You don't like him?'

'He can't captivate everyone, that's all. It's enough for him that Nastasya Karpovna's fallen in love with him.'

The poor widow was utterly confounded.

'What're you saying, Marfa Timofeyevna! Have you no fear of God!' she exclaimed, and a hectic flush spread instantly over her face and neck.

'And he knows, the rascal does,' Marfa Timofeyevna interrupted her, 'he knows what to flatter her with: he's given her a little snuff-box. Fedya, ask her for some snuff and you'll see what a splendid snuff-box it is: the lid's decorated with a hussar on horseback. You'd better not try to explain it all away, my dear.'

Nastasya Karpovna could only flutter her hands in confusion.

'Well, and Liza,' asked Lavretsky, 'is she indifferent to him?'

'She's fond of him, it seems, but then God alone knows what she really feels! Another's heart is like a dark forest, you know, especially a young girl's. Take Shurochka's – just you try and make that out! Why's she been hiding herself away and not gone out since you arrived?'

Shurochka gave a snort of suppressed laughter and skipped out of the room just as Lavretsky rose from his place.

'Yes,' he said, pausing between the words, 'there's no accounting for a young girl's heart.'

He began to say good-bye.

'So? Will we be seeing you soon?' asked Marfa Timofeyevna.

'As the occasion arises, auntie: it's not far away, after all.'

'Yes, of course, you're going to Vasilyevskoye. You don't want to live in Lavriki – well, that's your business. Only be sure to pay a visit to your mother's grave, and to your grandmother's while you're about it. You must've picked up a lot of learning over there, in foreign countries, and – who knows – perhaps they'll feel in their graves that you've come to visit them. And don't forget, Fedya, to have a service said for Glafira Petrovna; here's a rouble. Take it, take it, it's because I want to have a service said for her. I didn't love her when she was alive, but there's no denying she was a woman with a character. A clever one, she was, and she didn't treat you badly. But now be off with you in God's name, or I'll be boring you to tears.'

And Marfa Timofeyevna embraced her nephew.

'Liza won't be marrying Panshin, don't you worry; he's not the sort of husband she deserves.'

'I don't worry in the least,' answered Lavretsky and took his leave.

XVIII

FOUR hours later he was on his way home. His tarantass bowled briskly along the soft surface of a country road. There had been dry weather for a couple of weeks; a faint mist pervaded the air like milk and hid the far woods; it had a fragrance of burning. A mass of darkling clouds with vaguely defined edges crawled across the pale blue sky; a fairly strong breeze hurried in a dry uninterrupted stream over the land, but did not disperse the heat. Laying his head back on a cushion and folding his arms, Lavretsky gazed at the rows of fields which passed in a fan-wise movement, at the willows which slowly passed into and out of sight, at the stupid rooks and crows which looked out of the corners of their eyes in dull suspiciousness at the passing carriage, at the long boundaries between the fields overgrown with ragwort, wormwood and field rowans; he gazed . . . and this fresh, lush nakedness and wilderness of the steppe, this greenery, these long low hills, the ravines with their ground-hugging clumps of oak trees, the grey little villages, the flowing shapes of birches – the whole of this picture of Russia, which he had not seen for so long, evoked in him sweet and simultaneously anguished feelings and oppressed his heart with a kind of pleasant sadness. His thoughts took a slow wandering course; their outlines were as vague and troubled as the outlines of those high and also seemingly wandering clouds. He recalled his childhood, his mother, recalled how, as she lay dying, they had brought him to her and how she, pressing his head to her breast, had just begun a feeble lamenting over him, but had glanced up at Glafira Petrovna – and stopped. He remembered his father, at first hale and hearty, dissatisfied with everything, speaking in his brassy voice, and then blind and querulous, with an untidy grey beard; he remembered how once at table, having drunk a glass too much of wine and spilt the gravy over his napkin, his father had suddenly burst out laughing and begun, winking his sightless eyes and blushing, to speak of his conquests; he remembered Varvara Pavlovna – and winced despite himself, as a man winces from a momentary internal pain, and shook his head. Then his thoughts concentrated on Liza.

'Here,' he thought, 'is a new being just entering on life. A splendid girl, what will she make of herself? She is good-looking. A pale, fresh-complexioned face, such serious eyes and mouth, and a look of honesty and innocence. It's a pity

82

that she seems a little too serious-minded. She has a splendid figure, walks so lightly and has a quiet voice. I like it very much when she suddenly stops, listens attentively without smiling, becomes thoughtful and tosses back her hair. It occurs to me that Panshin is not worthy of her. And yet what's wrong with him? Still, what am I dreaming like this for? She'll run along the same primrose path they all run along. I'd better go to sleep.' And Lavretsky closed his eyes.

He was unable to sleep, but he sank into a drowsy travel-weary numbness. Images of the past rose as before, unhurriedly, and floated into his mind's eye, mingling and becoming confused with other memories. Lavretsky, God knows why, began to think about Robert Peel, about the history of France, about how he would have won a battle if he had been a general; he imagined the gunfire and the shouting. . . . His head slid sideways and he opened his eyes. . . . The same fields, the same views of the steppe; the well-worn hooves of the trace-horses flickered one after another through the waves of dust; the driver's shirt, yellow, with red gussets, bellied in the wind. . . . 'Much good being like this when I'm returning home,' Lavretsky thought in a flash, and he cried out: 'Get along there!' and drew his cloak more tightly round him and pressed his head back all the more firmly into the cushion. The tarantass gave a jolt: Lavretsky straightened up and opened his eyes wide. Before him on a rise in the land stretched a small village; a little to the right could be seen an antiquated manor house with closed shutters and a crooked little entrance porch; the broad courtyard, right up to the very gates, was overgrown with nettles as green and thick as hemp; there also stood a small barn, built stoutly of oak. This was Vasilyevskoye.

The driver turned towards the gates and stopped the horses; Lavretsky's servant raised himself on the box and, as if in readiness to jump down, shouted: 'Hey!' Hoarse, muffled barking ensued, but not even a dog appeared; the servant again prepared to jump down and again cried out: 'Hey!'

The croaky barking occurred again and an instant later there ran out into the yard, Heaven knows from where, a man in a nankeen caftan with a head as white as snow; he looked at the tarantass, shading his eyes from the sun, struck both hands against his thighs, hovered about uncertainly for an instant or so and then rushed to open the gates. The tarantass entered the courtyard, its wheels rustling through the nettles, and came to a halt before the entrance porch. The white-haired man, to all appearances extremely nimble, was already standing with his bow legs set wide apart on the bottom step of the porch. He undid the detachable front cover of the tarantass, jerkingly holding the leather up, and, in helping his master to set foot on the ground, kissed him on the hand.

'Good to see you, my good chap,' said Lavretsky. 'You're called Anton, aren't you? Can you still be alive?'

The old man bowed silently and ran off to get the keys. While he was gone, the driver sat motionlessly, his arms at his sides, giving looks at the closed door; while Lavretsky's servant, having jumped down, remained in exactly that picturesque pose with one hand thrown over the box. The old man brought the keys and, quite needlessly writhing like a snake, unlocked the door holding up his elbows high, stood aside and again gave a low bow from the waist.

'Here I am at home, here I am back at last,' thought Lavretsky, entering the tiny hall as the shutters were opened one after another with a clattering and a creaking and daylight penetrated into the desolate rooms.

XIX

THE small house to which Lavretsky had come and where two years ago Glafira Petrovna had died was built in the last century of solid pinewood; in appearance it seemed decrepit, but it could well stand another fifty years or more. Lavretsky went through all the rooms and, to the great discomfort of the ancient, enfeebled flies with their backs covered in white dust who were sitting motionless under the lintels, ordered that all the windows should be opened: from the moment of Glafira Petrovna's death no one had unlatched them. Everything in the house had remained as it was. In the drawing-room little white divans standing on elegant legs and upholstered in sheeny grey damask, frayed and holed, were a lively reminder of the times of Catherine[1]; there also stood the mistress's favourite armchair with its high straight back, against which she did not lean even in old age. On the main wall hung an ancient portrait of Fyodor's great-grandfather, Andrey Lavretsky; the dark, bad-tempered face was scarcely distinguishable from the warped and blackened background; small malicious eyes gazed morosely from beneath drooping and literally swollen lids; black unpowdered hair rose in bristles above a heavy furrowed brow. On one corner of the portrait hung a dusty wreath of everlasting flowers. 'Glafira Petrovna herself saw to the making of the wreath,' Anton announced. In the bedroom stood a lofty narrow bed under a canopy of old-fashioned but very good-quality striped material; a pile of faded pillows and a threadbare quilted counterpane lay on the bed, at the head of which hung an icon, 'The Blessed Virgin entering the Temple' – the very same icon to which the old maiden lady, dying alone and forgotten by the world, pressed her already cold lips for the last time. By the window stood a little inlaid dressing-table with brass fittings and a crooked mirror in a tarnished gilt frame. Next to the bedroom was an icon-room, a tiny place with bare walls and a heavy icon-case set in one corner; on the floor lay a worn, wax-stained piece of carpet where Glafira Petrovna used to make her obeisances. Anton left with Lavretsky's servant to unlock the stables and coach-house; in his place there appeared an old woman, almost his coeval, with a kerchief bound round her head to the level of her eyebrows; her head shook and her eyes stared vacantly, but she still contrived to express diligence, the long-term habit of unquestioning service and – at the same time – a kind of respectful regret. She approached Lavretsky's hand and then stopped by the door in anticipation of orders. He simply could not remember what she was called, and did not even remember whether he had ever seen her before; it transpired that she was called Apraxia; some forty years ago Glafira Petrovna had despatched her from the house and ordered her to be a poultry-keeper; she spoke little, as if she had outlived her wits, but still gazed at him deferentially. Apart from these two old people and three pot-bellied children in long shirts, Anton's great-grandchildren, there also lived at the house a little one-armed peasant who had been released from his obligations as a serf; he groused away to himself all day and was incapable of doing a thing; hardly more useful was the decrepit dog that had greeted Lavretsky's return with its barking: it had spent ten years on a heavy chain bought on Glafira Petrovna's orders and was barely in any condition to move about and drag its heavy burden. Having looked over the house, Lavretsky went into the garden and was satisfied by what he saw. It was entirely overgrown with thick weeds and burdock and gooseberry and raspberry bushes; but there was much shade and many old limes which were striking for their hugeness and the curious arrangements of their boughs, the result of having been planted too close together and – perhaps a hundred years ago – severely pruned back. The garden ended in a small bright pond with a fringe of tall reddish reeds. Traces of human life vanish very quickly: Glafira Petrovna's estate had not yet gone wild, but it seemed already to have sunk into that quiet repose which possesses everything on earth wherever there is no restless human infection to affect it. Fyodor Ivanych also took a walk through the village; women gazed at him from the doorways of their huts, hands resting on their cheeks; the menfolk bowed from a distance, children ran off and dogs barked indifferently. Finally he wanted to have a meal, but he could not expect the rest of his servants and his cook before evening, and the waggons with supplies from Lavriki had not yet arrived – so he had to fall back on Anton. Anton at once made the arrangements: he caught, killed and plucked an old chicken; Apraxia took a long time rubbing and washing and belabouring it, as though it were linen, before putting it in a saucepan; when it was at last cooked, Anton spread a cloth and laid the table, setting before his master's place a blackened plated salt-cellar on three legs and a cut-glass decanter with a round glass stopper and a thin neck; then he announced to Lavretsky in a sing-song voice that dinner was served and positioned himself behind Lavretsky's chair with a napkin wrapped round his right fist and exuding a strong antique odour similar to that of cypress wood. Lavretsky dealt with the soup and then addressed himself to the chicken; its skin was covered all over with large pimples; a large tendon ran down each leg and the meat had an alkaline, woody taste. Having dined, Lavretsky said that he would like some tea if . . . 'I'll bring it, sir, this very minute, sir,' the old man interrupted and was as good as his word. A pinch of tea was sought out, wrapped in a twist of red paper; a small but exceedingly fiery and noisy samovar was unearthed, along with sugar in very small lumps which looked as if they had been melted. Lavretsky drank his tea from a big cup; he remembered this cup from his child-hood: it had playing cards painted on it and only guests were allowed to drink out of it – and he drank out of it now as if he were a guest. His servants arrived towards evening; Lav-retsky did not want to sleep in his aunt's bed; he ordered that a bed be made up for him in the dining-room. When he had put out the candle he gazed around him for a long while and thought unhappy thoughts; he experienced the feeling, familiar to anyone who has had to spend a night for the first time in a long uninhabited place, that the darkness surrounding him on all sides could not, as it were, accustom itself to this new inhabitant, that the very walls of the house were baffled by him. Eventually he sighed, drew the blanket over him and fell asleep. Anton remained on his feet longer than anyone else; he spent a long time whispering with Apraxia, groaning under his breath and crossing himself a couple of times; neither of them had expected that the master would settle in Vasilyevskoye when he had nearby such a splendid estate with an admirably laid-out house and garden; they did not suspect that that very estate was repugnant to Lavretsky and aroused in him nothing but oppressive memories. Having whispered to his heart's content, Anton took a stick and struck the watchman's board which had long hung silent by the barn, and huddled down then and there out in the yard, without bothering to cover his white head. The May night was quiet and mild, and the old man slept sweetly.

XX

THE next day Lavretsky rose fairly early, chatted with the village elder, visited the threshing-floor, ordered the chain to be taken off the dog in the yard, who only barked a little but did not even leave his kennel, and then returned home to sink into a kind of peaceful torpor from which he did not emerge all day. 'Here's the point where I've fallen to the bottom of the river,' he said to himself more than once. He sat at the window without stirring a muscle, literally absorbed in listening to the flow of the quiet life surrounding him and the occasional sounds of the peaceful rural world. Somewhere beyond the nettles someone hummed a melody in the finest of thin voices, and a gnat seemed to take up the refrain. The voice ceased, but the gnat continued to hum: through the concerted, naggingly plaintive buzzing of flies there resounded the droning of a fat bumble-bee which now and then tapped against the ceiling; a cock started crowing in the street, wheezily prolonging its final crowing note; a cart rattled by and in the village a gate creaked. 'What'sat?' a woman's voice suddenly screeched. 'Oh, you're a little madam!' said Anton to the two-year-old girl he was dandling in his arms. 'Bring the kvass,' repeated the same woman's voice – and suddenly dead silence ensued; nothing tapped, nothing stirred; one by one swallows swooped along the ground without a murmur, and the very silence of their flight made the heart sad. 'Here am I as though I were at the bottom of a river,' Lavretsky thought again. 'And here always, at all times, life is quiet and unhurried,' he reflected. 'Whoever enters its charmed circle must submit to it: here there is nothing to worry about, nothing to disturb one; here success comes only to him who carves out his own unhurried path as the ploughman carves out the furrows with his plough. And what strength there is everywhere, what vigour in this static peace! Just there, beneath the window, a rugged burdock shoves its way through the thick grass; above it lovage stretches its juicy stalk, angels' tears unfurls its rosy curls higher still; and there, further off, in the fields, the rye gleams brightly burnished, and the oats have formed their little trumpet ears, and every leaf on every tree, and every blade of grass on its stalk, has broadened out to its fullest breadth. My best years have passed in loving a woman,' Lavretsky continued to reflect. 'Now let this boredom bring me to my senses, let it calm me and prepare me to take up my task without hurry.' And once again he began to listen to the silence, awaiting nothing – and yet at the same time endlessly expectant: the silence engulfed him on every side; the sun ran its course across the tranquil blue of the sky, and the clouds floated silently upon it; it seemed as if they knew why and where they were going. At that very time, in other places on the earth, life was seething, hurrying, roaring on its way; here the same life flowed by inaudibly, like water through marshy grass; and until evening Lavretsky could not tear himself away from contemplation of this receding, out-flowing life; anguish for the past was melting in his soul like spring snow and – strangest of all! – never before had he felt so deep and strong a feeling for his country.

XXI

In the course of a fortnight Fyodor Ivanych put Glafira Petrovna's little house in order and cleaned up the courtyard and the garden; comfortable furniture was brought from Lavriki, wine, books and journals from the town; in a word, Fyodor Ivanych surrounded himself with all he needed and began to live the life of the cross between a landowner and a hermit. One day passed much like another; he was not bored although he had no visitors; he diligently and carefully attended to the estate, rode on horseback through the surrounding region and did some reading. However, he did not read much: he found it pleasanter to listen to old Anton's stories. Usually Lavretsky would sit down with a pipe of tobacco and a cup of cold tea by the window; Anton would position himself at the door, his hands behind his back, and begin his unhurried stories about times long past, about those fairytale times when oats and rye were sold not in measures but in large sacks, for two or three copecks a sack; when on all sides, even in the vicinity of the town, there stretched impenetrable forests and untouched steppeland. 'But now,' the old man complained (he was already more than eighty), 'everything's cut down and ploughed up so much you can't go anywhere.' Anton also had many tales to tell about his mistress, Glafira Petrovna: how she had been so sensible and economical; how a certain gentleman, a young neighbour, had made up to her and come on frequent visits, and how she had even honoured him by wearing her Sunday bonnet with dark-red ribbons and a yellow dress of tru-tru-levantine; but how later, infuriated by the neighbouring gentleman's indelicate question: 'Pray, madam, how much capital would you say you have?', banned him from the house and then and there gave orders that after her death everything, down to the smallest rag, should be left to Fyodor Ivanych. And Lavretsky did indeed find all his aunt's worldly goods left intact, not excluding the Sunday bonnet with dark-red ribbons and the yellow dress of tru-tru-levantine. Of old papers and interesting documents, on which Lavretsky had counted, there remained nothing, apart from one ancient notebook into which his grandfather, Pyotr Andreyich, had copied 'The Celebration in St Petersburg of the Peace Concluded with the Empire of Turkey by His Excellency Prince Alexander Alexandrovich Prozorovsky,' a recipe for a *décoction* for relief of chest ailments with the attached note: 'This Instruction was given to the General's wife Praskovya Fyodorovna Saltykov by Fyodor Avksentyevich, Archpriest of Holy Trinity Church,' political news of the following kind: 'Things have quietened a bit about the French tigers,' and beside this: 'In the *Moscow News* it is announced that First Major Mikhail Petrovich Kolychev has died. Is this not Pyotr Vasilyevich Kolychev's son?' Lavretsky also found several old calendars and dreambooks and the mysterious work by Mr Ambodik; many memories were aroused in him by the long-forgotten but still familiar *Symbols and Emblems*. In Glafira Petrovna's dressing-table Lavretsky found a small packet tied with a black ribbon, sealed with black wax and shoved to the very back of the drawer. In the packet there lay face to face a pastel portrait of his father in his youth, with soft curls spilt over his temples, long languid eyes and a half-open mouth, and an almost completely faded portrait of a pale woman in a white dress, holding a white rose – his mother. Glafira Petrovna never allowed a portrait to be made of herself. 'I, sir, Fyodor Ivanych,' Anton would say to Lavretsky, 'though in them days I weren't livin' in t' master's house, I can still call to mind your great-granfer, Andrey Afanasyevich, seein' as I were just gone eighteen when 'ee died. Once I met 'im, I did, in the garden – an' fair shivered in me shoes, I did, but 'ee didn't do nothin', just asked me who I were an' sent me off to 'is room to fetch 'im a 'ankerchief. A real master 'ee were, no sayin' otherwise – an' 'ee wouldn't 'ave nobody over 'im, 'ee wouldn't. I'll tell you why, 'cos your great-granfer 'ad a sort of trinket, magical-like it were, what a monk gave 'im from Mount Athos. And this monk did tell 'im: "I give you this, sir, for your cordiality towards me; wear it and never be afraid." Well, sir, it's well known what times were like in those days: whatever the master might want, that 'ee would 'ave. It might be that one of the local gents even thought to contradict 'im, so 'ee'd just look at 'im and say: "You're small fry" – an' that was 'is favourite sayin'. An' your great-granfer, of blessed memory, did live in a small wooden house; and what goods 'ee left behind 'im – silver an' what 'ave you, all the cellars stuffed with 'em, they were! A grand manager of 'is affairs, 'ee were. That there decanter, what you were good enough to praise, was 'is: 'ee would drink 'is vodka from it. But your granfer, Pyotr Andreyich, build a brick house 'ee might but 'ee never did do no good; everything 'ee did went wrong; an' 'ee lived worse than 'is father, an' 'ee never 'ad no real pleasure – lost all 'is money, so there's nothin' to remember 'im by, not even a silver spoon's remained, an' what there is remainin' is thanks to Glafira Petrovna.'

'Is it true', Lavretsky interrupted him, 'that they used to call her a browbeating old bitch?'

'But who used to call her that!' Anton replied with displeasure.

'An' what, sir,' the old man on one occasion made to ask, 'what of our mistress, where will she be stayin'?'

'I have divorced my wife,' Lavretsky said with an effort. 'Please do not ask about her.'

'Very good, sir,' the old man responded sadly.

When three weeks had passed, Lavretsky rode into O . . . to the Kalitins and spent the evening at their house. Lemm was there; Lavretsky liked him very much. Although, through the kindness of his father, he could not play a single instrument, he was passionately fond of music – real music, classical music. Panshin was not at the Kalitins that evening. The Governor had sent him somewhere out of town. Liza played on her own and very precisely; Lemm became animated and expansive, rolling a piece of paper into a baton and conducting. Marya Dmitrievna laughed at first, seeing him do this, and then went off to bed; in her own words, Beethoven agitated her nerves too much. At midnight Lavretsky accompanied Lemm to his lodgings and sat with him there until three in the morning. Lemm talked a great deal; his bent back grew straight, his eyes widened and grew bright; even his hair rose more firmly above his temples. It was such a long time since anyone had taken any interest in him, and Lavretsky showed evident interest in him, asking him so many solicitous and attentive questions. The old man was touched; he ended by showing his guest his music, playing and even singing in a lifeless voice certain items from his works, among other things the whole of Schiller's ballad 'Fridolin'[1] which he had set to music. Lavretsky complimented him, made him repeat certain pieces and, on leaving, invited him to be his guest for a few days. Lemm, who accompanied him down to the street, agreed at once and firmly clasped his hand; but when he was left standing alone in the fresh, raw air of imminent dawn he looked round him, frowned, was assailed by an attack of goose-flesh and crept back into his own room like a criminal. '*Ich bin wohl nicht klug*' (I am not in my right mind), he muttered as he lay down in his short, hard bed. He attempted to cry off on the grounds of illness when, a few days later, Lavretsky called on him in a carriage, but Fyodor Ivanych went up to his room and persuaded him to come. What affected Lemm most strongly was the fact that Lavretsky had personally arranged for a piano to be brought out to his house from the town. Together they went off to the Kalitins and spent the evening with them, but not as pleasantly as on the last occasion. Panshin was there with a great deal to tell about his travels, and he very entertainingly imitated and parodied the landowners he had met; Lavretsky laughed, but Lemm never left his corner, never spoke, quietly spun his restless web like a spider, looked gloomy and morose and only came to life when Lavretsky began to say good-bye. Even sitting in the carriage, the old man continued to sulk and bristle; but the calm warm air, the light breeze, the faint shadows, the scent of grass and birch buds, the peaceful glow of the moonless starlit sky, the concerted hoofbeats and the snorts of the horses, all the enchantments of the road, the spring and the night sank into the soul of the poor German, and he was the first to talk.

XXII

He began to talk about music, about Liza, and again about music. He seemed to pronounce his words more slowly when he talked about Liza. Lavretsky directed the conversation to Lemm's work and, half jokingly, suggested he would write a libretto for him.

'Hm, a libretto!' Lemm responded. 'No, that's not for me: I haven't any longer got the vivacity or the play of imagination which are necessary for opera; I've already lost my powers now. . . . But if I could still do something, I'd be content with a romance; of course, I'd want the words to be good . . .'

He fell silent and sat motionless for a long while with his eyes raised to the sky.

'For instance,' he said eventually, 'something on the lines of: "You, O stars, pure stars! . . ."'

Lavretsky turned his head slightly and began looking at him.

'You, O stars, pure stars,' Lemm repeated, 'you look down equally on the just and the unjust, but only the innocent at heart – or something of that kind – understand you, that is to say, no – love you. Besides, I'm not a poet, not likely! But something in that line, something exalted.'

Lemm pushed his hat back on to the nape of his neck; in the

delicate shadows of the bright night his face seemed paler and younger.

'And you also,' he continued in a gradually dying voice, 'you also know who loves, who is capable of loving, for you, pure stars, you alone can bring comfort. . . . No, that's not what I mean at all! I'm not a poet,' he declared, 'but something in that line . . .'

'I'm sorry that I'm also not a poet,' Lavretsky remarked.

'Empty dreams!' rejoined Lemm and settled back into the corner of the carriage. He closed his eyes, as if preparing to go to sleep.

Several instants passed. Lavretsky pricked up his ears. ' "Stars, pure stars, love," ' the old man was whispering.

' "Love",' Lavretsky repeated to himself, becoming thoughtful, and there was a heaviness in his soul.

'You have written beautiful music for "Fridolin", Christopher Fyodorych,' he said aloud. 'But what do you feel – surely this Fridolin, after the count had led him to his wife, became her lover, didn't he?'[1]

'You think that', Lemm said, 'because experience has probably . . .' He stopped suddenly and turned away in confusion. Lavretsky gave a forced laugh and also turned away, and began to gaze at the road.

The stars were already beginning to pale and the sky had grown grey by the time the carriage drove up to the porch of the little house in Vasilyevskoye. Lavretsky showed his guest to his room, returned to his study and sat down before the window. In the garden a nightingale was singing its final song before the dawn. Lavretsky remembered that a nightingale had sung in the Kalitins' garden; he remembered also the quiet movement of Liza's eyes when, at the first sounds of the nightingale's song, they had turned towards the dark window. He began thinking about her, and his heart grew calm within him. 'Pure girl,' he murmured in a low voice; 'pure stars,' he added with a smile, and peacefully lay down to sleep.

But Lemm sat for a long time on his bed with a music workbook on his knees. It seemed that some improbably sweet melody was about to visit him: he was already seized by the fire, the excitement of it, he already felt the wearisome sweetness of its coming . . . but he could not quite grasp it . . .

'Not a poet and not a musician!' he muttered finally.

And his tired head dropped back heavily on to his pillow

XXIII

THE next morning host and guest had their tea out in the garden under an old lime.

'Maestro!' said Lavretsky during the course of their talk, 'you'll soon have to compose a triumphal cantata.'

'For what occasion?'

'The occasion of the marriage of Mr Panshin and Liza. Didn't you notice how he was courting her yesterday? It seems that everything's going along fine between them.'

'It will not happen!' exclaimed Lemm.

'Why not?'

'Because it's impossible. However,' he added after a short pause, 'anything's possible. Especially among you, here in Russia.'

'We'll leave Russia out of it for the time being; but what do you find wrong in such a marriage?'

'Everything's wrong, everything. Lizaveta Mikhaylovna is a right-minded, serious girl of noble feelings and he's – he's a dilettante, to put it in a nutshell.'

'But surely she's in love with him?'

Lemm rose from the garden bench.

'No, she's not in love with him – that is to say, she's pure in heart and does not know herself what it means to be in love. Madame von Kalitin tells her that he is a good young man, and she listens to Madame von Kalitin because she's still quite a child even though she's nineteen, saying her prayers night and morning as she does, which is very praiseworthy; but she's not in love with him. She can love only what is beautiful, and he is not beautiful – that's to say, he hasn't got a beautiful soul.'

Lemm delivered this speech fluently and heatedly, taking little steps backwards and forwards in front of the tea table and darting his eyes about on the ground.

'My most precious maestro,' exclaimed Lavretsky suddenly, 'I think you're in love with my cousin yourself!'

Lemm stopped suddenly.

'Please,' he began in an unsteady voice, 'don't make fun of me. I'm not out of my mind: I look forward to a dark grave, not to a rosy future.'

Lavretsky felt pity for the old man and asked his forgiveness. After tea Lemm played him his cantata, and over dinner, provoked into doing so by Lavretsky himself, he again spoke about Liza. Lavretsky listened to him with attention and curiosity.

'How do you think, Christopher Fyodorych,' he said eventually, 'everything here's in order, it seems, with the garden in full bloom – couldn't we invite her here for the day with her mother and my old auntie, eh? Would that please you?'

Lemm bent his head over his plate.

'Invite them,' he said barely audibly.

'But without Panshin?'

'Without Panshin,' replied the old man with an almost childlike smile.

Two days later Fyodor Ivanych set off for town to see the Kalitins.

XXIV

HE found everybody at home, but he did not announce his intention at once; he wanted first to discuss the matter alone with Liza. An occasion helped him: they were left alone together in the drawing-room. They struck up a conversation; she had already grown used to him – indeed, she was generally socially at her ease with anyone. He listened to her, gazed into her face and mentally repeated Lemm's words about her, agreeing with him. It sometimes happens that two already familiar, but not intimate, people suddenly and rapidly draw closer to each other in the course of a few moments – and an awareness of this intimacy is immediately expressed in their looks, in their calm and friendly smiles, and in their very movements. This is precisely what happened to Lavretsky and Liza. 'So that's what he's like,' she thought, looking fondly at him; 'so that's what you're like,' he thought as well. So that he was not very surprised when she, not of course without a little hesitation, announced to him that she had long had it in her heart to say something to him, but had been frightened of annoying him.

'Don't be frightened, say it,' he said and stopped in front of her.

Liza raised her clear eyes to his face.

'You are so kind,' she began, and at that very moment she thought: 'Yes, he really is kind . . .' 'You must forgive me, I shouldn't dare to speak about this to you . . . but how could you . . . why did you leave your wife?'

Lavretsky shuddered, glanced at Liza and sat down beside her.

'My child,' he said, 'please don't touch that wound. Your fingers are soft, but it will still be painful to me.'

'I know', Liza continued, as if she had misheard him, 'she has wronged you and I don't want to justify her; but how can one separate what God has joined together?'

'Our convictions on that account are too far apart, Lizaveta Mikhaylovna,' said Lavretsky rather sharply. 'We will not understand each other.'

Liza went pale; her whole body gave a slight shudder, but she did not fall silent.

'You must forgive,' she said quietly, 'if you wish to be forgiven as well.'

'Forgive!' Lavretsky chimed in. 'You should start by

recognizing whom you're asking to forgive. Forgive that woman, take her back into my house, her, that empty, heartless creature! And who told you that she wants to return to me? Besides, she is quite content with her lot. . . . There's no point in talking about it! Her name should not even be uttered by you. You're too pure and you're not even in a position to understand such a creature.'

'How insulting to her!' Liza said with an effort. Her hands were noticeably shaking. 'You were the one who left her, Fyodor Ivanych.'

'But I'm telling you,' Lavretsky countered with an involuntary burst of impatience, 'you don't know what sort of a creature she is!'

'So why did you marry her?' Liza whispered and lowered her eyes.

Lavretsky rose abruptly from his chair.

'Why did I marry? I was young then, and inexperienced; I was deceived, I was carried away by beautiful looks. I did not know women, I did not know anything. God grant that you make a happier match! But believe me, you can't be sure of anything beforehand.'

'I could also be unfortunate,' said Liza (her voice was beginning to break), 'but in that case it'd be necessary to submit to one's fate; I don't know how to say this, but if we will not submit . . .'

Lavretsky clenched his fists and tapped his foot.

'Don't be angry, forgive me,' Liza uttered hurriedly.

At that moment Marya Dmitrievna entered. Liza stood up and wanted to leave.

'Wait a minute,' Lavretsky unexpectedly called after her. 'I have a great favour to ask you and your mother. Visit me for my house-warming. You know I've had a piano installed; Lemm is staying with me; the lilac is now in bloom; you can have a breath of country air and return the same day – do you agree?'

Liza glanced at her mother, while Marya Dmitrievna assumed a pained look; but Lavretsky gave her no chance to open her mouth and there and then kissed her on both hands. Marya Dmitrievna, always susceptible to endearments and by no means anticipating such courtesy from 'the fat seal', softened her heart and agreed. While she was considering which day to choose, Lavretsky went up to Liza and, still overwrought, furtively whispered to her: 'Thank you, you're a kind girl; I'm to blame . . .' And her pale face crimsoned with a happy, ashamed smile; her eyes also smiled – until that moment she was afraid she had offended him.

'Can Vladimir Nikolaich come with us?' asked Marya Dmitrievna.

'Of course,' Lavretsky replied, 'but wouldn't it be best to keep it just in the family?'

'Surely, though, it seems . . .' Marya Dmitrievna began. 'However, as you wish,' she added.

It was decided to take Lenochka and Shurochka. Marfa Timofeyevna declined to make the trip.

'Too hard for me, my dear,' she said, 'it'd break my old bones; and probably there's nowhere at your place where I could spend the night; besides, I can't sleep in a strange bed. Let the young ones go for the ride.'

Lavretsky did not succeed in being alone with Liza again; but he looked at her in such a way that she began to feel happy and a little ashamed and sorry for him. In saying good-bye to her he pressed her hand firmly; she became thoughtful when she was alone.

XXV

WHEN Lavretsky returned home he was met on the threshold of the drawing-room by a tall, thin man in a worn blue coat, with a wrinkled but animated face, dishevelled grey side-whiskers, a long straight nose and small inflamed eyes. This was Mikhalevich, his former university comrade. Lavretsky did not recognize him at first, but embraced him warmly when the latter announced himself. They had not seen each other since their Moscow days. Exclamations and questions poured out; long dead memories broke into the light of day. Hurriedly smoking pipe after pipe, swallowing mouthfuls of tea and waving his long arms, Mikhalevich told Lavretsky of his adventures; there was nothing very gay about them, and he could not boast of success in what he had done – yet he ceaselessly laughed his hoarse, nervous laugh. A month ago he had obtained a position in the private office of a rich tax-farmer some two hundred miles from the town of O . . . and, having learned of Lavretsky's return from abroad, had made a detour to see his old friend. Mikhalevich talked just as impulsively as he had done in his youth, with just as much sound and fury. Lavretsky was on the point of mentioning his circumstances, but Mikhalevich interrupted him by hurriedly muttering: 'I heard about it, my dear chap – who would've expected such a thing?' – and at once directed the conversation to matters of general interest.

'My dear fellow,' he said, 'I must be off tomorrow; today – you must forgive me – we will go to bed late. I simply must know what you've been up to, what your opinions and convictions are, what you've become, what life has taught you.' (Mikhalevich adhered to the phraseology of the thirties.) 'So far as I'm concerned, I've changed a great deal, my dear chap. The waves of life have broken o'er my breast – by the way, who said that? – although in all the important and essential things I have not changed; I believe as ever in goodness and truth; but I not only believe in them, I now have faith – yes, I have faith in them, I have faith in them. Listen a moment – you know I scribble verses; there's no poetry in them, but there is truth. I'll read you my latest piece: in it I've expressed my most heartfelt convictions. Listen.'

Mikhalevich set about reading his poem; it was fairly long and ended with the following lines:

> To new feelings with all my heart I'm given,
> As a child have I become in soul:
> And I've burnt all to which I once was given,
> And bow down to all I burnt of old.

Speaking the last two lines, Mikhalevich almost broke down and cried; slight quiverings – the sign of strong feeling – flitted across his broad lips and his unattractive face lit up. Lavretsky listened and listened to him – and a spirit of opposition stirred within him: he was irritated by the ever-ready, continuously effervescent exultation of the Moscow student. A quarter of an hour had hardly passed before an argument sprang up between them, one of those interminable arguments of which only Russians are capable. From the outset, after many years of separation spent in two different worlds, without clearly understanding others' or even their own ideas, latching on to words and bandying words about, they became embroiled in an argument about the most abstract matters – and they argued as if it were a matter of life and death for both of them: literally bayed and howled, so that everyone in the house was in a state of commotion, and the wretched Lemm, who ever since Mikhalevich's arrival had locked himself in his room, felt quite put out and even began to be vaguely frightened.

'What are you after this – disillusioned?' shouted Mikhalevich after midnight.

'Is this how disillusioned people are?' Lavretsky protested. 'They're usually pale and sickly, but if you like I'll lift you up with one hand.'

'Well, then, if you're not *disillusioned*, you're a *scepteek*, which is still worse.' (Mikhalevich's pronunciation smacked of his Little Russian homeland.) 'What right have you to be a sceptic? Granted that you've not been lucky in your life; you weren't to blame for that: you were born with a passionate and loving soul, and yet you were forcibly kept from women; the first woman who came along was bound to deceive you.'

'She deceived you as well,' Lavretsky remarked gloomily.

'Granted, granted; I was an instrument of fate – but I'm talking nonsense, fate had nothing to do with it; it's my old habit of expressing myself imprecisely. But what does that prove?'

'It proves I've been all wrong since my childhood.'

'Put yourself right then! That's why you were born, that's why you're a man; you don't need to borrow energy to do that! But, however that may be, is it possible, is it permissible to elevate a private fact, as it were, into the status of a general law, of an unalterable rule?'

'What rule?' Lavretsky broke in. 'I don't see . . .'

'No, it's your rule, your rule,' Mikhalevich interrupted him in his turn.

'You're an egoist, that's what you are!' he thundered an hour later. 'You wanted self-indulgence, you wanted happiness in life, you wanted to live only for yourself . . .'

'What is self-indulgence?'

'And everything deceived you; everything collapsed under your feet.'

'What is self-indulgence, I'm asking you?'

'And it was bound to collapse. Since you looked for support where it was impossible to find it, since you built your house on shifting sands . . .'

'Speak more clearly, without analogies, *since* I do not understand you.'

'Since – laugh if you like – since you have no faith, no heartfelt warmth, just intellect, nothing but tuppeny-ha'penny intellect – you're simply a miserable, old-fashioned Voltairean, that's what you are!'

'Who – I, a Voltairean?'

'Yes, just like your father, and yet you don't even suspect it.'

'After that,' Lavretsky exclaimed, 'I've the right to call you a fanatic!'

'Hey!' Mikhalevich protested in a spirit of contrition.

'Unfortunately I haven't yet earned the right to such a lofty title . . .'

'Now I've found what to call you,' shouted Mikhalevich, the same as ever, after two in the morning. 'You're not a sceptic, not disillusioned, not a Voltairean, you're a layabout, a vicious layabout, consciously a layabout, not the naïve type. Naïve layabouts lie on the stove and do nothing, because they don't know how to do anything; and they don't think, but you're a thinking man – and yet you lie around; you could do something – and yet you do nothing; you lie with your full stomach sticking up in the air and say: This is how it must be, lying about like this, because no matter what people do, everything's nonsense, it's all a lot of rubbish leading to nothing.'

'Where have you got the idea from that I'm lying about?' Lavretsky asked. 'Why do you ascribe such ideas to me?'

'But above all, you're like all, all your gentry sort,' continued the indefatigable Mikhalevich, 'you're all well-read layabouts. You know the Achilles' heel of the Germans, you know what's wrong with the English and the French, and this pitiful knowledge of yours is your mainstay and is a justification of your shameful apathy and your disgusting inactivity. Some of you even take pride in the fact that you're so clever, you're just going to go on lying there, while some other fools do all the work. Yes, indeed! Or there are some gents among us – however, I'm not saying this on your account – who spend their whole lives in an absolute ecstasy of boredom, who grow so used to it they wallow in it like . . . like a mushroom in sour cream.' Mikhalevich burst out laughing at his own analogy. 'Oh, this ecstasy of boredom is the ruin of the Russian people! The crass layabout spends his whole life making up his mind to start work . . .'

'What's all this scolding!' Lavretsky howled in his turn. 'Work . . . activity. . . . Just you say what ought to be done, and stop scolding, you Poltavan Demosthenes!'

'See what he wants now! I'm not going to tell you that, my

good chap, because everyone should know that,' said the Demosthenes with irony. 'A landowner, a member of the gentry – and he doesn't know what to do! You'd know well enough if you had faith; no faith – and no vision to go with it.'

'Give me a chance to get my breath back at least, you devil, give me a chance to take stock of things,' begged Lavretsky.

'Not a minute's rest, not a second's!' protested Mikhalevich with an authoritarian wave of the hand. 'Not a single second's! Death doesn't wait, and life shouldn't be allowed to.'

'And when and where have people taken it into their heads to become layabouts?' he cried at four o'clock in the morning, but in a voice already grown hoarse. 'Among us! Now! In Russia! when each individual person has a duty, a great responsibility before God, before the people and before himself! We're sleeping while time's passing away; we're sleeping . . .'

'Permit me to point out to you,' Lavretsky said, 'that we're not sleeping now at all, but rather not giving the others a chance to sleep. We're straining our throats like crowing cocks. Listen, there's the cock crowing thrice.'

This joke delighted and quietened Mikhalevich. 'Till to-morrow,' he said with a smile and put his pipe away in his pouch. 'Till tomorrow,' Lavretsky repeated. But the friends went on chatting for more than an hour. Still, their voices were not raised any more, and their talk was quiet, wistful and kindly.

Mikhalevich left the next day, notwithstanding Lavretsky's attempts to keep him there. Fyodor Ivanych did not succeed in persuading him to remain; but he talked to him to his heart's content. It transpired that Mikhalevich had not got a penny to his name. On the previous day Lavretsky had noticed in him with regret all the signs and habits of long-standing poverty: his shoes were down at heel, a button was missing from the back of his coat, his hands were strangers to gloves and there was fluff in his hair; when he arrived he did not think of asking to wash, and at dinner he ate like a shark, tearing the meat with his hands and crunching the bones in his strong black teeth. It also transpired that government service had done him no good and that all his hopes were now placed on the tax-farmer, who had employed him solely in order to have 'an educated man' in his office. Despite this, Mikhalevich was not dispirited and lived to his liking the roles of cynic, idealist and poet, sincerely delighting in, and grieving for, the fate of mankind and his own vocation – and taking very little care about whether or not he died from hunger. Mikhalevich was unmarried, but he had fallen in love countless times and wrote poems to all his beloveds; he celebrated particularly ardently one mysterious black-curled 'Polish lady'. . . . True, there were rumours that this Polish lady was no more than a Jewess well known to many cavalry officers. . . . But when you come to think of it, does that make any difference?

Mikhalevich did not get on with Lemm: not being used to them, the German was apprehensive of his exceedingly noisy talk and brusque manners. Victims of misfortune are quick to sense another of their kind from a distance, but in old age they rarely become friends, which is in no way surprising: they have nothing to share together – not even hopes.

Before his departure Mikhalevich again had a long talk with Lavretsky, prophesied his doom if he did not mend his ways, begged him to occupy himself seriously with the life and conditions of his peasants, set himself up as an example to him, saying that he had been purified in the crucible of misfortune – and yet more than once called himself a happy man, compared himself with the birds of the air and the lilies of the valley . . .

'A black lily, in any case,' remarked Lavretsky.

'My dear fellow, don't come the aristocrat,' Mikhalevich responded with magnanimity, 'but rather thank God you've got honest plebeian blood flowing in your veins as well. But I can see that what you need now is some pure, heavenly creature who would drag you out of your apathy . . .'

'Thank you, my dear chap,' Lavretsky said, 'I've had enough of these heavenly creatures.'

'Don't talk like that, you *seeneek*!' Mikhalevich exclaimed.

'Cynic,' Lavretsky corrected him.

'Precisely, *seeneek*,' repeated Mikhalevich unperturbed.

Even sitting in the tarantass, to which his flat, yellow, strangely light trunk had been carried out, he still went on talking; shrouded in a kind of Spanish cloak with a rust-red collar and lions' claws instead of clasps, he went on amplifying his views on the fate of Russia and waving his swarthy hands about in the air as though he were distributing the seeds of future prosperity. The horses finally started away. 'Remember my last three words,' he shouted, doing a balancing act with his whole body thrust out of the tarantass, 'religion, progress, humanity! ... Farewell!' His head, with his cap pulled down over his eyes, disappeared from view. Lavretsky remained standing alone on the porch and gazed intently away along the road until the tarantass was lost from sight. 'Probably he's right,' he thought, turning back to the house, 'probably I am a layabout.' Many of Mikhalevich's words had entered irresistibly into his soul, although he had argued and disagreed with him. So long as a man is good-natured, no one can resist him.

XXVI

Two days later Marya Dmitrievna, according to her promise, arrived in Vasilyevskoye with all her young people. The little girls at once ran into the garden, while Marya Dmitrievna made a languid tour of the rooms and languidly praised everything. Her visit to Lavretsky she regarded as a mark of her great condescension, almost as an act of virtue. She graciously smiled when Anton and Apraxia, in the old-fashioned house-serf style, kissed her hand, and in a limp voice, nasally, asked if she might have some tea. To the profound annoyance of Anton, who had put on white knitted gloves for the occasion, tea was poured for the lady visitor not by him but by Lavretsky's hired man who had no understanding, in the old man's words, of the proper order of things. However, he came into his own at lunch-time: with a firm step he took his place by Marya Dmitrievna's chair and would not surrender his place to anyone. The long unfamiliar arrival of guests at Vasilyevskoye both alarmed and delighted the old man: it pleased him to see that people of such good standing knew his master. Yet he was not the only one to be excited that day: Lemm was also excited. He had put on a short tobacco-coloured swallow-tail coat and tied his neck-tie tightly round his neck, and he ceaselessly cleared his throat and made way for people with a pleasantly welcoming expression. Lavretsky noted with satisfaction that the intimacy between him and Liza was continuing: as soon as she had entered the house she had amicably offered him her hand. After the meal Lemm extracted from the rear pocket of his coat, where he had from time to time been putting his hand, a small rolled-up sheet of music and, pursing his lips, silently laid it on the piano. It was a romance, composed by him the previous day to old-fashioned German words which made mention of the stars. Liza at once sat down at the piano and started to play. Alas! the music turned out to be involved and unpleasantly strained; it was apparent that the composer had striven to express something passionate and profound, but nothing had come of it: the striving remained striving and nothing more. Lavretsky and Liza both felt this – and Lemm understood: without a word, he replaced his romance in his pocket and, in response to Liza's proposal that he should play it over again, simply gave a shake of the head, said significantly: 'Now – that's all!', hunched his shoulders, cringed into himself and left the room.

In the afternoon everyone went fishing. In the pond at the bottom of the garden there were many carp and roach. Marya

Dmitrievna was esconced in an armchair beside the bank, in a shady part, a rug was spread at her feet and she was given the best fishing-rod; Anton, as an old and experienced fisherman, offered her his services. He assiduously baited the hook with worms, slapped them with his hand, spat on them and even cast the line himself, elegantly bending his whole body forward as he did so. That very day Marya Dmitrievna expressed herself about him to Fyodor Ivanych with the following phrase in her schoolgirl French: '*Il n'y a plus maintenant de ces gens comme ça comme autrefois.*' Lemm and the two little girls went further on, to the dam; Lavretsky settled himself beside Liza. The fish were biting all the time; time and again carp hooked out of the water flashed their golden or silver sides in the air; the joyous cries of the girls never ceased; Marya Dmitrievna herself screeched delicately a couple of times. Lavretsky and Liza made catches less frequently than the others; no doubt this was because they paid less attention to their fishing than the others and let their floats drift right up to the bank. The reddish tall reeds rustled quietly all round them, the motionless water shone softly in front of them, and their conversation took a peaceful course. Liza stood on a small raft; Lavretsky sat on the overhanging trunk of a willow; Liza wore a white dress caught in at the waist by a broad ribbon, also white; a straw hat hung on one arm, while the other arm was holding up with some effort the pliant rod. Lavretsky gazed at her pure, rather severe profile, at her hair thrown back behind the ears, at her soft cheeks which were as sunburned as a child's, and thought: 'Oh, how charming you look standing at my pond!' Liza did not turn towards him, but looked at the water and was either smiling or frowning, it was difficult to tell which. The shade from a nearby lime-tree fell upon both of them.

'You know,' Lavretsky began, 'I've been thinking about our last conversation a great deal and I've come to the conclusion that you have an exceedingly kind nature.'

'I didn't intend that at all ...' Liza began to protest, and became confused.

'You have a kind nature,' Lavretsky repeated. 'I'm an uncouth sort of chap, but I feel that everyone is bound to love you. Take Lemm, for example; he's quite simply in love with you.'

Liza's eyebrows did not so much pucker as quiver; this always happened when she heard something unpleasant.

'I thought him very pitiful today,' Lavretsky added hastily, 'with his unsuccessful romance. To be young and not to know how, is bearable; to be old and not to have the strength, is too great a weight to carry. And what's so painful is you can't sense your powers leaving you. It's hard for an old man to endure such blows! Careful, one's biting! I've heard', Lavretsky added after a short pause, 'that Vladimir Nikolaich has written a very charming romance.'

'Yes,' answered Liza, 'it's a trifle, but not bad.'

'In your opinion,' asked Lavretsky, 'is he a good musician?'

'It seems to me that he has a great capacity for music, but so far he hasn't studied it as much as he should.'

'I see. Is he a nice man?'

Liza laughed and glanced quickly at Fyodor Ivanych.

'What a strange question!' she exclaimed, drawing the line out of the water and casting it again.

'Why strange? I'm asking you about him as a recent arrival and a relative.'

'As a relative?'

'Yes. Surely don't I qualify as an uncle of yours?'

'Vladimir Nikolaich has a kind heart,' Liza said, 'and he's clever; maman likes him very much.'

'Do you like him?'

'He's a nice man; why shouldn't I like him?'

'Ah!' Lavretsky said and was silent. A half-melancholy, half-amused expression passed across his face. His intent gaze embarrassed Liza, but she continued to smile. 'Well, God grant them happiness!' he muttered at last, as if to himself, and turned his head away.

Liza blushed.

'You're mistaken, Fyodor Ivanych,' she said, 'you needn't think. . . . But don't you like Vladimir Nikolaich?' she asked suddenly.

'No.'

'Why?'

'It seems to me he has no heart at all.'

The smile left Liza's face.

'You've grown used to judging people severely,' she said after a long silence.

'I have? No, I don't think so. What right have I to judge others severely, I ask you, when I myself am in need of charity? Or have you forgotten that it's only the lazy who don't laugh at me? By the way,' he added, 'did you keep your promise?'

'What promise?'

'Did you say a prayer for me?'

'Yes, I did pray for you and I pray for you each day. But please don't speak lightly about it.'

Lavretsky began to assure Liza that such a thing had never entered his head, that he had a profound respect for any and every conviction; then he embarked on a discussion of religion, its significance in the history of mankind and the significance of Christianity.

'One must be a Christian,' said Liza, not without a certain effort, 'not in order to perceive the divine . . . there . . . or the earthly, but because every man must die.'

Lavretsky raised his eyes to Liza in astonishment and met her gaze.

'What a thing to have said!' he remarked.

'They're not my words,' she answered.

'Not yours. . . . But why did you talk about death?'

'I don't know. I often think about it.'

'Often?'

'Yes.'

'One wouldn't think that, looking at you now: you've such a happy, bright face, you're smiling . . .'

'Yes, I'm very happy now,' Liza replied naïvely.

Lavretsky wanted to take both her hands and press them tightly, tightly . . .

'Liza, Liza,' cried Marya Dmitrievna, 'come and have a look at the carp I've caught!'

'Coming, maman,' Liza answered and went to her, while Lavretsky remained sitting on his willow. 'I talk to her just as if I weren't a man whose life is finished,' he thought. As she went, Liza had hung her hat on a branch; with an unfamiliar, almost tender, feeling Lavretsky looked at the hat and its long, slightly creased ribbons. Liza quickly returned to him and again stood on the raft.

'Why do you think Vladimir Nikolaich has no heart?' she asked a few moments later.

'I told you I could be mistaken; however, time will show.'

Liza became thoughtful. Lavretsky began talking about his day-to-day existence in Vasilyevskoye, about Mikhalevich and Anton; he felt a need to talk to Liza, to tell her everything he thought and felt: she listened to him so charmingly and attentively; her occasional remarks and objections seemed to him so unaffected and intelligent. He even told her so.

Liza was astonished.

'Do you really think so?' she said. 'I'd thought that, like my maid Nastya, I hadn't got any words of my own. She once told her boy-friend he'd be bored because he could talk about all sorts of things but she "hadn't got any words of her own".'

'And thank God!' thought Lavretsky.

XXVII

MEANWHILE, evening was approaching and Marya Dmitrievna expressed a desire to return home. The little girls were torn away from the pond only with difficulty and spruced up for the journey. Lavretsky announced that he would accompany his guests to the halfway point, and ordered his horse to be saddled. As he was assisting Marya Dmitrievna into the carriage, he suddenly missed Lemm; but the old man was nowhere to be found. He had disappeared as soon as the fishing was over. Anton, with remarkable force for his age, banged shut both the doors and shouted fiercely: 'Be off, driver!' The carriage started away. The back seat was occupied by Marya Dmitrievna and Liza, the front seat by the girls and the maid. The evening was warm and peaceful, and the carriage windows on both sides were lowered. Lavretsky trotted beside the carriage on Liza's side, resting his hand on the door – he had thrown the reins over the neck of his smoothly trotting horse – and occasionally exchanging two or three words with the young girl. The rays of the sunset vanished and night approached, but the air became even warmer. Marya Dmitrievna quickly fell into a doze; the little girls and the maid also slept. The carriage rolled along at a quick, even pace; Liza leaned forward; the newly risen moon shone in her face, a fragrant nocturnal breeze brushed her eyes and cheeks. She was happy. Her hand rested on the carriage door next to Lavretsky's hand. And he was happy, being carried along through the still and balmy night without lowering his eyes from the kindly young face and hearing the young and melodious voice whispering good and simple things; he did not even notice that he had ridden halfway. Not wishing to awaken Marya Dmitrievna, he lightly pressed Liza's hand and said: 'We're friends now, aren't we?' She nodded her head and he stopped his horse. The carriage rolled off on its way, ever so gently swaying and plunging; Lavretsky turned homewards at a walk. The charm of the summer night possessed him; everything around him seemed so unexpectedly strange and at the same time so long and so sweetly familiar to him; near and far – and one could see a long way, although the eye could not distinguish much of what it saw – everything was at peace; this very peace was redolent of youth bursting with life. Lavretsky's horse stepped out, rocking him evenly from side to side; its large black shadow moved along beside it; there was something secretly pleasing in the tramp of its hooves, something joyous and wonderful in the ringing cries of the quail. The stars disappeared in a bright haze; the moon, not yet full, shone with a hard glow; its light flowed in a pale-blue stream across the sky and fell in patches of smoky gold on the light clouds which passed close to it; the freshness of the air brought a slight moisture to the eyes, gently caressed the limbs and flowed freely into the lungs. Lavretsky was enjoying himself and revelled in his enjoyment. 'Well, we'll keep on living,' he thought, 'we're not yet completely eaten up by . . .' He did not say who or what. . . . Then he began thinking about Liza, about the fact that she could hardly be in love with Panshin; that had he met her in other circumstances, God knows what would have come of it; that he agreed with Lemm, although she had no words of her own. And yet that wasn't true: she did have words of her own. . . . He was reminded of her saying: 'Don't speak lightly about it.' For a long while he rode with lowered head, then straightened his back, uttered slowly:

> And I've burnt all to which I once was given,
> And bow down to all I burnt of old . . .

but at once whipped up his horse and galloped home.

Slipping off his horse, he looked round him for the last time with an involuntary smile of thankfulness. The night lay in a silent caress upon the hills and valleys; from afar, out of its perfumed deeps, God knows from where – whether from the sky or from the earth – stretched a calm and gentle warmth. Lavretsky made a final bow to Liza and ran up the porch steps.

The next day passed fairly dully. From morning on there was rain; Lemm glared from beneath his brows and pursed his lips so tightly it was as if he had given himself a promise never to open them again. When he went to bed, Lavretsky took with him a whole heap of French journals which had been lying unopened on his desk for more than a fortnight. Disinterestedly he began ripping off the covers and glancing through the columns of newspapers in which, however, there was nothing new. He was about to cast them aside when he suddenly leapt up from the bed as though stung. In a report in one of the newspapers M. Jules, who is already familiar to us, informed his readers of 'a sad piece of news': that delightful, fascinating Moscow lady, he wrote, one of the queens of fashion and an adornment of the Paris salons, Madame de Lavretzki, had died most suddenly – and this news, regrettably all too true, had only just reached him, M. Jules. He was, he continued, a friend of the deceased, one might say . . .

Lavretsky dressed, went out into the garden and until morning walked up and down the same pathway.

XXVIII

THE next morning, over tea, Lemm asked Lavretsky to let him have horses in order to return to town. 'It's time for me to get back to work – to giving my lessons, that's to say,' the old man remarked. 'Here I'm only wasting my time.' Lavretsky did not respond at once: he seemed distracted. 'All right,' he said finally, 'I'll be coming with you.' Without the help of a servant, groaning and losing his temper, Lemm packed his small trunk and tore up and burnt several sheets of music paper. The horses were got ready. Coming out of his study, Lavretsky placed the copy of the newspaper he had read yesterday in his pocket. Throughout the journey Lemm and Lavretsky spoke little: each was preoccupied with his own thoughts and was glad not to be disturbed. They parted rather drily, which, however, frequently happens among friends in Russia. Lavretsky took the old man to his little house; the old man alighted, got out his small trunk and, without offering a hand to his friend (he was holding his small trunk with both hands in front of him) and without even looking at him, said in Russian: 'Good-bye, sir!' 'Good-bye,' Lavretsky repeated and ordered his driver to take him to his rooms. He had already taken rooms in the town of O . . . for just such an occasion. After writing a few letters and having a hasty dinner, Lavretsky went to the Kalitins. In their drawing-room he found only Panshin, who announced that Marya Dmitrievna would be coming shortly and at once began talking to him with the most cordial affability. Until now Panshin had treated Lavretsky not so much haughtily as condescendingly; but Liza, in telling Panshin of her trip the previous day, spoke of Lavretsky as an excellent and intelligent person; this was sufficient: the 'excellent' person had to be won over. Panshin began with compliments, describing the enthusiasm with which, in his own words, Marya Dmitrievna's entire family had spoken about Vasilyevskoye, and then, in his customary way, skilfully turning to himself, he began to talk about his own affairs and his views on life, high society and government service; he said a couple of words about the future destiny of Russia and how governors were to be kept in check; at which he gaily made fun of himself and added that, among other things, in St Petersburg he had been given the task '*de populariser l'idée du cadastre*'.[1] He spoke for a rather long time, with careless self-assurance resolving all difficulties and juggling with the most important administrative and political questions. Expressions such as: 'That's what I'd do if I were the government' and 'You, as an intelligent man, will be bound to agree with me' slipped off his tongue. Lavretsky listened coldly to Panshin's exhortations: he did not like this handsome, clever man with his unforced elegance, his bright smile, his polite voice and probing eyes. Panshin soon guessed, with his habitual quick understanding of another's feelings, that he was not giving his listener particular pleasure and on a favourable pretext absented himself, having decided for his own part that Lavretsky might be an excellent person, but he was also unsympathetic, *aigri* and, *en somme*, slightly ridiculous. Marya Dmitrievna appeared in the company of Gedeonovsky; then came Marfa Timofeyevna and Liza, and after them the remaining members of the household; then came the music-lover, Mrs Belenitsyn, a small, thin woman, with an almost childish little face, wan and pretty, in a rustling black dress, with a colourful fan and fat gold bracelets; her husband also came, a red-cheeked, puffy man with large feet and hands, with white eyelashes and a fixed smile on his thick lips; when they were guests his wife never spoke to him, but at home, in moments of tenderness, she called him her little porker. Panshin returned; the rooms became very noisy and full of people. Such a mass of people did not suit Lavretsky's purpose; he was particularly irritated by Mrs Belenitsyn, who continually looked at him through her lorgnette. He would have left at once, had it not been for Liza: he wanted to have a word with her alone, but for a long time he could not find a suitable moment and had to content himself with the secret delight of following her with his eyes; her face had never seemed to him more noble or charming. She gained much through being close to Mrs Belenitsyn. That lady ceaselessly fidgeted on her chair, shrugged her narrow little shoulders, gave affected laughs and either screwed up her eyes or suddenly opened them wide. Liza sat quietly looking straight ahead of her and not laughing at all. The hostess sat down to play cards with Marfa Timofeyevna, Belenitsyn and Gedeonovsky, who played exceedingly slowly, made endless mistakes, blinked his eyes and wiped his face with a handkerchief. Panshin assumed a melancholy air, expressed himself briefly, pointedly and gravely – for all the world like a misunderstood artist – but notwithstanding the entreaties of Mrs Belenitsyn, who flirted with him outrageously, declined to sing his romance, since Lavretsky's presence embarrassed him. Fyodor Ivanych also spoke little; the special look on his face had struck Liza as soon as he had entered the room; she sensed at once that he had something to tell her, but she was frightened of asking him, without knowing exactly why. Finally, as she was crossing into the main room to pour the tea, she turned her head in his direction despite herself. At once he followed her.

'What is wrong with you?' she asked, placing the teapot on the samovar.

'Have you noticed something wrong?' he said.

'Today you are not the same as I have seen you up till now.'

Lavretsky leaned over the table.

'I wanted', he began, 'to let you have a piece of news, but it's not possible now. But read what's marked with a pencil in this newspaper report,' he added, handing her the copy of the paper he had brought with him. 'I beg you to keep it secret. I'll come round tomorrow.'

Liza was taken aback. . . . Panshin appeared in the doorway: she put the newspaper in her pocket.

'Have you read *Obermann*[2], Lizaveta Mikhaylovna?' Panshin asked her thoughtfully.

Liza muttered an answer in passing and left the room to go upstairs. Lavretsky returned to the drawing-room and went up to the card table. Marfa Timofeyevna, red in the face, with her cap-ribbons undone, began to complain to him about her partner Gedeonovsky who, according to her, had no idea what card to lead with.

'Evidently playing cards', she said, 'is not the same as telling stories.'

Gedeonovsky continued to blink his eyes and wipe his face. Liza came into the drawing-room and sat down in one corner; Lavretsky looked at her and she looked at him – and both experienced tremors of fright. He read perplexity and a kind of secret reproach on her face. No matter how much he wanted to, he could not speak to her; it was equally hard for him to remain in the same room with her as a guest among other guests: he decided to leave. Saying good-bye to her, he managed to repeat that he would call again tomorrow and added that he looked forward to her friendship.

'Please come,' she answered with the same perplexed look on her face.

After Lavretsky's departure Panshin came alive; he began to give advice to Gedeonovsky, exchanged jocular pleasantries with Mrs Belenitsyn and finally sang his romance. But with Liza he spoke and exchanged looks as he had done previously: pointedly and rather gravely.

But again Lavretsky did not sleep the whole night. He was neither sad, nor excited, he was quite calm; but he could not sleep. He did not even think about the past; he simply surveyed his life; his heart beat heavily and evenly, and the hours flew by without a thought of sleep. At times only there would float into his mind the thought: 'It's untrue, it's all nonsense,' and he would stop and lower his head and again begin the probing survey of his life.

XXIX

MARYA DMITRIEVNA received Lavretsky none too kindly when he made his appearance the following day. 'It looks as if he's making a habit of coming,' she thought. She had no very strong liking for him in any event, and Panshin, what is more, under whose spell she was, had sung his praises exceedingly craftily and slightingly the previous day. Since she did not consider him a guest and thought it unnecessary to entertain a relative who was almost one of the household, it was less than half an hour before he was strolling along a garden path with Liza. Lenochka and Shurochka were running about among the flowerbeds a few steps away.

Liza was calm and composed as usual, but more than usually pale. She took from her pocket and handed to Lavretsky the tightly folded sheet of newspaper.

'It's awful!' she said.

Lavretsky made no reply.

'And perhaps it's also not true,' Liza added.

'That's why I asked you not to speak to anyone about it.' Liza walked on a little way.

'Tell me,' she began, 'aren't you saddened? Even a little?'

'I don't know what I feel,' Lavretsky answered.

'But surely you loved her earlier?'

'I did.'

'Very much?'

'Very much.'

'And you're not saddened by her death?'

'She died for me before now.'

'What you say is sinful. . . . Don't be angry with me. You call me your friend: a friend can say anything. I really do feel terrible about it. . . . Yesterday there was such an unpleasant look on your face. . . . Do you remember how you railed against her recently? – and perhaps she was no longer on the earth at that moment. It's terrible. It's just as if it had been sent to you as a punishment.'

Lavretsky grinned bitterly.

'Do you think so? . . . At least I'm now free.'

Liza shuddered slightly.

'That's enough, you mustn't talk like that. What good to you is your freedom? You oughtn't to think about that now, but about forgiveness . . .'

'I forgave her long ago,' Lavretsky interrupted with a wave of the hand.

'No, not that,' Liza protested and reddened. 'You've mis-understood me. You ought to be worried that you're for-given . . .'

'Who's going to forgive me?'

'Who? God. Who can forgive you if not God?'

Lavretsky seized her by the hand.

'Ah, Lizaveta Mikhaylovna, believe me,' he exclaimed, 'I've already been punished enough! I've already expiated everything, believe me.'

'You can't know that for sure,' Liza said in a low voice. 'You're forgetting that quite recently, when you were talking to me, you didn't want to forgive her.'

They both walked a short way in silence.

'What about your daughter?' Liza asked suddenly, and stopped.

Lavretsky was startled.

'Oh, don't worry! I've already sent letters to all the neces-sary places. The future of my daughter, as you call her . . . as you say . . . is ensured. Don't worry.'

Liza smiled sadly.

'But you're right,' Lavretsky continued, 'what am I to do with my freedom? What good's it to me?'

'When did you get this newspaper?' asked Liza without answering his question.

'The day after your visit.'

'And didn't you . . . didn't you even cry?'

'No. I was staggered; but where was I to get tears from? There was no point in crying over the past when it had all been burnt out of me! Her misconduct did not destroy my hap-piness, but simply proved to me that it had never existed. What was there to cry about? However, who knows? I might have been more saddened if I'd received this news a fortnight earlier . . .'

'A fortnight?' Liza asked. 'What's happened during the last fortnight?'

Lavretsky did not answer, and Liza suddenly reddened more deeply than before.

'Yes, yes, you've guessed,' Lavretsky chimed in suddenly. 'In the course of this fortnight I have learned the significance of a pure woman's soul, and my past has retreated from me still further.'

Liza was embarrassed and moved quietly towards Lenochka and Shurochka among the flowerbeds.

'I'm happy I showed you that newspaper,' said Lavretsky, following behind her. 'I've become accustomed not to hide anything from you and I hope you'll repay me with the same trustfulness.'

'You think I should?' said Liza and stopped. 'In that case I ought to.... No! That's impossible.'

'What is it? Speak, speak.'

'It really seems to me I shouldn't.... But then,' added Liza and turned towards Lavretsky with a smile, 'what's the point of being frank by halves? Do you know something? Today I received a letter.'

'From Panshin?'

'Yes.... How did you know?'

'He asks for your hand?'

'Yes,' uttered Liza and looked at Lavretsky directly and seriously in the eyes.

Lavretsky, in his turn, looked seriously at Liza.

'Well, what answer did you give him?' he asked her finally.

'I don't know what answer to give,' Liza replied and lowered her clasped hands.

'Why not? Surely you love him?'

'Yes, I like him; he seems to be a nice person.'

'You told me the same thing in the same terms three days ago. I want to know whether you love him with that strong, passionate feeling which we are accustomed to call love?'

'As *you* understand it – no.'

'You're not in love with him?'

'No. But is that essential?'

'What do you mean?'

'My mama likes him,' Liza continued. 'He's kind and I haven't anything against him.'

'However, you haven't made up your mind?'

'Yes ... and perhaps you and your words are the reason why. Do you remember what you said the day before yesterday? But this is weakness ...'

'Oh, my child!' Lavretsky suddenly exclaimed, and his voice was shaking, 'don't deceive yourself with words, don't call weakness the cry of your heart that does not wish to give itself up without love. Don't take on yourself such a terrible responsibility to someone you don't love and yet wish to belong to ...'

'I'm obedient, I don't take anything on myself,' Liza started to say.

'Be obedient to your heart; it alone will tell you the truth,' Lavretsky interrupted her. 'Experience, reason – all that is dust and vanity! Do not deprive yourself of the best, the only happiness on earth.'

'Is it you saying this, Fyodor Ivanych? You yourself married for love – and were you happy?'

Lavretsky flung his arms wide.

'Ah, don't talk about me! You can have no idea of everything that a young, inexperienced and grotesquely ill-educated boy can take for love! ... Yet why should I tell lies about myself? I told you just now that I did not know happiness. ... That's not true! I was happy!'

'It seems to me, Fyodor Ivanych,' Liza said, lowering her voice (when she disagreed with her interlocutor she always lowered her voice; besides, she was in a state of great excitement), 'happiness on earth does not depend on us.'

'It depends on us and on you, believe me,' (he seized both her hands in his; Liza grew pale and almost in fright, if attentively, gazed at him) 'so long as we haven't ourselves spoiled our lives. For some people a love-match can be a misfortune; but not for you, with your calm temperament and your lucid soul! I implore you, don't get married without love, through a feeling of duty or renunciation or something of the kind. ... That's the same as lack of faith, the same as marrying for money and even worse. Believe me – I have a right to say this because I paid dearly for this right. And if your God ...'

At that moment Lavretsky noticed that Lenochka and Shurochka were standing beside Liza and staring at him with dumb amazement. He released Liza's hands and said hurriedly: 'Please forgive me,' and turned towards the house.

'I ask you only one thing,' he said, turning back to Liza, 'don't decide at once, wait a bit, think over what I've said to you. Even if you haven't believed me, even if you should decide to marry for reasons of expediency – don't, in that case, marry Mr Panshin: he is not the husband for you. ... You will promise me, won't you, not to hurry?'

Liza wanted to answer Lavretsky – and did not utter a word, not because she had decided to 'hurry', but because her heart was beating too fast and a feeling akin to terror stifled her breathing.

XXX

ON leaving the Kalitins, Lavretsky met Panshin; they bowed coldly to each other. Lavretsky returned to his rooms and locked himself in. He was experiencing feelings which he had hardly ever experienced before. Was it so long ago that he had been in a state of 'peaceful torpor'? Was it so long ago that he had thought of himself as being at the bottom of a river? What had made his position change? What had brought him to the surface? Was it the most ordinary, inevitable, though always unexpected accident of death? Yes; but he was thinking not so much about the death of his wife and his own freedom, as about what answer Liza would give to Panshin. He felt that in the course of the last three days he had begun to look at her with different eyes; he recalled how, returning home and thinking about her in the silence of the night, he had said to himself: 'If only!...' That 'if only', related by him to the past and the impossible, had now come to pass, if not exactly as he had supposed – but his freedom alone was not enough. 'She'll obey her mother,' he thought, 'and marry Panshin; but even if she refuses him – isn't it all the same to me?' Passing in front of a mirror, he glanced into his face and gave a shrug.

The day passed quickly in these reflections, and it became evening. Lavretsky went to the Kalitins. He walked hurriedly, but he approached their house with slower steps. Panshin's droshky stood before the porch. 'Well,' thought Lavretsky, 'I'm not going to be an egoist,' and he went into the house. He met no one inside, and there was no sound from the drawing-room; he opened the door and saw Marya Dmitrievna playing picquet with Panshin. Panshin bowed to him without speaking, and the mistress of the house exclaimed: 'What a surprise!' and slightly knitted her brows. Lavretsky sat down beside her and began looking at her cards.

'Do you know how to play?' she asked him with a kind of veiled annoyance and at once laid her cards on the table.

Panshin totted his score up to ninety and then began politely and composedly taking tricks, with a stern and dignified expression on his face. That is how diplomats should play; no doubt he had played like that in St Petersburg with some powerful high-up whom he wished to impress with a good opinion of his solidity and maturity. 'A hundred and one, a hundred and two, hearts, a hundred and three,' his voice resounded with monotonous regularity, and Lavretsky could not make up his mind whether it sounded reproachful or self-satisfied.

'May I see Marfa Timofeyevna?' he asked, when he noticed that Panshin had started shuffling the cards with even greater dignity. There was no inkling of the artist in him at that moment.

'Yes, I think so. She is in her room upstairs,' answered Marya Dmitrievna. 'Go and find out.'

Lavretsky went upstairs. And he also found Marfa Timofeyevna playing cards: she was playing Old Maid with Nastasya Karpovna. Roska began barking at him; but both the old ladies welcomed his arrival, particularly Marfa Timofeyevna, who seemed in excellent spirits.

'Ah! Fedya! Do come in,' she said, 'and sit down, my dear. We'll be finished with our game in a moment. Would you like some jam? Shurochka, get him the pot of strawberry. You wouldn't like that? Well, then, sit there just as you are; as for smoking – don't smoke: I can't stand your tobacco and it makes Sailor sneeze.'

Lavretsky hastened to announce that he had no wish to smoke.

'Were you downstairs?' the old lady continued. 'Who did you see there? Is Panshin still about the place? Have you seen Liza? No? She said she'd come here. . . . And there she is; no sooner said than done.'

Liza entered the room and, catching sight of Lavretsky, blushed.

'I was coming to you just for a minute, Marfa Timofeyevna,' she began.

'Why just for a minute?' protested the old lady. 'Why is it that all you young girls are such fidgets? You see I've got a guest: have a chat with him, keep him entertained.'

Liza sat down on the edge of a chair, raised her eyes to Lavretsky and felt at once that it was impossible for her not to let him know the result of her meeting with Panshin. But how was it to be done? She felt both ashamed and awkward. It was no time at all since she had got to know him, this man who rarely went to church and was so indifferent to the death of his wife, and yet she was now telling him her secrets. . . .

True, he was taking an interest in her; she also trusted him and felt an attraction for him; but nevertheless she felt ashamed, as though a stranger had entered her pure, virginal world.

Marfa Timofeyevna came to her aid.

'If you won't keep him entertained,' she said, 'who will, the poor fellow? I'm too old for him, he's too clever for me, and he's too old for Nastasya Karpovna: it's only the young ones for her.'

'How can I entertain Fyodor Ivanych?' asked Liza. 'If he likes, I'll play him something on the piano,' she added indecisively.

'And a very good idea, too; you're my clever one,' said Marfa Timofeyevna. 'Be off with you down below, my dears; when you're finished, come back up here; I'm ashamed to say I've been left an Old Maid and I want to get my revenge.'

Liza stood up. Lavretsky followed her. Going down the stairs, Liza stopped.

'They tell the truth,' she began, 'when they say the human heart is full of contradictions. Your example should frighten me, it should make me distrust love matches, but I . . .'

'You refused him?' Lavretsky interrupted.

'No; but I also didn't agree. I told him everything, everything I felt, and I asked him to wait. Are you satisfied?' she asked with a quick smile and, lightly touching the bannister rail with her hand, ran down the stairs.

'What shall I play you?' she asked, raising the piano lid.

'Whatever you like,' Lavretsky answered and sat down so that he could see her.

Liza began to play and for a long while did not lift her eyes from her fingers. She looked, finally, at Lavretsky and stopped: his face looked so strange and wonderful.

'What's wrong with you?' she asked.

'Nothing,' he replied, 'I feel very happy. I'm glad for you and glad to see you. Please go on playing.'

'It seems to me', Liza said a few moments later, 'that if he really loved me, he wouldn't have written me that letter; he should have felt that I couldn't answer him now.'

'That's not important,' said Lavretsky. 'What's important is that you don't love him.'

'Stop talking like that! I have visions of your dead wife, and you terrify me.'

'How charmingly my Lisette plays, Woldemar, doesn't she?' Marya Dmitrievna was saying to Panshin at that moment.

'Yes,' answered Panshin, 'very charmingly.'

Marya Dmitrievna looked with tenderness at her young partner; but the latter assumed a still more important and preoccupied look and declared a fourteen of kings.

XXXI

LAVRETSKY was not a young man; he could not deceive himself for long about the feeling induced in him by Liza; that day he was finally convinced he loved her. This conviction brought him no great happiness. 'Can it be', he thought, 'that at thirty-five years of age I have nothing better to do than once again relinquish my soul to a woman? But Liza is not to be compared with *her*: she would not demand degrading sacrifices; she would not distract me from my studies; she would herself inspire me to honest, disciplined labour, and we would go forward together towards a beautiful ideal. Yes,' he ended his reflections, 'all this is good, but the bad part is that she has no wish to go with me. She meant it when she said I terrified her. Still she doesn't love Panshin . . . a poor consolation!'

Lavretsky drove to Vasilyevskoye; but he was there less than four days – it seemed to him so boring. He was fretted also by expectation: the news given by M. Jules needed confirmation, and he had received no letters. He returned to the town and sat out the evening at the Kalitins. It was easy for him to see that Marya Dmitrievna was ranged against him; but he succeeded in ingratiating himself with her to some extent by losing fifteen roubles to her at picquet, and he spent about half an hour almost alone with Liza despite the fact that her mother had advised her the previous day not to be too familiar with someone *'qui a un si grand ridicule'*. He found a change in her: she had apparently become more thoughtful, reproached him for his absence and asked him whether he would be going to church the next day. (The next day was Sunday.)

'Come to church,' she said before he could answer, 'and we'll pray together for the peace of *her* soul.' Then she added that she did not know what to do, not knowing whether she had the right to make Panshin wait any longer for her decision.

'Why exactly?' asked Lavretsky.

'Because,' she said, 'I'm already beginning to suspect what that decision will be.'

She announced that she had a headache and went upstairs to her room, irresolutely holding out to Lavretsky the tips of her fingers.

The next day Lavretsky went to church. Liza was already there when he arrived. She noticed him although she did not turn towards him. She prayed with great devotion; her eyes radiated a quiet reverence, with quiet reverence she bowed and raised her head. He felt that she was praying for him as well, and he felt wonderfully uplifted in his soul. It was a feeling both happy and a little conscience-stricken. The people standing there in their Sunday best, the familiar faces, the harmonious singing, the smell of incense, the long oblique rays of sunlight from the windows, the very darkness of the walls and vaulted ceiling – everything spoke directly to his heart. It was a long time since he had been in a church, a long time since he had addressed himself to God; he uttered no words of prayer now – and he did not pray even wordlessly –

but if only for an instant, if not with his body, then with all his being, he cast himself down and bowed in humility to the ground. He was reminded how in his childhood, on each visit to the church, he would pray until such time as he felt upon his brow the touch of something sent to refresh him; that, he used to think, was his guardian angel taking him into his keeping and setting upon him the seal of grace. He glanced at Liza. . . . 'You've brought me here,' he thought, 'stretch out your hand and touch me, touch my soul.' She still prayed with the same quiet reverence; her face seemed to him radiant with joy, and again he was uplifted, and he begged peace for another person's soul and forgiveness for his own . . .

They met at the entrance to the church; she greeted him with a fond and cheerful gravity. The sun shone brightly on the young grass in front of the church and the colourful dresses and headwear of the women; the bells of neighbouring churches boomed high above; sparrows chattered on the fences. Lavretsky stood smiling with uncovered head; a light breeze flicked up his hair and the ends of the ribbons of Liza's hat. He helped Liza, and Lenochka who was accompanying her, into the carriage, distributed all the money he had with him to the beggars and went quietly home.

XXXII

DIFFICULT days set in for Fyodor Ivanych. He was in a constant fever of excitement. Each morning he went to the post office and excitedly tore open letters and journals – and yet nowhere did he find anything to confirm or deny the fateful rumour. Sometimes he became repugnant to himself: 'Here I wait,' he thought, 'like a vulture waiting for blood, for genuine news of my wife's death!' He visited the Kalitins each day; but things were no easier for him there: the mistress of the house was obviously huffy with him and received him only out of condescension; Panshin treated him with exaggerated politeness; Lemm had assumed his misanthropic air and scarcely bowed to him, but worst of all: Liza seemed to be avoiding him. Whenever the two of them happened to be alone together, in place of the former trustfulness she showed signs of being overwrought and confused; she had no idea what to say to him and he was himself covered in embarrassment. In the course of a few days Liza became unlike the girl he had known previously: her movements, her voice, even her laughter were marked by a secret alarm and a hitherto non-existent lack of moderation. Marya Dmitrievna, like the dyed-in-the-wool egoist she was, suspected nothing; but Marfa Timofeyevna began to keep a close watch on her favourite. More than once Lavretsky reproached himself for having shown Liza the newspaper: he could not fail to recognize that his spiritual condition contained something repugnant to one of pure feeling. He also supposed that the change in Liza was due to a struggle with herself and to her doubts about what answer to give to Panshin. One day she brought him a book, a novel by Walter Scott, which she had herself asked him for.

'Have you read this book?' he asked.

'No, I haven't any time for books now,' she answered, and wanted to go.

'Wait a minute; it's such a long time since we were alone. You seem to be frightened of me.'

'I am.'

'Why, may I ask?'

'I don't know.'

Lavretsky was silent a moment.

'Tell me,' he began, 'have you decided yet?'

'What do you mean?' she asked, without raising her eyes.

'You know what I mean ...'

Liza suddenly flared up.

'Don't ask me about anything!' she cried with animation. 'I don't know anything, I don't even know myself ...'

And she at once left the room.

On the following day Lavretsky drove to the Kalitins after dinner and found everything ready for the celebration of an evening service. In a corner of the dining-room was a square table covered with a clean cloth, upon which, leaning against the wall, were placed small icons in gold frames, with small lustreless diamonds set in the haloes. An old servant in a grey frock-coat and shoes walked unhurriedly and without making tapping noises with his heels the whole length of the room, placed two wax candles in delicate candlesticks before the icons, made the sign of the cross, bowed and quietly went out. The unlit drawing-room was empty. Lavretsky walked through the dining-room and inquired whether it was someone's Saint's Day? He was told in a whisper that it was not, but that the evening service had been ordered on the wishes of Lizaveta Mikhaylovna and Marfa Timofeyevna; that they had wanted to hold aloft a miracle-working icon, but it had gone twenty miles away for the benefit of a sick man. There soon appeared, along with the deacons, the priest, a man far from young, with a large bald patch, who coughed loudly in the entrance hall; the ladies at once filed out of the study and went up to him to receive his blessing; Lavretsky bowed to them in silence; they bowed back in silence. The priest remained standing there a short while, again coughed and asked in a deep undertone:

'Do you wish me to start?'

'Please start, father,' said Marya Dmitrievna.

He began to put on his vestments; a deacon in a surplice asked obsequiously for a live coal; the smell of incense arose. Household servants came in from the hall and stood in a dense crowd by the doors. Roska, who had never come downstairs before, suddenly appeared in the dining-room: they started to drive her out, but she grew frightened, dashed round and round and then sat down; a manservant picked her up and carried her away. The service began. Lavretsky pressed himself into a corner; his feelings were strange, almost sad; he had no very clear idea what he felt. Marya Dmitrievna stood at the front, before the armchairs; she made the sign of the cross with an affected nonchalance, in lordly fashion, either looking around her or suddenly raising her eyes to the ceiling: she was manifestly bored. Marfa Timofeyevna seemed preoccupied; Nastasya Karpovna bowed to the floor and rose again with a kind of soft and modest rustling; Liza stood on the one spot without moving or stirring; judging from the look of concentration on her face, it could be assumed that she was engaged in intent and fervent prayer. When the cross was placed to her lips at the end of the service, she also kissed the priest's large red hand. Marya Dmitrievna invited him to take tea; he removed his stole, took on a slightly worldly look and joined the ladies in the drawing-room. A not unduly lively conversation began. The priest drank four cups of tea, ceaselessly wiped his bald patch with a handkerchief, related among other things that the merchant Avoshnikov had given seven hundred roubles for the gilding of the church 'cupola' and informed them of a reliable means of getting rid of freckles. Lavretsky was about to sit next to Liza, but she held herself stiffly, almost severely, and did not once glance in his direction. She seemed deliberately not to notice him; she was possessed by a kind of cold, serious exaltation. Lavretsky for some reason felt a constant urge to smile and say amusing things; but there was confusion in his heart, and he left finally, secretly bewildered. . . . He felt that there was something in Liza which he could not fathom.

On another occasion Lavretsky, sitting in the drawing-room and listening to the insinuating, but oppressive, chatter of Gedeonovsky, suddenly, without knowing why, turned his head and caught a profound, attentive, questioning look in Liza's eyes. . . . It was directed straight at him, this enigmatic look. Lavretsky later thought about it the whole night. He was in love not like a boy, and sighs and longings did not suit him, nor did Liza herself arouse that kind of feeling; but love at any age has its sufferings, and he experienced them to the full.

XXXIII

ONCE Lavretsky, in his usual way, was sitting at the Kalitins. A tiresomely hot day had been succeeded by such a beautiful evening that Marya Dmitrievna, despite her aversion to draughts, had ordered all the windows and doors into the garden to be opened and announced that she would not play cards, that it was a sin to play cards in such weather and it was right to enjoy the beauties of nature. Panshin was the only guest. Inspired by the evening and yet unwilling to sing in front of Lavretsky, but experiencing an access of artistic feelings, he launched into poetry: he read well, but too deliberately and with unnecessary niceties, several poems by Lermontov[1] (in those days Pushkin had not yet come back into fashion) – and suddenly, as if ashamed of his outpourings, began, apropos of the well-known poem *Duma*, to attack the younger generation; added to which, he did not overlook the opportunity to expound how he would change everything if he had the power. 'Russia,' he said, 'has fallen behind Europe; we must catch up. People assert that we're young – that's nonsense; besides, we lack inventiveness; Khomyakov[2] himself has admitted that we did not even invent the mousetrap. Consequently, we must borrow willy-nilly from others. We're sick, says Lermontov, and I agree with him; but we're sick because we've only become half-European; we must cure ourselves with more of what's made us sick.' ('*Le cadastre*,' thought Lavretsky.) 'Among us', he continued, 'the best minds – *les meilleures têtes* – have long been convinced of this; all nations are in substance the same; you have only to introduce good institutions, and that's the end of the matter. Certainly the institutions can be modified to suit the existing national customs; that is our business, the business of men of ...' (he almost said: men of state) 'of government servants; but if the need arises, you needn't worry: the institutions will remake the national customs.' Marya Dmitrievna ranged herself admiringly on Panshin's side with nods of the head. 'What an intelligent talker I have in my house,' she thought; Liza was silent, leaning at the open window; Lavretsky was also silent; Marfa Timofeyevna, playing cards in one corner with her friend, mumbled something under her breath. Panshin walked up and down the room and spoke eloquently, but with secret exasperation, as if he was scolding not a whole generation but a few of those known to him. In the Kalitins' garden, in a large lilac bush, lived a nightingale; the first notes of its evening song resounded during pauses in the eloquent speech; the first stars were alight in the rosy sky above the motionless tips of the limes. Lavretsky stood up and began to counter Panshin's words; a controversy developed. Lavretsky upheld the youth and independence of Russia; he sacrificed himself and his own generation, but he interceded for the new men, for their convictions and desires; Panshin made bad-tempered and sharp rejoinders, declared that intelligent people must change everything and was finally carried away to the point where, forgetting his court status and civil service career, he called Lavretsky an outdated conservative and even hinted – true, very remotely – at his false position in society. Lavretsky did not lose his temper, did not raise his voice (he remembered that Mikhalevich had also called him outdated, only a Voltairean) and calmly defeated Panshin on all points. He demonstrated to him the impossibility of progress by leaps and bounds or making high-handed changes from above through officialdom – changes justified neither by a knowledge of one's native land, nor by genuine belief in an ideal, even a negative one; he cited his own education as an example and he demanded first of all a recognition of Russia's own popular 'truth' and reconciliation with it – that reconciliation, without which opposition to falsehood is impossible; finally, he did not attempt to evade the – in his opinion – deserved reproach of having lightmindedly wasted his time and energies.

'All that is admirable!' exclaimed Panshin, furious at last. 'So here you are, you've returned to Russia – what precisely do you intend to do?'

'To plough the land,' answered Lavretsky, 'and to strive to plough it as well as possible.'

'That's very praiseworthy, no doubt of it,' retorted Panshin, 'and I'm told you've already made great strides in that direction; but you will agree that not everyone is capable of that kind of activity.'

'*Une nature poétique*,' said Marya Dmitrievna, 'of course, cannot plough . . . *et puis*, Vladimir Nikolaich, you are called to do everything *en grand*.'

This was too much for Panshin; he stopped short – and curtailed the conversation. He attempted to redirect the talk to the beauties of the starlit sky and the music of Schubert – all to no avail; he ended by suggesting that Marya Dmitrievna should play picquet. 'What! On such an evening?' she protested weakly; however, she ordered the cards to be brought.

Panshin tore open a new pack with a crackling sound, while Liza and Lavretsky, as if literally in collusion, both rose and took their places beside Marfa Timofeyevna. Both of them suddenly became so happy they were even frightened of staying together, and simultaneously they both felt that their recent mutual embarrassment had vanished and would not return. The old lady tapped Lavretsky slyly on the cheek, knowingly screwed up her eyes and shook her head several times, whispering: 'Thank you for dealing with the smart aleck.' Everything grew quiet in the room; only the faint crackling of the wax candles could be heard, and occasionally a hand tapping the table, an exclamation or a reckoning of the score, and, in a broad wave of sound pouring in through the windows together with the dewy night air, the powerful, audaciously resonant song of the nightingale.

XXXIV

LIZA did not utter a word during the controversy between Lavretsky and Panshin, but she followed it closely and was entirely on Lavretsky's side. Politics interested her very little; but the high-handed tone of the worldly government official (he had never let himself go like that before) repelled her; his contempt for Russia deeply offended her. It had never occurred to Liza that she was a patriot; but she was spiritually at home with Russian people; the Russian cast of mind delighted her; she would spend hours unselfconsciously talking to the village elder from her mother's estate whenever he came into town, and she talked to him as an equal, without any lordly condescension. Lavretsky felt all this: he would not have spoken simply to counter Panshin's arguments; he spoke only for Liza. They said nothing to each other, even their eyes met only occasionally; but they both understood that they had come closely together that evening, understood that they liked and disliked the same things. They differed only on one matter; but Liza secretly hoped to bring him to God. They sat beside Marfa Timofeyevna and seemed to be following her game; and they were in fact following it – yet meanwhile their hearts were expanding, nothing was lost on them: for them the nightingale sang, the stars burned and the trees whispered softly, cradled in sleep by summer softness and summer warmth. Lavretsky surrendered himself utterly to the wave of feeling that swept him away – and was filled with joy; but no words can express what was happening in the pure soul of the girl: it was a secret for her; let it remain a secret for all and everyone. No one can know, no one has seen or will ever see how the seed summoned to life and fruition swells and ripens in the bosom of the earth.

It struck ten. Marfa Timofeyevna went upstairs to her room with Nastasya Karpovna; Lavretsky and Liza crossed the room, stopped before the open door into the garden, glanced into the outer darkness and then at each other – and smiled; they were about to take each other's hands, it seemed, and talk to their heart's content. They turned back to Marya Dmitrievna and Panshin, whose game of picquet was going on and on. The final king was called, and the mistress of the house rose, groaning and sighing, from the cushion-filled armchair; Panshin seized his hat, kissed Marya Dmitrievna's hand, remarked that nothing now prevented the lucky ones from going to sleep or enjoying the night air, but he had to sit until morning poring over a lot of stupid papers, coldly exchanged bows with Liza (he had not expected that in answer to his proposal she would ask him to wait, and consequently he was in a huff with her) – and left. Lavretsky followed him to the gate, where they parted. Panshin woke his driver by poking him in the neck with the end of his stick, sat in his droshky and drove away. Lavretsky was unwilling to go home: he went out of town into the field. The night was calm and bright, although there was no moon; Lavretsky wandered for a long while through the dewy grass; he came upon a narrow path and followed it. It led him to a long fence and a small gate; he tried pushing it, not knowing why: it creaked faintly and opened just as if it had been waiting for the touch of his hand. Lavretsky found himself in a garden, took a few steps along an avenue of limes and suddenly stopped in amazement: he recognized the Kalitins' garden.

He at once entered a black patch of shadow cast by a thick hazelnut bush and stood there for a long time, shrugging his shoulders in wonder.

'This was intended,' he thought.

All was quiet around him; no sound came from the direction of the house. He stepped cautiously forward. There, at the turn in the avenue, the whole house suddenly turned its dark face towards him: a light glimmered only in two upper windows: in Liza's a candle burned behind the white curtain, and in Marfa Timofeyevna's bedroom the little red flame of the lamp burning before the icon was reflected in an even radiance over the gold of the frame; downstairs the door on to the balcony yawned wide open. Lavretsky sat down on a little wooden bench, leaned his head on his hand and began to watch that door and Liza's window. It struck midnight in the town; in the house small clocks delicately chimed midnight; a watchman struck a tattoo on his board. Lavretsky had no thoughts, no expectations; it was pleasant to feel himself close to Liza, to sit in her garden on a bench where she had sat more than once. . . . The light went out in Liza's room. 'Good night, my darling,' whispered Lavretsky, still sitting motionless without taking his eyes off the darkened window.

Suddenly a light appeared in one of the lower-floor windows, moved to another, then to a third. . . . Someone was walking with a candle from room to room. 'Surely it's not Liza? It can't be! . . .' Lavretsky half rose. . . . A familiar figure momentarily flashed by and Liza appeared in the drawing-room. In a white dress, with plaited hair falling to her shoulders, she quietly approached the table, leaned over it, put down the candle and looked for something; then, turning her face towards the garden, she came up to the open door and, all in white, airy, slender, stopped in the doorway. A quiver ran through Lavretsky's limbs.

'Liza!' was hardly audible from his lips.

She was startled and began peering into the darkness.

'Liza!' Lavretsky repeated more loudly and stepped out of the shadows of the avenue.

Liza stretched back her head in fright and rocked on her heels: she had recognized him. He called her name a third time and stretched out his hands to her. She left the doorway and stepped into the garden.

'You?' she said. 'You here?'

'It's me ... me. ... Hear what I've got to say,' Lavretsky whispered and, seizing her hand, led her to the bench.

She followed him without resistance; her pale face, fixed eyes, all her movements reflected her unspeakable astonishment. Lavretsky made her sit down on the bench and himself stood in front of her.

'I did not think of coming here,' he began. 'Something brought me here ... I ... I ... I love you,' he uttered with horror, despite himself.

Liza looked slowly up at him; it seemed she had only that instant realized where she was and what was happening to her. She wanted to get up, couldn't make herself and covered her face with her hands.

'Liza,' Lavretsky uttered. 'Liza,' he repeated, and bowed down to her feet ...

Her shoulders began to shake slightly and the fingers of her pale hands pressed more tightly to her face.

'What's wrong?' asked Lavretsky and heard her quiet weeping. His heart missed a beat. He realized what these tears meant. 'You're in love with me, aren't you?' he whispered and touched her knees.

'Get up,' he heard her say. 'Get up, Fyodor Ivanych. What are you and I doing this for?'

He stood up and sat down next to her on the bench. She had stopped crying and was looking closely at him with her moist eyes.

'I'm frightened; what are we doing this for?' she repeated.

'I love you,' he said again. 'I'm ready to give up my life for you.'

Again she shuddered, as though the words had stung her, and raised her eyes to the sky.

'It is all in God's hands,' she said.

'But you love me, Liza? We'll be happy, won't we?'

She lowered her eyes; he quietly drew her to him, and her

head dropped on to his shoulder. . . . He moved his head a little to one side and touched her pale lips.

Half an hour later Lavretsky was already standing by the garden gate. He found it locked and was obliged to jump over the fence. He returned to town and walked through the sleeping streets. A feeling of great and unexpected joy filled his soul; all his doubts had perished. 'Be gone, dark shade of the past,' he thought. 'She loves me and will be mine.' Suddenly he was invaded by a feeling that the air above him poured with enchanting, exultant sound; he stopped short: the sounds rang out still more magnificently; they flowed in a strong, full-throated flood – and they spoke and sang, it seemed, of all his happiness. He looked around: the sounds came from the two upper windows of a small house.

'Lemm!' Lavretsky shouted and ran up to the house. 'Lemm! Lemm!' he repeated loudly.

The sounds stopped and the figure of an old man in a night-shirt, bare-chested, with dishevelled hair, appeared in the window.

'Aha!' he said with dignity. 'It's you, is it?'

'Christopher Fyodorych, what marvellous music! For God's sake, let me in.'

The old man, without saying a word, made a grandiose movement of the hand and threw a key from the window into the street. Lavretsky ran briskly upstairs, dashed into the room and was on the point of embracing Lemm when the latter directed him imperiously to a chair and said in brokenly curt Russian: 'Sit and lizten!', seated himself before the piano, looked arrogantly and sternly round him and began to play. It was a long time since Lavretsky had heard anything similar: the sweet, passionate melody captivated his heart from the first note; it was full of radiance, full of the tender throbbing of inspiration and happiness and beauty, continually growing and melting away; it rumoured of everything on earth that is dear and secret and sacred to mankind; it breathed of immortal sadness and it departed from the earth to die in the heavens. Lavretsky straightened himself and stood, chill and pale with the ecstasy of it. These sounds literally sank into his soul, so recently shaken by the happiness of love; they themselves blazed with love. 'Again,' he whispered, as soon as the final chord was played. The old man looked at him with his eagle eyes, struck his breast with his hand and said slowly in his native language: 'I have done this, for I am a great musician' – and played his wonderful composition once more. There were no candles in the room; the light of the risen moon fell obliquely through the windows; the air, so finely attuned, quivered vibrantly; the tiny, wretched room seemed a holy sanctuary, where the old man's head rose high and inspired in a silvery haze. Lavretsky went up to him and embraced him. At first Lemm did not respond to his embrace, even elbowed him away; for a long time, still in every limb, he gazed ahead of him in the same stern, almost uncouth way, and once or twice grunted: 'Aha!' At last his transfigured face lost its severity, relaxed, and in response to Lavretsky's enthusiastic congratulations he at first smiled a little, then burst into tears, weakly sobbing like a child.

'It's astonishing,' he said, 'you should come precisely at this time; but I know everything, everything.'

'You know everything?' Lavretsky said in a confused voice.

'You heard me,' Lemm replied. 'Haven't you realized I know everything?'

Lavretsky could not sleep until morning; all night he sat on his bed. And Liza did not sleep: she was praying.

XXXV

THE reader knows how Lavretsky grew up and developed; we will say a few words about Liza's upbringing. She was ten years old when her father died; but he had had little time for

142

her. Overwhelmed with business matters, constantly pre-occupied with making money, embittered, sharp-tongued, impatient, he had spent money unsparingly on teachers, tutors, clothes and other children's needs; but he could not stand, as he put it, 'being nursemaid to the brats' – and indeed there was no occasion for him to be nursemaid to them: he worked, busied himself with his affairs, slept little, played an occasional game of cards and again worked; he compared himself to a horse harnessed to a threshing machine. 'My life's slipped away all too quickly,' he murmured on his death-bed, with a bitter smile on his dried-up lips. Marya Dmitrievna, to all intents and purposes, had no more time for Liza than her husband, although she had boasted to Lavretsky that she had brought her children up by herself; she used to dress Liza up like a doll, stroked her on the head in the presence of guests and called her to her face a clever girl and her darling – and that was all: any permanent care would utterly exhaust the indolent lady. During her father's lifetime Liza was in the hands of a governess, a Mademoiselle Moreau from Paris; after his death she passed into Marfa Timofeyevna's keeping. The reader already knows Marfa Timofeyevna; but Mademoiselle Moreau was a tiny wrinkled creature with bird-like ways and a bird-like brain. In her youth she had led a very disorderly life, but in old age she had retained only two passions – for sweet things and for cards. When she had eaten amply, was not playing cards or chattering, her face would instantly acquire an expression that was almost moribund: she would sit, gaze and breathe, but one could literally see that there was not a single thought in her head. She could not even be called kindly: birds, after all, are not kind-hearted. Whether as a consequence of a youth passed in frivolity or of the Parisian air which she had breathed since childhood, there had been fostered in her a kind of cheap and nasty, universal scepticism, which expressed itself usually in the words: '*Tout ça c'est des bêtises.*' She spoke an incorrect but purely Parisian jargon, did not gossip and was not given to caprices – what more can one ask of a governess? She had little influence on Liza; all the stronger, then, was the influence of her nurse, Agafya Vlasyevna.

This woman's story was remarkable. She came of a peasant family; at sixteen she was married to a muzhik; but she was in sharp contrast to her peasant sisters. Her father had been a village elder for twenty years, had accumulated a good deal of money and spoiled her. She was extraordinarily good-looking, the best-dressed woman in the whole region, clever, talkative and bold. Her master, Dmitry Pestov, Marya Dmitrievna's father, a quiet and modest man, saw her once during the threshing, talked to her and fell passionately in love with her. She was soon widowed; Pestov, although a married man, took her into his house and dressed her like a house-serf. Agafya at once acclimatized herself to her new position, just as if she had never lived otherwise. She grew paler and fuller; her arms beneath her muslin sleeves grew 'white as wheaten flour', like those of a merchant's wife; the samovar was never off the table; she would wear nothing but silk and velvet and slept on feather beds. This life of bliss lasted about five years, until Dmitry Pestov died; his widow, a kindly woman, in deference to the dead man's memory, had no wish to deal dishonourably with her rival, more especially since Agafya had never been disrespectful to her; however, she married her off to a cowherd and banished her from sight. Three years or so passed. One hot summer's day the mistress paid a visit to her cowsheds. Agafya offered her such excellent cold dairy cream, carried herself so modestly and was so neatly dressed, happy and contented with everything, that her mistress forgave her and allowed her to return to the house; and within six months had become so attached to her that she made her a housekeeper and entrusted the management of the household to her. Agafya again came into her own, grew plump and white-skinned; her mistress had implicit confidence in her. So

144

passed another five years. Misfortune broke over Agafya's head a second time. Her husband, whom she had raised into a man-servant, took to drink, started absenting himself from the house and ended by stealing six of the mistress's silver spoons and hiding them – for the time being – in his wife's trunk. The theft was discovered. He was again turned into a cow-herd, but Agafya suffered the worse indignity of disgrace; though she was not driven from the house, she was down-graded from housekeeper to seamstress and ordered to wear a kerchief instead of a cap. To everyone's surprise, Agafya accepted the blow that had fallen on her with meek humility. She was already more than thirty, all her children had died and her husband did not live long. The time had come for her to take stock; and take stock she did. She became very taciturn and religious, never missed a single morning or evening ser-vice, and gave away all her pretty dresses. Fifteen years she spent quietly, humbly, sedately, quarrelling with no one, acquiescent in all things. If people insulted her, she would simply bow her head and be grateful for the lesson. Her mis-tress had long since forgiven her, removed the disgrace from her and made her a gift of her own cap; but she herself had no wish to doff her kerchief and habitually went about in a dark dress; and after the death of her mistress she became still quieter and more humble. A Russian is always apprehensive and easily befriended; but it is hard to earn his respect: it is not given readily and not to everyone. Agafya was very much respected by everyone in the house; no one remembered her past sins, as if they had literally been buried in the earth along with the old master.

Having become Marya Dmitrievna's husband, Kalitin wanted to entrust the management of the household to Agafya; but she refused 'for fear of temptation'; he tried to get his way by shouting at her: she bowed low and went out. The intelligent Kalitin understood people; he also understood Agafya and did not forget her. When he moved into town, with her agreement he gave her a place as nurse to Liza, who had just passed her fifth year.

Liza was at first frightened by the stern and serious face of her new nurse; but she soon grew used to her and developed a strong attachment for her. She was herself a serious child; her features took after the sharp and regular face of her father; only her eyes were different: they shone with a calm attentiveness and goodness rare in children. She did not enjoy playing with dolls, had a laugh that was not loud or long, and was always on her best behaviour. She did not often become thoughtful, but when she did it was almost always to good effect: after a short silence she would usually end up by turning to a grown-up with a question which showed that her mind had been at work on some new impression. She stopped lisping very early and could pronounce words quite clearly before she was four. She was frightened of her father; her feeling for her mother was less well defined – she was not frightened of her and yet was not overtly fond of her; for that matter, she showed no overt fondness for Agafya, although it was only Agafya she really loved. She and Agafya were inseparable. They presented an odd sight both together. There would be Agafya, all in black, with a dark kerchief on her head, with her lean, waxenly translucent, but still beautiful and expressive face, sitting upright and knitting a stocking; at her feet, in a little armchair, would be Liza, also working at something or, with seriously raised bright little eyes, listening to what Agafya was telling her; and Agafya would not be telling her fairytales: in an even, level voice she would tell of the Virgin Mary, the lives of hermits, saints and holy martyrs; she would tell Liza how saints had dwelt in waste places, how they had been saved, how they had endured hunger and need, had not feared the wrath of kings and had confessed their faith in Christ; how birds of the air had brought them food and wild beasts were obedient to them; how on the places where their blood had fallen flowers had sprung up. 'Wallflowers?'

Liza, who was very fond of flowers, asked once. . . . Agafya spoke to Liza in serious and humble tones, as if she herself felt that it was not for her to pronounce such exalted and sacred words. Liza listened to her – and the image of an ever-present, omniscient God stole with a kind of sweet force into her soul, filled her with a pure, worshipful awe, and Christ became something close, familiar, almost kindred to her. Agafya also taught her how to pray. Sometimes she would wake Liza at dawn, hastily dress her and carry her off in secret to early service; Liza would follow her on tiptoe, hardly breathing; the cold and half-light of morning, the freshness and emptiness of the church, the very mysteriousness of these unexpected absences from home, the cautious return to the house and to bed – all this mixture of the forbidden, strange and holy shook the very foundations of the young girl's life and penetrated into the very depths of her being. Agafya never passed judgement on anyone and did not scold Liza for being naughty. When she was dissatisfied, she simply kept quiet; and Liza understood this silence; with the quick insight of a child she understood equally well when Agafya was dissatisfied with others – whether with Marya Dmitrievna or with Kalitin himself. Agafya looked after Liza for more than three years; Mademoiselle Moreau took her place; but the frivolous Frenchwoman with her dry ways and her exclamation: '*Tout ça c'est des bêtises*,' could not drive from Liza's heart her beloved nurse: the seeds she had sown had put down roots far too deep for that. Moreover Agafya, although she had ceased to look after Liza, remained in the house and had frequent occasion to see her pupil, who trusted her as before.

Agafya, however, did not get on with Marfa Timofeyevna when the latter moved into the Kalitin house. The stern solemnity of the former 'peasant' had no appeal for the self-willed and impatient old lady. Agafya asked to be allowed to go on a pilgrimage and did not return. Dark rumours circulated that she had joined a sect of Raskolniks. But the trace left by her in Liza's soul was not erased. She went as before to Mass, as if going on an outing, and said her prayers with enjoyment, with a kind of restrained and shamefaced excess of feeling which was a source of no little secret wonder to Marya Dmitrievna, and Marfa Timofeyevna herself, although she did not inhibit Liza in any way, tried to make her moderate her fervour and would not allow her to make too many obeisances to the ground: that, she said, was not the way the gentry did things. Liza learned her lessons well, that is to say assiduously; God had not endowed her with particularly remarkable capabilities or great cleverness; nothing came easily to her. She played the piano well; but Lemm alone knew how much that had cost her. She read little; she had no 'words of her own', but she had her own ideas and she went her own way. It was not for nothing that she resembled her father: she also never asked others what to do. So she grew up, calmly and unhurriedly, and had reached nineteen years of age. She was very charming without knowing it. Her every movement bespoke an involuntary, slightly awkward gracefulness; her voice rang with the silvery ring of immaculate youth; the slightest sensation of happiness brought an attractive smile to her lips and endowed her brightening eyes with a profound lustre and a kind of secret kindliness. Permeated with a feeling of duty, with a fear of offending anyone, with a kindness and meekness of heart, she loved the whole world and no one in particular; God alone she loved exultantly, shyly, tenderly. Lavretsky was the first person to disturb her calm inner life.

Such was Liza.

XXXVI

THE next day, at about twelve o'clock, Lavretsky went to the Kalitins. On the way he met Panshin, who galloped past him on horseback with his hat pulled down over his eyebrows. At the Kalitins he was not received – for the first time since he had made their acquaintance. Marya Dmitrievna was 'resting', or so the footman announced; 'her ladyship' had a headache. Marfa Timofeyevna and Lizaveta Mikhaylovna were not at home. Lavretsky took a stroll round the garden in the faint hope of meeting Liza, but saw no one. He returned two hours later and received the same answer, added to which the footman looked at him somewhat askance. It seemed improper to Lavretsky to pay a third call the same day – and he decided to go to Vasilyevskoye, where there were matters enough to be seen to. On the way he made various plans, each one more splendid than the next; but in his aunt's little village he was attacked by melancholy; he broached a conversation with Anton; the old man, as if deliberately, had only dismal thoughts on his mind. He told Lavretsky how Glafira Petrovna before her death had bitten her own hand – and, after a short silence, said with a sigh: 'Ev'ry man, master, sir, is destined to eat 'isself.' It was already late when Lavretsky set out for the return journey. The previous day's music captivated him, the image of Liza rose in his soul in all its meek lucidity; he was touched at the thought that she loved him – and he drove up to his little town house in a calm and happy mood.

The first thing that struck him on entering the hallway was the – to him – very repugnant smell of patchouli; and there stood there several tall trunks and boxes. The face of his valet, who came skipping out to meet him, looked odd. Without taking account of his impressions, he entered the doorway of the drawing-room. . . . There rose to meet him from the divan a lady in a black silk dress with flounces who, raising a cambric handkerchief to her pale face, took a few steps across the room, bent her exquisitely coiffured and perfumed head – and fell at his feet. . . . Only then did he recognize her: this lady was his wife.

His breathing failed him. . . . He leaned back against the wall.

'Theodore, do not drive me away!' she said in French, and her voice cut through his heart like a knife.

He gazed at her senselessly and yet at once noted, despite himself, that she had grown white and stout.

'Theodore!' she continued, occasionally casting up her eyes and carefully wringing her surprisingly beautiful hands with their pink polished nails. 'Theodore, I'm to blame, deeply to blame – I will say more, I've committed a crime against you; but you must hear me out, remorse is torturing me, I've become a burden to myself, I couldn't endure my position any longer; so many times I thought of turning to you, but I was frightened of your anger; I decided to break every connexion with the past . . . *puis, j'ai été si malade*, I was so ill,' she added, and drew a hand over her temples and cheek. 'I took advantage of the rumour that had been spread about my death and abandoned everything; without stopping, day and night I hurried here; I've hesitated a long time before coming before you, my judge – *paraître devant vous, mon juge*; but I decided finally to come to you, remembering your former goodness; I learned your address in Moscow. Believe me,' she continued, very quietly rising from the floor and sitting on the very edge of an armchair, 'I often thought about death, and I would've found enough courage in myself to take my own life – ah, life for me now is an unbearable burden! – but the thought of my daughter, of my Adochka, made me stop; she is here, she is asleep in the next room, poor child! She is tired – you will see her: she at least is not to blame, but I'm so wretched, so wretched!' exclaimed Mrs Lavretsky and burst into tears.

Lavretsky finally came to his senses; he moved away from the wall and turned towards the door.

'You're leaving?' his wife said with desperation. 'Oh, that's cruel! Without a single word to me, not even a reproach. . . . This contempt is killing me, it's terrible!'

Lavretsky stopped.

'What do you want to hear from me?' he uttered in a toneless voice.

'Nothing, nothing,' she chimed in animatedly. 'I know I have no right to demand anything; I'm not out of my mind, believe me; I don't hope, I don't dare to hope for your forgiveness; I only want to be bold enough to beg you to tell me what I should do and where I should live. Like a slave I will obey your command, whatever it may be.'

'It's not my business to give you orders,' Lavretsky retorted in the same voice. 'You know that everything's finished between us . . . and now more than ever. You can live wherever you like; and if your allowance seems to you too small . . .'

'Ah, don't say such terrible things,' Varvara Pavlovna interrupted him. 'Have pity on me, if only for . . . if only for the sake of this angel . . .' And, so saying, Varvara Pavlovna dashed headlong into the other room and instantly returned with a small, very elegantly dressed little girl in her arms. Large auburn curls fell about her pretty, rosy little face and on her large, black, sleepy eyes; she was both smiling and screwing up her eyes from the firelight and leaning with one fat little hand on her mother's neck.

'*Ada, vois, c'est ton père,*' said Varvara Pavlovna, lifting the curls from her eyes and robustly kissing her, '*prie-le avec moi.*'

'*C'est ça papa,*' the little girl lisped.

'*Oui, mon enfant, n'est-ce pas que tu l'aimes?*'

But this was too much for Lavretsky.

'In what melodrama is there just such a scene?' he muttered and went out.

Varvara Pavlovna stood for a while where she was, gave a slight shrug of the shoulders, carried the little girl into the other room, undressed her and put her to bed. Then she got out a book, sat down by the lamp, waited about an hour and eventually went to bed herself.

'*Eh bien, madame?*' asked her French maid, who had been brought by her from Paris, as she was taking off her corset.

'*Eh bien, Justine,*' she replied, 'he has grown much older in appearance, but it seems to me he's still the same kind-hearted man. Give me my gloves for the night and lay out my grey dress for tomorrow; and don't forget the mutton chops for Ada. . . . True, they may not be easy to find here; but one must try.'

'*À la guerre comme à la guerre,*' Justine replied and blew out the candle.

XXXVII

FOR more than two hours Lavretsky wandered about the streets of the town. He recalled to mind the night spent on the outskirts of Paris. His heart was breaking and in his head, empty and literally stunned, swarmed over and over the same thoughts, dark, senseless, wicked. 'She's alive, she's here,' he whispered with ever growing amazement. He felt that he had lost Liza. Bitterness choked him; this blow had fallen on him all too suddenly. How could he so readily have believed the rubbishy gossip of a newspaper report, a mere scrap of paper? 'Well, if I hadn't believed it,' he thought, 'what would've been the difference? I wouldn't have known that Liza loved me, nor would she have known it herself.' He could not drive out of his mind the image, the voice, the eyes of his wife. . . . And he cursed himself, cursed everything on earth.

Tormented by exhaustion, before morning he arrived at Lemm's. It took a while for his knocking to evoke a response; finally there appeared at the window the nightcapped head of the old man looking sour and wrinkled and quite unlike that stern, inspired head which, twenty-four hours before, had looked down upon Lavretsky majestically from the heights of its artistic magnificence.

'What do you want?' Lemm asked. 'I can't play every night, I've taken a decoction.'

But evidently Lavretsky's face had a strange look: the old man cupped a hand over his eyes, peered at his nocturnal visitor and admitted him.

Lavretsky entered the room and sank down on to a chair; the old man stopped in front of him and drew the skirts of his threadbare, colourful dressing-gown round him, hugging himself and gnawing his lips.

'My wife has arrived,' said Lavretsky, raising his head and suddenly, despite himself, burst into laughter.

Lemm's face expressed amazement, but he did not even smile, simply pulled the dressing-gown more tightly round him.

'Of course, you don't know,' Lavretsky continued, 'I imagined . . . I read in a newspaper that she was no longer alive.'

'O-oh, did you read this recently?' asked Lemm.

'Yes.'

'O-oh,' the old man repeated and raised his eyebrows high. 'And she's arrived here?'

'Yes. She's at my place now; and I'm . . . I'm an unlucky man.'

And again he gave a short laugh.

'You are an unlucky man,' Lemm repeated slowly.

'Christopher Fyodorych,' Lavretsky began, 'will you undertake to deliver a note?'

'Hm. May one know to whom?'

'Lizav . . .'

'Yes, yes, I understand. All right. But when should the note be delivered?'

'Tomorrow, as early as possible.'

'Hm. I could send Katrin, my cook. No, I'll go myself.'

'And you'll bring me back an answer?'

'And I'll bring you back an answer.'

Lemm gave a sigh.

'Yes, my poor young friend, you are indeed an unlucky young man.'

Lavretsky wrote a couple of words to Liza: he informed her of his wife's arrival and begged her to let him see her – and flung himself down on the narrow divan with his face to the wall; and the old man lay down on his bed and was restless for a long time, coughing and taking mouthfuls of his decoction.

Morning came; they both got up. They looked at each other with strange eyes. At that moment Lavretsky wanted to kill himself. Katrin, the cook, brought them some dreadful coffee. It struck eight o'clock. Lemm put on his hat and went out, saying that his lesson at the Kalitins was not until ten but that he would find a suitable excuse. Lavretsky again flung himself down on the little divan, and again bitter laughter rose from the depths of his soul. He thought how his wife had driven him out of his house; he imagined to himself Liza's position, closed his eyes and folded his hands behind his head. Eventually Lemm returned and brought him a scrap of paper on which Liza had pencilled the following words: 'We can't see each other today; perhaps tomorrow evening. Good-bye.' Lavretsky gave Lemm his dry, confused thanks and went off to his own house.

He found his wife at breakfast; Ada, her hair a mass of curls, dressed in a pale-white frock with pale-blue ribbons, was eating her mutton cutlet. Varvara Pavlovna rose the instant Lavretsky came into the room and approached him with a look of submissiveness on her face. He asked her to follow him into his study, locked the door behind him and began walking to and fro; she sat down, placing one hand modestly upon the other, and proceeded to follow him with her still beautiful, though slightly touched-up eyes.

It took Lavretsky some while to begin speaking: he felt that he had no control of himself and he clearly saw that

Varvara Pavlovna was not in the least frightened of him, though she pretended to be on the point of fainting.

'Please listen, madam,' he began at last, breathing heavily and from time to time clenching his teeth. 'We have no need to pretend to each other; I don't believe in your repentance; and even if it were sincere, to go back to you again, to live with you – that is impossible for me.'

Varvara Pavlovna pursed her lips and narrowed her eyes. 'This is repugnance,' she thought. 'It's all over! I'm not even a woman for him.'

'Impossible,' Lavretsky repeated and buttoned his coat up to the top. 'I don't know why it pleased you to come here; probably you had no more money.'

'Oh! You're insulting me,' Varvara Pavlovna whispered.

'However that may be – you are, alas, still my wife. I can't turn you out . . . and so this is what I propose to you. This very day, if you like, you can go to Lavriki and live there; there is a good house there, you know; you will receive all you need, over and above the allowance. . . . Do you agree?'

Varvara Pavlovna raised an embroidered handkerchief to her face.

'I've already told you,' she said, her lips working nervously, 'that I'll agree to whatever you think fit to do with me; on this occasion it remains for me to ask you: will you allow me at least to thank you for your magnanimity?'

'Without thanks, I beg you, that way it's better,' Lavretsky said hurriedly. 'So,' he continued, going to the door, 'I can count on . . .'

'Tomorrow I will be in Lavriki,' said Varvara Pavlovna, rising respectfully from her chair. 'But, Fyodor Ivanych' (she no longer called him Theodore) . . .

'What is it?'

'I know I have done nothing yet to deserve your forgiveness; can I hope at least that with time . . .'

'Oh, Varvara Pavlovna,' Lavretsky interrupted her, 'you're

a clever woman, but I'm also no fool; I know you don't need that at all. I forgave you long ago; but between us there was always a bottomless pit.'

'I will learn how to be submissive,' Varvara Pavlovna responded and bowed her head. 'I haven't forgotten my guilt; I wouldn't have been surprised if I'd learned that you even took delight in the news of my death,' she added meekly, lightly indicating with her hand the newspaper lying forgotten on the table by Lavretsky.

Fyodor Ivanych shuddered: the report had been marked in pencil. Varvara Pavlovna looked at him with even greater self-abasement. She was very fine at that moment. The grey Parisian dress gracefully shaped itself to her supple, almost seventeen-year-old waist, her delicate, soft neck surrounded by a little white collar, her evenly breathing bosom, her hands bare of rings and bracelets – her whole figure, from her glossy hair down to the tip of her slightly exposed shoe, was so elegant ...

Lavretsky encompassed her with a look of disgust, almost exclaimed: 'Bravo!' and was on the point of crowning her with his fist – and went out. An hour later he had already set off for Vasilyevskoye, while two hours later Varvara Pavlovna ordered that the best carriage in town be hired for her, put on a simple straw hat with a black veil and a modest mantle, entrusted Ada to Justine and went to the Kalitins: by questioning her servants she had learned that her husband visited them every day.

XXXVIII

THE day of the arrival of Lavretsky's wife in the town of O ..., an unhappy day for him, was a hard day for Liza as well. She had not succeeded in going downstairs and saying good morning to her mother when the sound of horse's hooves could already be heard from below the window and with secret horror she saw Panshin ride into the courtyard. 'He has come so early for a final explanation,' she thought – and she was not mistaken; having chatted about this and that for a while in the drawing-room, he suggested that she accompany him into the garden and there demanded to know what his fate was to be. Liza took her courage into her hands and announced that she could not be his wife. He heard her out, standing sideways to her with his hat pulled down over his forehead; politely, but in a changed voice, he asked her whether this was her last word and whether he had given her any cause to change her mind in such a way. Then he pressed his hand to his eyes, sobbed briefly and brokenly, and withdrew his hand from his face.

'I did not want to follow the beaten track,' he said tonelessly. 'I wanted to find a wife according to the inclination of my heart, but evidently that was not to be. Good-bye, sweet dreams!' He bowed low to Liza and returned to the house.

She hoped that he would leave at once; but he went to the study to see Marya Dmitrievna and stayed there for about an hour. When he came out, he said to Liza: '*Votre mère vous appelle; adieu à jamais . . .*', sat astride his horse and started away from the porch at a gallop. Liza went in to Marya Dmitrievna and found her in tears: Panshin had told her of his misfortune.

'Why have you been the death of me? Why?' was how the embittered widow began her complaints. 'Who else do you need? What's wrong with him for a husband? He has a position at court! He doesn't need to marry for money! In St Petersburg he could marry any lady-in-waiting! But for me, for me, there were such hopes! And how long is it since your feeling for him has changed? This cloud's been blown up from somewhere, it didn't come of its own accord. Is it that idiot relative of mine? What an adviser you've found!'

'But he, my dear,' continued Marya Dmitrievna, 'how

honourable he is, how attentive even in his grief! He has promised not to abandon me. Oh, I'll not·survive this! Ah, this headache'll be the death of me! Send Palashka to me. You'll kill me if you don't think again, do you hear?' And having called her an ungrateful girl a couple more times, Marya Dmitrievna sent Liza away.

She went to her room. But she had not had time to recover from the scenes with Panshin and her mother before another storm broke over her head, and from a quarter where she had least of all expected it. Marfa Timofeyevna came into her room and at once banged the door behind her. The old lady's face was pale, her cap askew, her eyes flashed and her hands and lips were quivering. Liza was flabbergasted: she had never seen her clever and discreet aunt in such a state.

'Marvellous, my fine lady,' Marfa Timofeyevna began in a trembling and broken whisper, 'marvellous! Who did you learn it all from, my dear. . . . Give me some water; I can't say another word.'

'Calm yourself, auntie, what's wrong with you?' said Liza, offering her a glass of water. 'After all you yourself, it seems, were none too fond of Mr Panshin.'

Marfa Timofeyevna put down the glass.

'I can't drink a drop. If I do, I'll knock out what few teeth I've got left. What's this about Panshin? What's Panshin got to do with it? You'd much better tell me who taught you to go making assignations at night, my dear, eh?'

Liza went pale.

'Please don't try denying it,' Marfa Timofeyevna continued. 'Shurochka herself saw everything and has told me. I've told her not to chatter on so, but she's not a liar.'

'I'm not going to deny it, auntie,' Liza murmured scarcely audibly.

'Aha! So that's how it is, my dear: you did make an assignation with him, with that old sinner, with that meek-and-mild one, did you?'

'No, I didn't.'

'How did it happen, then?'

'I went down into the drawing-room for a book: he was in the garden – and he called to me.'

'And you went? Marvellous. Are you in love with him, is that it?'

'I'm in love with him,' Liza answered in a quiet voice.

'Heavens above! She's in love with him!' Marfa Timofeyevna pulled the cap off her head. 'She's in love with a married man! Eh? She's in love with him!'

'He told me . . .' Liza began.

'What was he saying to you, the darling man, wha-at?'

'He told me his wife had died.'

Marfa Timofeyevna crossed herself.

'God rest her soul,' she whispered. 'An empty-headed wench she was – not that she should be remembered for it. So that's it: he's become a widower. And I see he's not letting the grass grow under his feet. He's no sooner got rid of one wife than he's after another. He's a quiet one, isn't he? Only I'll tell you this, niece: in my time, when I was young, girls weren't let off lightly for such carryings-on. Don't you be angry with me, my dear; only fools get angry at the truth. I gave orders that he wasn't to be admitted today. I'm very fond of him, but I'll never forgive him for this. A widower, indeed! Give me some of that water. And as for you giving Panshin one on the nose, for that you're in my good books; only don't go spending your nights sitting about with that breed of goats called men; don't break my old lady's heart! Otherwise you'll find I can do more than mollycoddle, I can bite as well. . . . A widower!'

Marfa Timofeyevna went out and Liza sat down in one corner and burst into tears. Her soul was filled with bitterness; she had not deserved such humiliation. Love had not come to her as happiness: for the second time she was in tears since yesterday evening. Her heart had only just given birth to that new, unexpected feeling, and already how heavily she had been made to pay for it, how rudely had others' hands touched her dearest secret! She felt ashamed and bitter and hurt; but she felt neither doubt, nor fear – and Lavretsky grew even dearer to her. She had hesitated only so long as she did not understand; but after that meeting, after that kiss she could hesitate no longer: she knew she was in love – and had fallen in love honestly, seriously, had committed herself firmly, for the rest of her life – and had no fear of threats: she felt no force on earth could break this bond.

XXXIX

MARYA DMITRIEVNA was very alarmed when the arrival of Varvara Pavlovna Lavretsky was announced; she did not even know whether to receive her for fear of offending Fyodor Ivanych. Curiosity finally gained the upper hand. 'Well,' she thought, 'she's a relative, too,' and, seating herself in an armchair, said to the footman: 'Show her in!' A moment or so passed; the door opened; briskly, with barely audible steps, Varvara Pavlovna approached Marya Dmitrievna and, without giving her a chance to rise from the armchair, almost sank on to her knees before her.

'Most gracious thanks, my dear aunt,' she began in a low, poignant voice, in Russian, 'most gracious thanks. I did not hope for such condescension on your part. You're as kind as an angel.'

Having said these words, Varvara Pavlovna unexpectedly seized Marya Dmitrievna's hand and, lightly pressing it in her pale-lilac Jouvin gloves[1], obsequiously raised it to her full and rosy lips. Marya Dmitrievna was quite at a loss, seeing such a beautiful, exquisitely dressed woman almost at her feet; she had no idea what to do, wanting both to withdraw her hand, and offer her a seat, and say something affectionate to her; she ended by raising herself and kissing Varvara Pavlovna on her smooth and perfumed brow. Varvara Pavlovna was over-whelmed by this kiss.

'How do you do, *bonjour*,' said Marya Dmitrievna. 'Of course I hadn't imagined . . . mind you, I am of course glad to see you. You understand, my dear, that it's not for me to judge between husband and wife . . .'

'My husband is right in everything,' Varvara Pavlovna interrupted her. 'I alone am to blame.'

'Those are very praiseworthy feelings,' responded Marya Dmitrievna, 'very. Have you been here long? Have you seen him? Do sit down, please.'

'I arrived yesterday,' Varvara Pavlovna answered, self-effacingly taking a seat. 'I have seen Fyodor Ivanych and I have spoken to him.'

'Ah! Well, and what did he say?'

'I was frightened that my sudden arrival would arouse his anger,' Varvara Pavlovna continued, 'but he did not deprive me of his presence.'

'That's to say, he didn't. . . . Yes, yes, I understand,' Marya Dmitrievna said. 'He only gives the appearance of being a little uncouth, but he has a soft heart.'

'Fyodor Ivanych did not forgive me; he did not wish to hear me out. . . . But he was so kind that he assigned me Lavriki as a place to live.'

'Ah! A splendid estate!'

'I am going there tomorrow, in fulfilment of his wishes; but I considered it my duty to pay you a visit beforehand.'

'I am very, very grateful to you, my dear. One should never forget one's relatives. But do you know something, I am astonished how well you speak Russian. *C'est étonnant.*'

Varvara Pavlovna sighed.

'I have been too long abroad, Marya Dmitrievna, I know that; but my heart has always been Russian, and I have not forgotten my homeland.'

'Quite, quite; that is best of all. Fyodor Ivanych, however, was not expecting you at all. . . . Yes, trust in my experience of things: *la patrie avant tout*. Ah, do show me, please, what an exquisite mantle you have.'

'Do you like it?' Varvara Pavlovna quickly took it off her shoulders. 'It is very simple, from Madame Baudran.'

'You can tell that at once. From Madame Baudran. . . . How charming and what taste! I feel sure you've brought with you a great many fascinating things. I'd love to have a look.'

'My entire wardrobe is at your service, dearest aunt. If you'll permit it, I can show your maid some things. I have a servant with me from Paris – she's a remarkable dressmaker.'

'You're very kind. But, really, I have a bad conscience.'

'A bad conscience . . .' repeated Varvara Pavlovna reproachfully. 'If you want to make me happy, deal with me as with your own property!'

Marya Dmitrievna's heart melted.

'*Vous êtes charmante*,' she said. 'Come now, why not take off your hat and gloves?'

'Really? You permit me?' Varvara Pavlovna asked and lightly, with a show of emotion, clasped her hands.

'Of course. You'll have dinner with us, I hope. I . . . I'll introduce you to my daughter.' Marya Dmitrievna grew a little confused. 'Well, what's it matter!' she thought. 'She is not quite herself today.'

'Oh, *ma tante*, how kind of you!' exclaimed Varvara Pavlovna and raised a handkerchief to her eyes.

A page-boy announced Gedeonovsky's arrival. The old gossip entered, bowing low and smirking. Marya Dmitrievna introduced him to her guest. At first he made a show of being put out; but Varvara Pavlovna was so respectfully coquettish towards him that his ears turned a fiery red, and stories, gossip and compliments flowed like honey from his lips. Varvara Pavlovna listened to him, smiled with restraint and began gradually to join in the conversation. She spoke modestly about Paris, her travels and Baden; once or twice she made Marya Dmitrievna laugh and each time she sighed lightly afterwards and seemed mentally to scold herself for such inappropriate gaiety; she asked permission to bring Ada; after removing her gloves, she demonstrated with her smooth hands smelling of soap *à la guimauve* how and where flounces, frills, lace and choux were worn; she promised to bring a bottle of the new English scent, Victoria Essence[2], and was as pleased as a child when Marya Dmitrievna agreed to accept it as a present; she grew tearful when she recalled what she had felt on hearing Russian church bells for the first time: 'So deeply they struck me, in my very heart,' she murmured.

At that instant Liza entered.

Ever since the morning and that very moment when, cold with horror, she had read Lavretsky's note, Liza had been preparing herself to meet his wife; she had a presentiment that she would see her. She had resolved not to avoid her, in punishment for her – as she called them – criminal hopes. The sudden crisis in her destiny had shaken her to the core; in no more than a couple of hours her face had grown thin; yet she had not shed a single tear. 'It serves me right!' she had told herself, suppressing excitedly and with difficulty certain bitter, malicious eruptions of feeling which frightened even her. 'Well, I must go,' she thought, as soon as she heard of Mrs Lavretsky's arrival, and go she did . . . She stood for a long while in front of the drawing-room door before she could make up her mind to open it; with the thought 'I have wronged her', she entered the room and forced herself to look at her, to smile at her. Varvara Pavlovna came towards her as soon as she saw her and bowed slightly, but nevertheless politely. 'Allow me to introduce myself,' she began ingratiatingly. 'Your maman has been so gracious to me that I hope you will also be . . . kind.' The expression on Varvara Pavlovna's face when she said this last word, her insinuating smile, her cold and, at the same time, soft glance, the movement of her hands

163

and shoulders, what she was wearing and her whole being aroused such a feeling of repugnance in Liza that she could not answer and it was with an effort that she stretched out her hand. 'This young lady can't stand me,' thought Varvara Pavlovna, firmly pressing Liza's cold fingers, and, turning to Marya Dmitrievna, she said in a low voice: '*Mais elle est délicieuse!*' Liza coloured faintly at the mockery and insult which she heard in this exclamation; but she was determined not to trust her first impressions and sat down by the window with her embroidery. Varvara Pavlovna gave her no peace even there: she approached her, began praising her taste and her artistry. . . . Liza's heart beat violently and sickeningly: she could hardly contain herself, hardly stay where she was. It seemed to her that Varvara Pavlovna knew everything and, secretly triumphant, was making fun of her. Luckily for her, Gedeonovsky began talking to Varvara Pavlovna and distracted her attention. Liza bent over her embroidery and covertly observed her. 'This was the woman', she thought, 'that *he* loved.' But she at once banished from her head all thought of Lavretsky, for she was frightened of losing control of herself and felt her head quietly spinning. Marya Dmitrievna started talking about music.

'I have heard, my dear,' she began, 'that you're astonishingly gifted.'

'I haven't played for a long time,' Varvara Pavlovna responded, immediately seating herself at the piano, and she briskly ran her fingers over the keys. 'Would you like me to?'

'Please do.'

Varvara Pavlovna gave a masterly rendering of a brilliant and difficult étude by Herz[3]. She played with great power and agility.

'Sylph-like!' exclaimed Gedeonovsky.

'Extraordinary!' agreed Marya Dmitrievna. 'Well, Varvara Pavlovna, I confess', she said, calling her by her name for the first time, 'you've astonished me; you ought to give concerts. We have a musician here, an old man, a German, eccentric, very learned; he gives Liza lessons; he'd be simply thrilled to bits by you.'

'Lizaveta Mikhaylovna also plays?' asked Varvara Pavlovna, slightly turning her head towards her.

'Yes, she doesn't play badly and is fond of music; but what's that compared to you? But there is a young man here, whom you ought to get to know. He has the soul of an artist and composes very charmingly. He alone could appreciate you to the full.'

'A young man?' asked Varvara Pavlovna. 'Who is he? Is he some poor fellow?'

'Not at all. He's the most eligible young man we have, and not only here – *et à Pétersbourg*. He has a position at court and is received in the best society. You may have heard of him: Panshin, Vladimir Nikolaich. He is here on government business . . . a future minister for certain!'

'And an artist?'

'The soul of an artist, and so charming. You will see him. All the time he has been coming here very frequently; I invited him for this evening; I *do* hope he comes,' added Marya Dmitrievna with a short sigh and a bitter smile to one side.

Liza understood the meaning of this smile, but was unconcerned by it.

'And young?' asked Varvara Pavlovna again, modulating her voice slightly from one tone to another.

'Twenty-eight – and of most pleasant appearance. *Un jeune homme accompli*, believe me.'

'An exemplary young man, one might say,' remarked Gedeonovsky.

Varvara Pavlovna suddenly launched into a noisy Strauss waltz, beginning with such a strong and rapid trill that Gedeonovsky even jumped; in the middle of the waltz she suddenly changed to a sad melody and ended with the aria from *Lucia*, *Fra poco* ...[4] She surmised that gay music did not go with her position. The aria from *Lucia*, with its emphasis on emotive notes, touched Marya Dmitrievna very much.

'What soulfulness,' she remarked to Gedeonovsky in a low voice.

'Sylph-like!' repeated Gedeonovsky and raised his eyes to heaven.

Time for dinner arrived. Marfa Timofeyevna came downstairs when the soup was already on the table. She behaved very drily towards Varvara Pavlovna, answered her compliments in monosyllables and did not look at her. Varvara Pavlovna herself soon realized that nothing was to be got from this old lady and ceased talking to her; whereat Marya Dmitrievna became even more solicitous towards her guest: her aunt's rudeness infuriated her. However, it was not only at Varvara Pavlovna that Marfa Timofeyevna was not looking: she also did not look at Liza, although her eyes literally shone. She sat there as if made of stone, yellow and pale, with tightly closed lips, and ate nothing. Liza seemed calm; and she was. Her soul had grown calmer; a strange absence of feeling, the absence of feeling of a condemned man, had settled upon her. At dinner Varvara Pavlovna spoke little, as if she had grown shy once again, and spread upon her face an expression of modest melancholy. Gedeonovsky was the only one to enliven the conversation with his stories, although he now and then glanced apprehensively in Marfa Timofeyevna's direction and coughed – he always had a coughing fit when he was about to tell fibs in her presence – but she did not prevent or interrupt him. After dinner it transpired that Varvara Pavlovna was very fond of preference; Marya Dmitrievna was so pleased by this that she even became sentimental and thought to herself: 'What a fool Fyodor Ivanych must be, not to know how to understand a woman like this!'

She sat down to cards with her and Gedeonovsky, while

Marfa Timofeyevna led Liza upstairs to her room, saying that she was nothing to look at and most likely had a headache.

'Yes, she has an awful headache,' murmured Marya Dmitrievna, turning to Varvara Pavlovna and rolling her eyes. 'I also have such attacks of migraine . . .'

'You don't say!' responded Varvara Pavlovna.

Liza entered her aunt's room and sank exhausted into a chair. Marfa Timofeyevna gave her a long, silent look and quietly kneeled down before her – and began, silently as ever, to kiss each of her hands in turn. Liza leaned forward, reddened – and burst into tears, but did not make Marfa Timofeyevna rise and did not withdraw her hands: she felt she had no right to withdraw them, had no right to prevent the old woman from expressing her repentance and concern and asking forgiveness for what happened yesterday; and Marfa Timofeyevna could not have enough of kissing the poor, pale powerless hands – and noiseless tears flowed from her eyes and from Liza's; and Sailor, the cat, purred next to a ball of wool in the wide armchair, and the long, long flame of the lamp made a slight flickering and wavered before the icon; in the little neighbouring room, behind the door, stood Nastasya Karpovna and also furtively wiped her eyes with a checked handkerchief compressed into a little ball.

XL

MEANWHILE below, in the drawing-room, the game of preference was continuing; Marya Dmitrievna was winning and in high spirits. A footman entered and announced the arrival of Panshin.

Marya Dmitrievna dropped her cards and fussed about in her armchair; Varvara Pavlovna looked at her with a half-smile and then turned her eyes to the door. Panshin appeared in a black frock-coat with a high English collar buttoned up to the top. 'It was hard for me to comply but, as you can see,

I have come' – so said the expression on his unsmiling, newly shaven face.

'Really, Woldemar,' cried Marya Dmitrievna, 'you've always come in unannounced before!'

Panshin answered Marya Dmitrievna with no more than a glance, bowed politely to her, but did not kiss her hand. She introduced him to Varvara Pavlovna; he stepped back a pace, bowed to her just as politely, but with a suggestion of elegance and respect, and sat down at the card table. The game soon ended. Panshin asked about Lizaveta Mikhaylovna, learned that she was not quite well and expressed his regret; then he struck up a conversation with Varvara Pavlovna, diplomatically weighing and neatly rounding each word and respectfully hearing out her answers to the end. But the self-importance of his diplomatic tone did not have any effect on Varvara Pavlovna and was not even communicated to her. On the contrary, she looked him in the face with gay attentiveness, speaking without constraint, and her delicate nostrils quivered slightly as if from suppressed laughter. Marya Dmitrievna began to praise her talents; Panshin courteously bowed his head (as much as his collar would permit him), declared that 'he had been sure of that from the start' – and embarked on a discourse that led him almost to Metternich[1]. Varvara Pavlovna screwed up her velvety eyes and, saying in a low voice: 'Yes, you're an artist, too, *un confrère*,' added even more quietly: '*Venez!*' and nodded in the direction of the piano. This one casual word: '*Venez!*' instantly, as if by magic, changed Panshin's whole appearance. His preoccupied expression vanished; he smiled, grew animated, undid his coat and, repeating: 'What sort of an artist am I, indeed? But you, I hear, are a true artist,' followed Varvara Pavlovna to the piano.

'Make him sing his romance "The moon sails high …",' exclaimed Marya Dmitrievna.

'You sing, do you?' asked Varvara Pavlovna, flashing a bright, quick glance at him. 'Sit down.'

Panshin began to cry off.

'Sit down,' she repeated, insistently tapping the back of the chair.

He sat down, cleared his throat, tugged at his collar and sang his romance.

'*Charmant*,' said Varvara Pavlovna, 'you sing beautifully, *vous avez du style*. Sing it again.'

She went round the piano and stood directly opposite Panshin. He sang his romance again, giving his voice a melodramatic quavering. Varvara Pavlovna watched him intently, leaning on the piano and holding her white hands level with her lips. Panshin finished.

'*Charmant, idée charmante*,' she said with the calm assurance of an expert. 'Tell me, have you written anything for a woman's voice, for a mezzo-soprano?'

'I have written almost nothing,' Panshin replied. 'I only did this for amusement, in my spare time. . . . Do you sing?'

'I do.'

'Oh, do sing us something!' said Marya Dmitrievna.

Varvara Pavlovna drew her hair back from her crimsoning cheeks and gave a shake of the head.

'Our voices should go together,' she said, turning to Panshin. 'Let's sing a duet. Do you know "*Son geloso*" or "*La ci darem*" or "*Mira la bianca luna*"?'[2]

'I used to sing "*Mira la bianca luna*",' Panshin answered, 'but a long time ago, and I've forgotten it.'

'No matter. We'll rehearse it in a low voice. Allow me.'

Varvara Pavlovna sat down at the piano. Panshin stood beside her. They sang the duet in a low voice, with Varvara Pavlovna correcting him a number of times, and then they sang it aloud and twice repeated: '*Mira la bianca lu . . . u . . . una*.' Varvara Pavlovna's voice had lost its freshness, but she used it very cleverly. Panshin was diffident at first and slightly out of tune, then he came into his own and, if he did not sing irreproachably, he at least made his shoulders quiver, swayed his whole body and raised his hand from time to time like a real singer. Varvara Pavlovna played two or three pieces by Thalberg[3] and coquettishly 'spoke' a French ariette. Marya Dmitrievna had no idea how to express her pleasure; several times she wanted to send for Liza; Gedeonovsky also was at a loss for words and could only shake his head – but suddenly gave an unexpected yawn and barely succeeded in hiding his mouth with his hand. This yawn did not slip by Varvara Pavlovna; she suddenly turned her back on the piano, said: '*Assez de musique comme ça*, now we'll talk,' and folded her hands. '*Oui, assez de musique*,' Panshin gaily repeated and initiated a conversation with her in French that was dashing and light-hearted. 'Just as in the best Paris salon,' thought Marya Dmitrievna, listening to their devious and fanciful speeches. Panshin felt complete satisfaction; his eyes were radiant and he was smiling; to start with he had passed his hand across his face, knitted his brows and sighed abruptly whenever he happened to exchange glances with Marya Dmitrievna; but later he quite forgot about her and surrendered himself utterly to enjoyment of the semi-worldly, semi-artistic chatter. Varvara Pavlovna revealed herself as quite a thinking woman: she had a ready answer to everything, never wavered, never doubted; it was evident that she had conversed much and often with all manner of clever people. All her thoughts and feelings revolved about Paris. Panshin directed the conversation towards literature; it turned out that both of them read only French books; George Sand[4] made her indignant, Balzac she respected, although he bored her, in Sue and Scribe she saw great connoisseurs of the human heart, and she adored Dumas and Féval; in her soul she preferred Paul de Kock to all of them, but it goes without saying that she did not so much as mention his name. For her own part, literature did not interest her too much. Varvara Pavlovna very artfully avoided everything that could even remotely remind them of her position; no hint of love was there in her words; on the contrary, they were filled rather with severity towards the passions, with disillusionment and humility. Panshin made objections; she did not agree with him. . . . But – strange indeed! – at the same time as her lips uttered words of censure, often harsh, the sound of these words was soft and caressive, and her eyes said . . . it was difficult to say precisely what these beautiful eyes said, save that their message was not severe, not clear and sugary. Panshin tried to understand their secret meaning, and tried himself to say things with his eyes, but he felt that nothing came of it; he realized that Varvara Pavlovna, as a real foreign lioness, stood above him, and for this reason he was not fully in command of his powers. Varvara Pavlovna had a habit during conversation of lightly touching her interlocutor's sleeve; these momentary contacts excited Vladimir Nikolaich very much. Varvara Pavlovna had a capacity for being on easy terms with anyone; two hours had hardly passed before it seemed to Panshin he had known her all his life, while Liza, that very same Liza whom he had nevertheless loved and to whom he had proposed the previous day, had vanished as if in a mist. Tea was served; the talk became even less restrained. Marya Dmitrievna rang for the pageboy and ordered Liza to be told she should come down if her headache was better. Panshin, hearing Liza's name, began to discuss the subject of self-sacrifice and whether a man or a woman was more capable of making sacrifices. Marya Dmitrievna at once grew excited and began to insist that a woman was more capable, declared that she could demonstrate this in a couple of words, got tied up in what she was saying and ended by making a rather unsuccessful comparison. Varvara Pavlovna took a music-book, half hid her face behind it and, leaning towards Panshin and nibbling a biscuit, said in a low voice with a calm smile of her lips and eyes: 'Elle n'a pas inventé la poudre, la bonne dame.' Panshin was a trifle frightened and astonished at Varvara Pavlovna's audacity; but he did not understand how much loathing for himself was secreted in this unexpected outburst and, forgetting the kindness and devotion of Marya Dmitrievna, forgetting the dinners she had given him and the money she had loaned him, he (the wretch!) responded with the same little smile and tone of voice: '*Je crois bien*' – and not even: '*Je crois bien*', but '*J'crois ben!*'

Varvara Pavlovna threw him a friendly glance and rose. Liza came in; Marfa Timofeyevna had not succeeded in preventing her from coming down, and she was determined to endure her ordeal to the end. Varvara Pavlovna went to meet her together with Panshin, whose face wore his former diplomatic expression.

'How are you feeling?' he asked Liza.

'I feel better now, thank you,' she answered.

'And we have been occupying ourselves with a little music. It's a pity you didn't hear Varvara Pavlovna. She sings beautifully, *en artiste consommée*.'

'Come here, *ma chère*,' resounded Marya Dmitrievna's voice.

Varvara Pavlovna immediately, with the obedience of a child, went up to her and sat down on a little stool at her feet. Marya Dmitrievna had called her over in order to leave her daughter alone with Panshin, if only for a moment, since she still secretly hoped that Liza would think again. Apart from that, an idea had entered her head which she wanted to discuss without delay.

'You know,' she whispered to Varvara Pavlovna, 'I want to try and reconcile you with your husband. I don't guarantee success, but I will try. He has great respect for me, you know.'

Varvara Pavlovna slowly raised her eyes to Marya Dmitrievna and prettily folded her hands.

'You would be the saviour of me, *ma tante*,' she said in a melancholy voice. 'I don't know how to thank you for all your kindness. But I am too much to blame in Fyodor Ivanych's eyes; he cannot forgive me.'

'Surely you . . . is that so . . .', Marya Dmitrievna was on the point of saying, out of curiosity.

'Don't ask me,' Varvara Pavlovna interrupted her and bowed her head. 'I was young and thoughtless . . . Besides, I don't want to justify myself.'

'Well, still, is there any harm in trying? Don't despair,' said Marya Dmitrievna and wanted to tap her on the cheek, but glanced in her face and grew shy. 'Modest, modest,' she thought, 'but she's a veritable lioness.'

'You're unwell?' Panshin meanwhile asked Liza.

'Yes, I am.'

'I understand you,' he said after a rather prolonged silence. 'Yes, I understand you.'

'How?'

'I understand you,' repeated Panshin significantly, simply not knowing what to say.

Liza was embarrassed, and then thought: 'Let it be!' Panshin assumed a mysterious look and fell silent, looking sternly to one side.

'It's already gone eleven, it seems,' remarked Marya Dmitrievna.

The guests took the hint and began to say good-bye. Varvara Pavlovna had to promise that she would come to dinner the next day and bring Ada; Gedeonovsky, who had almost fallen asleep sitting in the corner, was called on to accompany her home. Panshin bowed ceremoniously to everyone and on the front steps, as he helped Varvara Pavlovna into the carriage, squeezed her hand and cried out as she left: '*Au revoir!*' Gedeonovsky sat beside her; she entertained herself the whole journey by placing the tip of her foot apparently unintentionally against his leg; he was confused and paid her compliments; she giggled and made eyes at him when the light from a street lamp fell into the carriage. The waltz which she had played rang in her head and excited her; no matter where she was, she had only to imagine to herself lights, a ballroom and rapid circling to the sound of music for her soul literally to catch fire, her eyes to become strangely glassy, a smile to hover on her lips and something elegantly Bacchanalian to pervade her whole body. Reaching home, Varvara Pavlovna skipped lightly out of the carriage – only lionesses can skip out like that – swung round to Gedeonovsky and suddenly burst into ringing laughter right under his nose.

'A charming person,' the councillor thought, making his way up to his apartment where his servant was waiting for him with a bottle of opodeldoc. 'It's a good thing I'm a respectable man. . . . Only what on earth was she laughing at?'

Marfa Timofeyevna sat the whole night at Liza's bedside.

XLI

LAVRETSKY spent a day and a half in Vasilyevskoye and almost all the time wandered about the place. He could never stay long in one place: regret gnawed at him; he experienced all the torments of never-ending, impetuous and impotent passion. He remembered the feeling that overwhelmed him the day after his arrival in the country; he remembered his intentions at that time and felt utterly disgusted with himself. What could have torn him away from what he considered his duty, the one and only task of his future life? The thirst for happiness, that same old thirst for happiness! 'Evidently Mikhalevich was right,' he thought. 'What you wanted', he said to himself, 'was to know happiness for the second time in your life, and you forgot that it is a luxury, an undeserved favour, when it visits a man's life even once. It was not full happiness, it was false happiness, you will say – then show what right you have to full and perfect happiness! Look about you and see who is happy, who enjoys life. Look, there's a peasant on the way to mowing, perhaps he's happy with his fate. . . . Do you want to change places with him, eh? Remember your mother and how triflingly small were her demands, yet what was her share of life's happiness? You were evidently only boasting to Panshin when you told him that you'd come to Russia to plough the land; you had come in your old age to go chasing after young girls. No sooner had news come that you were free than you cast everything aside, forgot everything and ran off like a boy after a butterfly . . .' The image of Liza endlessly rose before him in the midst of his cogitations; he banished it from him with an effort, as he did that other importunate image, those other nonchalantly calculating, beautiful, despicable features. Old Anton noticed that his master was preoccupied; sighing several times behind the door, and several times in the doorway, he made up his mind to approach him and proffered the advice that he should drink something warming. Lavretsky shouted at him, ordered him out and then begged his pardon; but Anton became even more crestfallen as a result. Lavretsky could not sit in the drawing-room, for he gained the quite literal impression that his great-grandfather Andrey looked despisingly from the canvas at this gutless descendant of his. 'Hey, you, you small fry!' his side-ways twisted lips seemed to be saying. 'Will I, though,' Lavretsky thought, 'be unable to get myself right, will I give in to this . . . nonsense?' (Severely wounded soldiers always call their wounds 'nonsense'. Without deceiving himself a man cannot live.) 'What am I, in fact – just a little boy? Well, yes: I saw within reach, almost held in my hands, the possibility of lifelong happiness – and then it suddenly vanished; just as in roulette, the wheel has only to turn a fraction more and the beggar perhaps becomes a rich man. But if it's not to be, it's not to be – and that's the end of it. I will do what I have to do with clenched teeth, and tell myself to keep quiet; one blessing is that it's not the first time I've had to take myself in hand. And why did I run away, why am I sitting here with my head in the sand like an ostrich? They say it's terrible to look catastrophe in the face – nonsense!' 'Anton,' he cried loudly, 'order the tarantass to be got ready at once!' 'Yes,' he thought again, 'I must tell myself to keep quiet, I must rule myself with a rod of iron . . .'

By such arguments Lavretsky strove to ease his sorrow, but it was great and powerful; and Apraxia herself, who had gone not so much out of her mind as out of all her feelings, shook her head and sadly followed him with her eyes as he sat down in the tarantass to go into town. The horses galloped away; he sat motionless and straight, and motionlessly he gazed ahead of him at the road.

XLII

THE previous day Liza had written to Lavretsky, asking him to come that evening; but he went first to his own apartments. He found neither his wife, nor his daughter, at home; from the servants he learned that she had taken his daughter to the Kalitins. This news both amazed and infuriated him. 'Obviously Varvara Pavlovna has decided to leave me nothing to live for,' he thought with an access of malice in his heart. He began to walk backwards and forwards, ceaselessly kicking and casting aside the children's toys, books and various female belongings that got in his way; he summoned Justine and ordered her to clear away all this 'trash'. '*Oui, monsieur,*' she said, making a face, and proceeded to tidy the room, bending elegantly and giving Lavretsky to understand with every movement that she considered him an uneducated bear of a man. He looked with loathing at her raddled but still 'piquant', supercilious Parisian face, at her white cuffs, silk pinafore and little cap. He dismissed her eventually, and after much hesitation (Varvara Pavlovna had still not returned) made up his mind to go to the Kalitins – not to Marya Dmitrievna (nothing on earth would have made him enter her drawing-room, the drawing-room where his wife was), but to Marfa Timofeyevna; he remembered that a back staircase from the servants' entrance led directly to her room. This is what Lavretsky did.

He was helped by circumstances: Shurochka was in the courtyard and took him to Marfa Timofeyevna. He found her, contrary to custom, alone; she was sitting in a corner, bent, capless and with her arms folded. Seeing Lavretsky, the old lady got in a tizzy, jumped to her feet and began walking to and fro about the room as if looking for her cap.

'Ah, so there you are, there you are,' she began, avoiding his eyes and pretending to busy herself, 'well, how are you? What is it, then? What's to be done? Where were you yesterday? Yes, she's come, she's come. Well, it must be . . . somehow or other it must be . . .'

Lavretsky sank into a chair.

'Yes, do sit down, do sit down,' the old lady continued. 'Did you come straight upstairs? Well, of course you did. What for? Did you come to have a look at me? Thank you very much.'

The old lady fell silent; Lavretsky did not know what to say to her; but she understood him.

'Liza. . . . Yes, Liza was here a moment ago,' Marfa Timofeyevna went on, tying and untying the cords of her pocketbag. 'She is not very well. Shurochka, where are you? Come here, my dear. Why can't you sit still? And my head's aching, too. Probably it's all because of *that* – that singing and that music.'

'From what singing, auntie?'

'How can you ask? They've been having – how do you call them? – those . . . those duets here. And all in Italian: *chi-chi* and *cha-cha*, carrying on like magpies. Then they start drawing the notes out as if they're sobbing out their souls. That Panshin and your wife. And how quickly everything's been ironed out: it's all in the family now, no formalities. Still, it has to be admitted: even a dog looks for a home and won't get lost, so long as people don't drive it away.'

'Nevertheless, I admit I hadn't expected this,' Lavretsky said. 'This needed great boldness.'

'No, my dear fellow, this isn't boldness, this is calculation. And God be with her! They say you're packing her off to Lavriki, is that true?'

'Yes, I am assigning that estate to her.'

'Has she asked for money?'

'Not so far.'

'Well, that won't be long now. I've only now had a chance to look at you. Are you well?'

'I am well.'

'Shurochka,' cried Marfa Timofeyevna suddenly, 'go and tell Lizaveta Mikhaylovna – that's to say, no, ask her. . . . She's downstairs, isn't she?'

'Yes, she is.'

'Well, then, go and ask her where she's put my book. She knows where.'

'At once.'

The old lady again began fussing about, opening and closing drawers. Lavretsky sat motionless in his chair.

Suddenly there were light footsteps on the stairs – and Liza entered.

Lavretsky stood up and bowed; Liza stopped by the door.

'Liza, my little Liza,' Marfa Timofeyevna started saying fussily, 'where did you put it, where did you put my book?'

'What book, auntie?'

'Well I never, there it is! But I didn't call you. . . . Still, it doesn't matter. What were you doing downstairs? You see, Fyodor Ivanych's come. How is your head?'

'It's nothing.'

'You always say it's nothing. What's happening downstairs – is it music again?'

'No, they're playing cards.'

'So she's not letting the grass grow under her feet. Shurochka, I see you want to run about the garden. Off with you!'

'But I don't, Marfa Timofeyevna . . .'

'Don't argue, please – off with you! Nastasya Karpovna

178

went into the garden by herself: you go and find her. Be respectful now to an old woman.' Shurochka went out. 'Now where's my cap? Where on earth's it got to?'

'Let me go and look for it,' said Liza.

'Sit down, sit down. My own legs haven't fallen off yet. It's probably there in my bedroom.'

And, casting a distrustful look at Lavretsky, Marfa Timofeyevna went out. She was on the point of leaving the door open, but suddenly turned back and closed it tight.

Liza leaned back in her chair and quietly raised her hands to her face; Lavretsky remained where he was.

'So this is how we had to see each other,' he said at last.

Liza took her hands from her face.

'Yes,' she said tonelessly, 'we've been quickly punished.'

'Punished,' said Lavretsky. 'What've you been punished for?'

Liza raised her eyes to his. They expressed neither grief nor anxiety; they looked smaller and dimmer. Her face was pale; the slightly open lips had also lost their colour.

Lavretsky's heart was shaken by feelings of pity and love.

'You wrote to me that it was all over,' he whispered. 'Yes, it was all over before it began.'

'It must all be forgotten,' said Liza. 'I'm glad you've come. I wanted to write to you, but it's better this way. Only we've got to make the most of these minutes. It remains for both of us now to do our duty. You, Fyodor Ivanych, must be reconciled with your wife.'

'Liza!'

'I beg you to do this. This alone can wipe out ... everything that's happened. You think about it – and don't refuse me.'

'Liza, for God's sake, you're asking the impossible. I'm ready to do everything you command; but to be reconciled with her *now*! ... I agree to everything, I've forgotten everything; but I cannot force my heart. ... No, that's cruel!'

'I don't ask of you . . . what you say. Don't live with her if you can't. But be reconciled,' Liza said and again raised her hands to her eyes. 'Remember your daughter; do this for my sake.'

'Very well,' uttered Lavretsky through his teeth, 'suppose I do this and in this way I do my duty – well, what about you – what's your duty to be?'

'That is my business.'

Lavretsky suddenly shuddered all over.

'You're not thinking of marrying Panshin?' he asked.

Liza gave a barely discernible smile.

'Oh, no!' she said.

'Ah, Liza, Liza,' Lavretsky cried out, 'how happy we could have been!'

Again Liza looked at him.

'Now you see for yourself, Fyodor Ivanych, that happiness depends not on us, but on God.'

'Yes, because you . . .'

The door from the next room was flung open and Marfa Timofeyevna entered with a cap in her hand.

'Got it,' she said, stopping between Lavretsky and Liza. 'I'd put it down myself. That's old age for you, more's the pity! Still, it's no better being young. So, are you going with your wife to Lavriki?' she added, turning to Fyodor Ivanych.

'With her to Lavriki? I? I don't know,' he said after a pause.

'Aren't you going downstairs?'

'Today – no.'

'Well, you know best; but I think you, Liza, ought to go down. Oh, saints above, I've forgotten to feed the bullfinch! Just wait a moment, I'll . . .'

And Marfa Timofeyevna rushed out without even putting on her cap.

Lavretsky quickly went up to Liza.

'Liza,' he began in a pleading voice, 'we're parting for ever and my heart is breaking – give me your hand in farewell.'

Liza raised her head. Her tired, almost exhausted eyes rested on him . . .

'No,' she said and drew back her already proffered hand, 'no, Lavretsky' (it was the first time she had called him that), 'I won't give you my hand. What's the point in it? Go away, I beg you. You know I love you. . . . Yes, I do love you,' she added with an effort, 'but no . . . no.'

And she raised a handkerchief to her lips.

'At least give me that handkerchief.'

The door creaked. . . . The handkerchief slipped on to Liza's knees. Lavretsky seized it before it could fall to the floor, quickly stuffed it into a side pocket and, turning about, encountered Marfa Timofeyevna's eyes.

'Liza, my dear, I think your mother's calling you,' the old lady said.

Liza at once rose and went out.

Marfa Timofeyevna again sat down in her corner. Lavretsky began to say good-bye.

'Fedya,' she said suddenly.

'What, auntie?'

'Are you an honest man?'

'What do you mean?'

'I'm asking you: are you an honest man?'

'I hope so, yes.'

'Hmm. Give me your word that you're an honest man.'

'As you wish. But what's this for?'

'I know what it's for. And you, my boy, if you take a little thought, for you're not stupid, will understand what I'm asking this for. But now, my dear, good-bye. Thank you for coming to see me; but remember what you've promised, Fedya, and give me a kiss. Oh, I know, my dear one, how hard it is for you; but, then, it's not easy for anyone. There was a time when I used to envy flies: that's a good way to live, I used to think; but then one night I heard a fly whining in a spider's clutches, and I thought: No, they've got to watch out, too. You can't do anything about it, Fedya; just keep your promise. Go now.'

Lavretsky went out by the back entrance and was already approaching the gates, when a footman caught up with him.

'Marya Dmitrievna asks you to come and see her,' he informed Lavretsky.

'Tell her, my good fellow, that I can't now . . .' Fyodor Ivanych began.

'She said especial-like to ask,' the footman went on. 'She said to say she was alone.'

'The guests have gone, have they?' asked Lavretsky.

'Yes-sir,' the footman replied and grinned.

Lavretsky shrugged his shoulders and followed him.

XLIII

MARYA DMITRIEVNA was alone in her study, sitting in a Voltairean armchair and sniffing eau-de-cologne; a glass of orange-flower water stood on a little table beside her. She was in an excitable state and seemed to be frightened of something.

Lavretsky entered.

'You wished to see me,' he said, coldly bowing.

'Yes,' said Marya Dmitrievna and drank a little of the water. 'I learned that you had gone straight up to auntie's room; I said that you should be asked to come and see me: I have something to discuss with you. Please sit down.' Marya Dmitrievna drew a deep breath. 'You know,' she went on, 'that your wife has arrived.'

'That is known to me,' said Lavretsky.

'Yes, well, what I meant was: she has come to me and I have received her; now this is what I want to talk to you about, Fyodor Ivanych. I, thank God, have earned, I can say, universal respect and I will not do something improper for anything in the world. Although I foresaw that it would not be pleasant for you, I could not resolve to refuse her, Fyodor Ivanych; she is related to me – through you; appreciate my position, what right had I to refuse her entry to my house? Do you agree?'

'You are worrying unnecessarily, Marya Dmitrievna,' Lavretsky answered. 'You behaved quite correctly; I am not in the least angry. I have no intention of depriving Varvara Pavlovna of the opportunity to see her friends; I did not come to you today simply because I did not wish to meet her, that's all.'

'Ah, I am so pleased to hear that from you, Fyodor Ivanych,' cried Marya Dmitrievna. 'However, I have always expected you to have noble feelings. But that I am worried is not surprising, for I am a woman and a mother. And your wife ... of course, I cannot judge you and her and I told her as much myself ... but she is such a charming person that she doesn't seem capable of giving anything save pleasure.'

Lavretsky gave a wry smile and played with his hat.

'And I have something more to tell you, Fyodor Ivanych,' continued Marya Dmitrievna, moving slightly closer to him, '– if only you'd seen how modestly she behaved, how respectfully! Truly, it was even touching. And if you'd heard what she said about you! I am wholly to blame, she said; I did not know how to appreciate him, she said; he's an angel, not a man, she said. Truly, that is just what she said: an angel. Her repentance is such that ... God is my witness, I've never seen such repentance!'

'Is it true, Marya Dmitrievna,' said Lavretsky, 'allow me to inquire, that Varvara Pavlovna has been singing in your house, that she has been singing during her period of repentance? Or what was it?'

'Ah, you ought to be ashamed of what you're saying! She sang and played simply to do me a favour, because I insisted she should, almost ordered her to. I saw that things were so hard for her, so very hard; I wondered how to distract her –

and I'd heard that she had such a splendid talent! Believe me, Fyodor Ivanych, she is quite shattered, ask Sergey Petrovich if you like – a broken woman, *tout à fait*. So how can you ask such a question?'

Lavretsky simply shrugged his shoulders.

'Then again, what a little angel your Ada is, what a charmer! How delightful she is, what a clever little thing! How well she speaks French, and she understands Russian – she called me auntie! And you know, she's not in the least shy, like most children of her age – not in the least. She looks so like you, Fyodor Ivanych, it's quite terrifying. Her eyes, her brows . . . well, they're you, just like yours. I confess I'm not very fond of such little children, but I've simply lost my heart to your little daughter.'

'Marya Dmitrievna,' Lavretsky suddenly said, 'allow me to ask you why you've been good enough to say all this to me?'

'Why?' Marya Dmitrievna again sniffed the eau-de-cologne and took a sip of water. 'I say this, Fyodor Ivanych, because . . . I am, after all, related to you, I take the closest interest in you. . . . I know you have the kindest of hearts. Listen, *mon cousin*, I am a woman of experience and I won't go on wasting breath! Forgive her, forgive your wife.' Marya Dmitrievna's eyes suddenly filled with tears. 'Just think: youth, inexperience . . . well, perhaps a bad example: she didn't have the kind of mother who could put her on the right path. Forgive her, Fyodor Ivanych, she has been punished enough.'

Tears began to run down Marya Dmitrievna's cheeks; she did not wipe them away: she loved crying. Lavretsky sat as if on live coals. 'My God,' he thought, 'what torture this is, what a day this has turned out to be for me!'

'You don't answer,' Marya Dmitrievna began again. 'How should I take that? Can you be so cruel? No, I don't want to believe that. I feel that my words have convinced you.

Fyodor Ivanych, God will reward you for your kindness, and now accept your wife from my hands . . .'

Lavretsky involuntarily rose from his chair; Marya Dmitrievna also stood up and, going briskly behind a screen, led Varvara Pavlovna out from behind it. Pale, half-alive, with lowered eyes, she seemed to have abdicated all thoughts of her own, all will-power – and to have given herself over wholly into Marya Dmitrievna's hands.

Lavretsky took a step back.

'You were here!' he exclaimed.

'Don't blame her,' Marya Dmitrievna said hurriedly, 'she didn't want to stay at all, but I ordered her to stay and it was I who put her behind the screen. She assured me that it would make you even angrier; I wouldn't listen to her; I know you better than she does. Accept your wife from my hands. Go on, Varya, don't be frightened, get on your knees to your husband' (she pulled her by the arm) ' – and my blessing . . .'

'Stop, Marya Dmitrievna,' Lavretsky interrupted her in a hollow but impressive voice. 'No doubt you're fond of emotional scenes' (Lavretsky was not mistaken: since her schooldays Marya Dmitrievna had retained a passion for theatricality); 'they amuse you; but others may come out of them badly. However, I don't intend to talk to you: in *this* scene you're not the principal character. What do *you* want from me, madam?' he added, turning to his wife. 'Haven't I done what I can for you? Don't retort that you were not the one who contrived this meeting – I won't believe you, and you know I can't believe you. What do you want? You're clever. You don't do anything without a purpose. You must understand that I have no inclination to live with you as I lived before, not because I am angry with you but because I have become a different person. I told you that the day after you returned, and in your soul, at this moment, you know you agree with me. But you want to rehabilitate yourself in the eyes of the world; it's not enough for you to live in my house, you want to live with me under the same roof – isn't that so?'

'I want you to forgive me,' said Varvara Pavlovna, without raising her eyes.

'She wants you to forgive her,' Marya Dmitrievna repeated.

'And not for my sake, for Ada's sake,' whispered Varvara Pavlovna.

'Not for her sake, for your Ada's sake,' repeated Marya Dmitrievna.

'Excellent. That's what you want, is it?' Lavretsky uttered with an effort. 'Then I agree to that, too.'

Varvara Pavlovna cast a quick glance in his direction, but Marya Dmitrievna exclaimed: 'Well, thank God!' and again drew Varvara Pavlovna by the arm: 'Now accept from me . . .'

'Stop, I tell you,' Lavretsky interrupted her. 'I agree to live with you, Varvara Pavlovna,' he continued, ' – that is, I will take you to Lavriki and live there with you as long as I have the strength to do so, but then I will leave – and will make occasional return visits. You see, I don't want to deceive you, but don't ask more than that. You would yourself burst out laughing if I were to fulfil the wish of our most respected relative and clasp you to my heart and start assuring you that . . . that the past was forgotten, that a felled tree can flourish again. But I see now that one must submit. You won't understand that . . . it doesn't matter. I repeat . . . I will live with you . . . or no, I cannot promise that . . . I will fall in with your wishes and again regard you as my wife . . .'

'At least give her your hand on that,' said Marya Dmitrievna, whose tears had long since dried up.

'I have never deceived Varvara Pavlovna,' Lavretsky retorted, 'and she'll trust my word. I will take her to Lavriki – and remember, Varvara Pavlovna: our pact will be considered broken the moment you leave there. And now allow me to go.'

He bowed to both of them and hurriedly went out.

'You're not taking her with you ...' Marya Dmitrievna shouted after him.

'Leave him alone,' Varvara Pavlovna whispered to her and at once embraced her, began thanking her, kissing her hands and calling her her saviour.

Marya Dmitrievna condescended to accept her advances, but inwardly she was dissatisfied with Lavretsky, with Varvara Pavlovna and with the whole scene she had prepared. Too little emotional effect had come of it; Varvara Pavlovna, in her opinion, should have thrown herself at her husband's feet.

'Why didn't you understand me?' she argued. 'I told you: get on your knees.'

'It's better like this, my dear aunt. Don't worry – everything's splendid,' Varvara Pavlovna insisted.

'Well, there it is – he's as cold as ice,' Marya Dmitrievna remarked. 'There it is – you didn't cry, while I streamed tears right in front of him. He wants to lock you up in Lavriki. Does that mean you won't even be able to come and see me? Men have no feelings,' she said in conclusion and significantly nodded her head.

'Women know all the more how to value kindness and generosity,' said Varvara Pavlovna and, dropping gently on to her knees before Marya Dmitrievna, enfolded her stout waist with her arms and pressed her face to her. This face slyly smiled, but in Marya Dmitrievna's case tears again began to flow.

Lavretsky went to his lodgings, locked himself in his valet's small room, flung himself on the sofa and lay there until morning.

XLIV

THE next day was Sunday. The sound of bells for early service did not waken Lavretsky – he had not closed his eyes all night – but reminded him of that other Sunday when he had gone to church on Liza's wishes. He rose hurriedly; some secret voice told him that he would see her there again today. He left the house without a sound, having left word for Varvara Pavlovna, who was still sleeping, that he would return for dinner, and with big strides set off in the direction to which the monotonously sad ringing called him. He arrived early: hardly anyone was yet in the church; a deacon was reading prayers in the chancel; his voice, occasionally interrupted by bouts of coughing, rose and fell in its measured deep intoning of the words. Lavretsky positioned himself not far from the entrance. Worshippers arrived one by one, stopped, crossed themselves and bowed on all sides; their footsteps made a ringing sound in the emptiness and quiet, clearly echoing in the vaulted roof. A decrepit old woman in a threadbare coat with a hood kneeled by Lavretsky and prayed diligently; her toothless, yellow, wrinkled face expressed intense exultation; her reddened eyes gazed immovably up at the icons on the iconostasis; her bony hand ceaselessly emerged from her coat and slowly and firmly made the sign of the cross in broad, large gestures. A peasant with a thick beard and despondent face, dishevelled and crumpled, entered the church, fell at once on both knees and instantly began hurriedly crossing himself, throwing back and shaking his head after each obeisance. Such bitter sorrow was written in his face and expressed in all his movements that Lavretsky decided to approach him and ask what was wrong. The peasant started back sternly and in fright, and looked at him. . . . 'My son has died,' he said in haste and again started making his obeisances. 'What can replace for them the comfort of the church?' thought Lavretsky and made his own attempt to pray; but his heart had become hard and embittered and his thoughts were far away. He kept on waiting for Liza, but Liza did not come. The church began to fill with people; still she wasn't there. The service began, and the deacon had already read the gospel, the bell had rung for the final devotion, when Lavretsky moved a little forward – and suddenly he saw Liza. She had come earlier than him, but he had not noticed her; pressed into the little space between the wall and the chancel, she did not look round and did not move. Lavretsky did not take his eyes off her until the very end of the service: he was saying good-bye to her. The people began to disperse, but she still remained there, as if she was waiting for Lavretsky to leave. Finally she crossed herself for the last time and went out without turning round; she had a maid with her. Lavretsky followed her out of the church and caught up with her in the street; she was walking very fast, with her head bent forward and a veil over her face.

'Good morning, Lizaveta Mikhaylovna,' he said loudly, with forced lack of restraint. 'May I accompany you?'

She said nothing; he walked along beside her.

'Are you satisfied with me?' he asked, lowering his voice. 'Have you heard what happened yesterday?'

'Yes, yes,' she answered in a whisper, 'that was good.' And she walked even more quickly.

'Are you satisfied?'

Liza simply nodded her head.

'Fyodor Ivanych,' she began in a calm but faint voice, 'I wanted to ask you something: Don't visit us any more, go away at once; we can see each other later – some time or other, a year from now. But do this now for me, do what I ask you, for God's sake.'

'I am ready to agree to anything you say, Lizaveta Mikhaylovna; but do we have to part like this? Can't you at least say something to me?'

'Fyodor Ivanych, you may be walking now beside me ... but already you're so far, far away from me. And it's not only you, but ...'

'Do finish, I beg you!' exclaimed Lavretsky. 'What did you want to say?'

'You will hear probably ... but no matter, forget ... no, please don't forget me, remember me.'

'I forget you! ...'

'Enough now, good-bye. Don't follow me.'

'Liza ...' Lavretsky began.

'Good-bye, good-bye!' she repeated, drew the veil further over her face and almost ran away from him.

Lavretsky watched her go and, bowing his head, turned back along the street. He bumped into Lemm who also walked along with his hat pulled down to his nose and his eyes fixed on his feet.

They exchanged looks in silence.

'Well, what d'you have to say?' Lavretsky asked eventually.

'What do I have to say?' Lemm replied gloomily. 'I have nothing to say. Everything is dead, and we're dead. (*Alles ist todt, und wir sind todt.*) You're going to the right, aren't you?'

'To the right.'

'And I'm going left. Good-bye.'

The next morning Fyodor Ivanych set off for Lavriki with his wife. She travelled ahead of him in a carriage, with Ada and Justine; he travelled behind in the tarantass. Throughout the whole journey the pretty little girl never left the carriage window; she marvelled at everything: the peasants, the peasant women, the peasant huts, the wells, the horses' yokes, the little bells and the multitudes of rooks; Justine shared her surprise; Varvara Pavlovna laughed at their remarks and exclamations. She was in high spirits; before leaving the town of O ... she had discussed things with her husband.

'I understand your position,' she told him – and, judging by the expression of her clever eyes, he could conclude that she understood his position fully. 'But you must at least do me the justice of agreeing that I am easy to live with; I won't impose myself on you or embarrass you; I wanted to ensure Ada's future; I need nothing more.'

'Yes, you have achieved your object,' said Fyodor Ivaných.

'I dream of only one thing now: of burying myself in the depths of the country; I will always remember your generosity . . .'

'Phew! Enough of that,' he interrupted her.

'And I will know how to respect your independence and your peace and quiet,' she said in completion of her prepared phrase.

Lavretsky bowed low to her. Varvara Pavlovna gathered that her husband was inwardly grateful to her.

Towards evening of the second day they arrived at Lavriki; a week later Lavretsky departed for Moscow, leaving his wife five thousand roubles to live on, and the day after Lavretsky's departure Panshin appeared, in answer to Varvara Pavlovna's summons not to forget her in her isolation. She received him in the most hospitable way possible, and until late at night the high-ceilinged rooms of the house and even the garden were resonant with the sound of music, singing and gay French conversation. Panshin spent three days as a guest of Varvara Pavlovna; firmly pressing her beautiful hands as he said good-bye, he promised to be back very soon – and he kept his promise.

XLV

LIZA had a small room of her own on the second floor of her mother's house, clean and bright, with a white bedstead, pots of flowers in the corners and under the windows, with a little writing-table, a small case of books and a crucifix on the wall. This little room was called the nursery; Liza had been born there. When she returned from the church, where Lavretsky had seen her, she tidied everything up more carefully than usual, dusted everywhere, looked through all her letters from girl-friends and all her notebooks and tied them up with ribbons, locked all her drawers, watered the flowers and touched each one lightly with her hand. All this she did unhurriedly, silently, with a look of intent and calm solicitude on her face. She stopped finally in the middle of the room, slowly looked round her and, going to the table, above which hung the crucifix, dropped on to her knees, placed her head on her clasped hands and remained motionless.

Marfa Timofeyevna entered and found her in that position. Liza did not notice her come in. The old lady went out through the door on tiptoe and coughed loudly several times. Liza rose abruptly and wiped her eyes which glistened with bright, unshed tears.

'I see you've been tidying up your little cell again,' said Marfa Timofeyevna, bending low to sniff a young rose in a pot. 'What a splendid scent!'

Liza looked thoughtfully at her aunt.

'What a word to use!' she whispered.

'What word, which one?' the old lady interrupted excitedly. 'What do you mean? It's awful,' she said, suddenly throwing down her cap and seating herself on Liza's bed, 'it's more than I can bear – today is the fourth day that I've been literally bubbling with worry; I can't go on pretending that I don't notice anything, that I can't see how pale you are, how dried up you are, how much you're crying – I can't, I can't.'

'What's happened to you, auntie?' Liza asked. 'It's nothing ...'

'Nothing?' cried Marfa Timofeyevna. 'You can say that to the others, but not to me! Nothing! Who's just been kneeling? Whose eyelashes are still wet with tears? Nothing! Just you take a look at yourself – what've you done to your face, what's happened to your eyes? Nothing! Do you think I don't know everything?'

'It will pass, auntie. Give it time.'

'It will pass – yes, but when? Oh, the Good Lord above! Did you really love him that much? After all, he's an old man, Lizochka. I don't dispute that he's a good man, that he won't bite, but is that something special? We're all good people; the world's not coming to an end, there'll always be plenty of that sort of goodness.'

'I tell you that it will all pass, that it's already all over.'

'Listen, Lizochka, to what I've got to say,' Marfa Timofeyevna said suddenly, making Liza sit down beside her on the bed and adjusting first Liza's hair, then her kerchief. 'It only seems to you now, when it's all so fresh, that there's no cure for your grief. Ah, my dearest, it's only for death that there's no remedy! You just say to yourself: "I won't give in, I'll forget him!" – and in a while you'll be truly amazed how quickly, how well it all passes. You just bide your time.'

'Auntie,' rejoined Liza, 'it's already over, it's all over.'

'It's all over! What's all over? See, your little nose is even looking peaky, and yet you say it's all over. All over, indeed!'

'Yes, it's all over, auntie, if only you'll be willing to help me,' Liza announced with sudden animation and flung herself on Marfa Timofeyevna's neck. 'Dearest auntie, be my friend, help me, don't be angry, try to understand me . . .'

'What is it, what is it, my dear? Don't frighten me so, please – I'll cry out this instant! Don't look at me like that – tell me at once what it is!'

'I . . . I want . . .' Liza hid her face in Marfa Timofeyevna's bosom. 'I want to go into a convent,' she said tonelessly.

The old lady gave a jump.

'Make the sign of the cross, Lizochka, my dear, and think what you're saying – may God be with you!' she eventually muttered. 'Lie down, my darling, and have a little sleep; this is all because you haven't been sleeping well, my dearest.'

Liza raised her head and her cheeks were on fire.

'No, auntie,' she said, 'don't talk like that. I have made up my mind, I have prayed, I have sought the advice of God; everything is finished, my life with you is finished. I haven't had to learn this lesson for nothing; and it's not the first time

I've thought about it. Happiness did not come to me; even when I had hopes of happiness, my heart was still full of pain. I know everything, both my own sins and others', and how papa made all our money; I know everything. It all has to be paid for by prayer, wiped away by prayer. I am sorry for you and for mama and for Lenochka; but it can't be helped; I feel there is no life for me here. I've already said good-bye to everything, said my last good-byes to everything in the house; something is calling me away, and I feel sick of it all and I want to lock myself away for ever. Don't try to stop me, don't try to dissuade me, help me, otherwise I'll go off alone . . .'

Marfa Timofeyevna listened with horror to what her niece had to say.

'She's sick, she's delirious,' she thought, 'and we must send for a doctor – but for which one? Gedeonovsky talked highly of one not long ago, but he always talks a lot of nonsense – still, perhaps he was telling the truth this time.' But when she had convinced herself that Liza was neither sick nor delirious, and when Liza persisted in giving the same answers despite all her protestations, Marfa Timofeyevna grew frightened and was genuinely distressed.

'My dearest one, you haven't any idea,' she began trying to persuade her, 'what life is like in a convent. After all, my very own dear one, they'll feed you on green hemp oil and they'll dress you up in clothing that's ever so thick and coarse; they'll make you walk about out in the cold; you won't be able to endure that, Liza dear. This is all the result of Agafya's influence; she's the one who put this nonsense in your head. After all, she began by living her life first, and she lived it for her own pleasure; you must too. At least let me die peacefully, and then you do what you want. And who ever heard of anyone going into a convent, God forgive me, on account of a bearded old goat, on account of a man? Well, if you're sick of it all, go away, make supplication to a saint, have prayers said,

194

but don't you go and put a black hood over your head, my dearest one, my darling . . .'

And Marfa Timofeyevna cried bitterly.

Liza comforted her, wiped away her tears, cried herself, but remained unmoved. In desperation Marfa Timofeyevna tried to employ the threat of telling her mother everything . . . but that did not help. It was only as a result of the old lady's even stronger pleading that Liza agreed to postpone fulfilment of her plans for six months; in exchange Marfa Timofeyevna had to give her word that she would help in obtaining Marya Dmitrievna's consent if at the end of the six months Liza had not changed her mind.

With the coming of the first cold weather Varvara Pavlovna, despite her promise to bury herself in the depths of the country, provided herself with the necessary money and moved to St Petersburg where she rented a modest but charming little apartment, discovered for her by Panshin, who had left O . . . Province even before she did. During the last part of his stay at O . . . he had been completely out of favour with Marya Dmitrievna; he suddenly ceased visiting her and was almost never away from Lavriki. Varvara Pavlovna had enslaved him, literally enslaved him: there is no other way of describing the limitless, irrevocable, irresistible power she exercised over him.

Lavretsky spent the winter in Moscow, and in the spring of the following year news reached him that Liza had taken the veil in the convent of B . . ., in one of the remotest parts of Russia.

Epilogue

EIGHT years passed. Spring had come again. . . . But before going any further we will say a few words about the fate of Mikhalevich, and of Panshin, and of Madame Lavretsky – and say good-bye to them. Mikhalevich, after prolonged wandering, has finally discovered his true vocation: he has obtained the post of senior superintendent in a government institute. He is very satisfied with his lot, and his pupils 'adore' him, although they make fun of him behind his back. Panshin has made good progress in the bureaucratic hierarchy and is already aiming to become a departmental director; he walks about slightly bent; perhaps the Cross of St Vladimir, which he wears round his neck, weighs him down. The official in him has achieved decisive ascendancy over the artist; his still young-looking face has a jaundiced complexion, his hair has thinned, and he neither sings nor draws any more, but secretly dabbles in literature: he has written a little comedy piece, a kind of theatrical 'proverb', and since nowadays all who write invariably 'take off' someone or something, so he has portrayed a coquette in it and he reads it to two or three well-wishing ladies of his acquaintance. He has not embarked on marriage, although many excellent opportunities have arisen; for that Varvara Pavlovna is to blame. So far as she is concerned, she resides permanently in Paris as she did before: Fyodor Ivanych has allocated her a fixed sum of money and thus bought himself freedom from the possibility of her landing on him unexpectedly a second time. She has grown older and stouter, but she is still charming and elegant. Everyone has an ideal: Varvara Pavlovna has found hers – in the dramatic works of Dumas *fils*. She assiduously visits the theatre, where consumptive and highly strung *dames aux camélias* are presented on the stage; to be Madame Doche[1] seems to her the summit of human bliss. She once declared that she could not wish a better fate for her daughter. It must be hoped that fate will preserve Mademoiselle Ada from such bliss: from a red-cheeked, plump child she has been turned into a weak-chested, pale little girl; she already has bad nerves. Varvara Pavlovna's admirers have diminished, but not disappeared; she will retain some, probably, until the end of her life. The most ardent of them recently has been a certain Zakurdalo-Skubyrnikov, a moustachioed retired guardsman, of about thirty-eight years of age and unusually powerful physique. French visitors at Madame Lavretsky's salon call him '*le gros taureau de l'Ukraine*'; Varvara Pavlovna never invites him to her fashionable evenings, but he enjoys her fullest benevolence.

There it is ... eight years have passed. The sky has again exuded the radiant happiness of spring; spring has again smiled on the earth and its people; once again at her fond touch everything has blossomed and fallen in love and begun singing. The town of O ... has changed little in the course of these eight years; but Marya Dmitrievna's house has become rejuvenated, as it were: its recently painted walls shine a welcoming white, and the glass of its open windows is pink-tinged and glittering from the setting sun; joyous, light-hearted sounds of resonant young voices and constant laughter pour from its windows into the street; the whole house, it seems, seethes with life and bubbles over with gaiety. The mistress of the house has long gone to her grave: Marya Dmitrievna died a couple of years after Liza took the veil; and Marfa Timofeyevna did not long survive her; they lie side by side in the town graveyard. Nastasya Karpovna has also gone; the loyal old lady for several years made weekly visits to pray over her friend's grave. ... Then her time came and her bones were laid to rest in the damp earth. But Marya Dmitrievna's house did not fall into strange hands, did not pass out of her family; the 'home' was not destroyed. Lenochka, who had turned into a slim and beautiful girl, and her fiancé, a fair-haired hussar officer; Marya Dmitrievna's son, just married in St Petersburg and spending the spring in O . . . with his young wife, his wife's sister, a sixteen-year-old schoolgirl with crimson cheeks and limpid eyes; Shurochka, also grown up and pretty – these were the young people who made the walls of the Kalitin house resound with laughter and talk. Everything in the house had changed, everything fitted in with the new inhabitants. Beardless house-boys, pranksters and jackanapes, had taken the place of the former sedate old men-servants; where once podgy Roska used to waddle solemnly, two setters raced frantically about, jumping over the sofas; the stables contained lean race-horses, dashing shaft-horses, spirited outriders with plaited manes, Don saddle-horses; the times for breakfast, dinner and supper were all mixed up and confused; 'unheard-of arrangements', as the neighbours called them, held sway.

On that evening, of which we have just spoken, the inhabitants of the Kalitin house (the eldest of them, Lenochka's fiancé, was only twenty-four years old) were engaged in a slightly complicated but, judging by their concerted laughter, to them extremely amusing game: they were running from room to room and catching each other; the dogs were also running about and barking, and the canaries in the cages hanging by the windows strained their throats to bursting, adding to the general commotion with the loud cacophony of their frantic trilling. At the very height of this deafening fun a muddy tarantass drove up to the gates and a man of about forty-five, in a travelling cloak, stepped out of it and stopped in astonishment. He stood there for a short while, encompassed the house with his attentive gaze, entered the courtyard through the little gate and slowly climbed the porch steps. He met nobody in the hall; but the door of the dining-room was flung open and out of it dashed a red-faced Shurochka, followed an instant later, with loud shouts, by the whole party of young people. They stopped suddenly and fell quiet at the sight of the stranger; but the bright eyes directed at him did not lose their kindly look and the fresh faces did not cease their laughter. Marya Dmitrievna's son approached the new arrival and hospitably asked him what he wanted.

'I am Lavretsky,' the new arrival replied.

A chorus of shouts resounded in response to this – not because the young people were overjoyed at the arrival of a distant and almost forgotten relative, but simply because they were ready to shout and enjoy themselves whenever there was a suitable opportunity. They at once surrounded Lavretsky: Lenochka, like a longstanding acquaintance, introduced herself first, assuring him that, given a moment or so, she would certainly have recognized him, and then she introduced the rest of them, calling each one, even her fiancé, by their familiar, shortened names. The whole crowd moved through the dining-room into the drawing-room. The wallpaper in both these rooms was different, but the furniture was the same; Lavretsky recognized the piano; even the same embroidery-frame stood in the same place by the window – and with practically the same unfinished embroidery in it as eight years before. He was given a seat in a deep armchair; they ranged themselves round him. Questions, exclamations, stories poured out one after another.

'We haven't seen you for such a long time,' Lenochka naïvely remarked, 'and we also haven't seen Varvara Pavlovna.'

'Hardly likely!' her brother hurriedly chimed in. 'I took you off to St Petersburg, while Fyodor Ivanych's lived in the country all the time.'

'Yes, and since then mama's died.'

'And Marfa Timofeyevna,' said Shurochka.

'And Nastasya Karpovna,' said Lenochka, 'and Monsieur Lemm . . .'

'What? Is Lemm dead, too?' asked Lavretsky.

'Yes,' young Kalitin answered. 'He went off to Odessa; they say someone enticed him there; and he died there.'

'Do you know whether he left any of his music behind?'

'I don't know; not very likely.'

They all grew quiet and exchanged looks. A small cloud of sorrow passed across their young faces.

'But Sailor's alive,' Lenochka suddenly said.

'And Gedeonovsky,' her brother added.

At the mention of Gedeonovsky there was a universal peal of laughter.

'Yes, he's alive and telling tall stories the same as ever,' Marya Dmitrievna's son went on. 'And just imagine, this crazy child here' (he indicated the school girl, his wife's sister) 'yesterday sprinkled pepper in his snuff-box.'

'How he sneezed!' exclaimed Lenochka, and again there was a peal of helpless laughter.

'We had news of Liza recently,' said young Kalitin, and again everyone grew quiet. 'She's all right, and her health's a little better now.'

'Is she still in the same convent?' asked Lavretsky, not without effort.

'In the same one.'

'Does she write to you?'

'No, never; we get news through other people.'

There was a sudden, profound silence; 'an angel has just flown by,' they all thought.

'Would you like to go into the garden?' Kalitin asked Lavretsky. 'It's very pretty now, although we've let it grow a bit wild.'

Lavretsky went into the garden, and the first thing that struck him was that very bench where he had once spent with Liza a few happy, never-to-be-repeated moments; it had grown blackened and bent; but he recognized it, and his soul was seized by a feeling which has no equal in its sweetness and bitterness – a feeling of living sorrow for vanished youth and for a happiness that was once possessed. Together with the young people he walked along the paths; the limes had aged a little and grown taller in the last eight years, their shade had become thicker; all the bushes had shot up, the raspberries were full-grown, the hazels had run riot and everywhere there was a fragrance of fresh wild growth, of woods and grass and lilac.

'This is a good place to play "I sent a letter to my love",' Lenochka suddenly cried, entering a small grassy area surrounded by limes. 'Besides, there are five of us.'

'Have you forgotten Fyodor Ivanych?' her brother asked. 'Or aren't you counting yourself?'

Lenochka blushed slightly.

'Surely Fyodor Ivanych, at his age, can . . .' she began.

'Please, do play,' Lavretsky said hurriedly. 'Don't pay any attention to me. It'll be much pleasanter for me if I know that I'm not in your way. Don't feel you have to entertain me; we old people have an entertainment of our own, which you don't know about yet and which can't be replaced by any other: our memories.'

The young people listened to Lavretsky with affable and slightly ironic respectfulness, as if a teacher had just read them a lesson, and suddenly scattered, dashing on to the grass; four of them took up places by the trees, one in the middle – and the fun began.

Lavretsky returned to the house, went into the dining-room, approached the piano and touched one of the keys. A faint but pure sound rang out and secretly reverberated in his heart: this was the note that began the inspired melody with which, long ago, on that happiest of nights, Lemm, the dead Lemm, had brought him to such a pitch of exultation. Then Lavretsky crossed into the drawing-room, and it was a long time before he left it: in this room, where he had seen Liza so frequently, her image rose more vividly before him; he seemed to feel traces of her presence around him; but his sadness for her was poignant and oppressive: there was none of the silence in it evocative of death. Liza still lived somewhere, shut away, far off; he tried to think of her as a living person and could not recognize the girl he had once loved in that blurred, pale ghost shrouded in her nun's habit and surrounded by smoky waves of incense. Lavretsky would not even have been able to recognize himself, if he looked at himself as he mentally looked at Liza. In the course of these eight years the crisis had finally occurred in his life, that crisis which many never experience but without which it's impossible to remain a decent man to the end: he had actually ceased to think about personal happiness, about venal ends. He had become tranquil and – what point is there in hiding the truth? – old, not in face and body alone, but in his soul as well; to keep the heart young into old age, as some claim they can, is difficult and almost comic; that man can be satisfied, who has not lost his faith in goodness, the constancy of the will, the desire to keep active. Lavretsky had a right to be satisfied: he had really made himself into a good proprietor, he had really learned how to plough the land, and he laboured not for himself alone; so far as was in his power, he tried to ensure and stabilize the livelihood of his peasants.

Lavretsky went out of the house into the garden, sat down on the bench that was so familiar to him – and in that dear place, face to face with the house where for the last time he had vainly stretched out his hands to the promised cup in which there bubbles and sparkles the golden wine of pleasure – he, a lonely, homeless wanderer, his ears filled with the gay shouts of a younger generation that had already taken his place, looked back upon his life. He grew sad at heart, but not oppressed and not ashamed: there were things to regret, nothing to be ashamed of. 'Play on, enjoy yourselves, grow up, forces of youth,' he thought, and there was no bitterness in his thoughts. 'Your life lies ahead of you, and for you it will be easier: you won't have to seek out your path as we have done, to struggle and fall and rise again in the midst of darkness; we had to strive to remain whole – and how many of us fell by the wayside? – but for you there are things to be done, there is work to do, and the blessing of us old men will go with you. But for me, after this day, after such sensations as these, it remains only to make you a final bow – and, if with sadness, but without envy, without any dark feelings, to say, in sight of the end, in sight of an ever-waiting God: "Welcome, lonely old age! Burn out, useless life!"'

Lavretsky rose quietly and quietly departed; nobody noticed him, nobody detained him; the gay shouts rang out still more loudly in the garden beyond the tall green screen of limes. He sat in the tarantass and ordered his driver to drive home and not to whip up the horses.

'And is that the end?' the dissatisfied reader may ask. 'What happened afterwards to Lavretsky? What happened to Liza?' But what can one say about people who may still be living but have passed from the walks of life, why return to them? They say that Lavretsky visited that remote nunnery where Liza had hidden from the world – and he saw her. Passing from choir to choir, she walked close by him, walking with the gliding, hurriedly meek step of a nun – and she did not look at him; only the lashes of the eye turned towards him fluttered very slightly and she bent still lower her wasted face, and the fingers of her clasped hands, entwined with the rosary, were pressed more tightly together. What did the two of them think, what did they feel? Who can know? Who can say? There are such moments in life, such feelings.... One can but point to them – and pass by.

Notes

(These notes are taken partly from I. S. Turgenev, *Sochineniya*. T. VII, izd. 'Nauka', M.-L., 1964, upon which this translation has been based.)

CHAPTER IV

1. *preference:* A card game similar to Boston. Cards are distributed as at whist. During every deal the player opposite the dealer should shuffle a pack to be cut by his right-hand neighbour and turn up a card for the first preference. The suit of the same colour, whether red or black, is styled the second preference, and the other two are common suits.
2. *Oberon:* The overture to the opera of 1826 by Karl Weber (1786–1826).
3. This poem, slightly modified, was originally written by Turgenev in 1840 and addressed to Alexandra Khovrina, whom he had met in Rome.

CHAPTER VIII

1. *. . . beginning of Alexander I's reign:* Alexander I, Emperor of Russia, reigned from 1801 to 1825.
2. *. . . crammed full of Voltaire:* Jean Voltaire (1694–1778), French sceptic; Denis Diderot (1713–84), Jean-Jacques Rousseau (1712–78), Guillaume Raynal (1713–96), Claude Helvétius (1715–71) – leading philosophical writers of the eighteenth-century Enlightenment.
3. *. . . à la Titus:* A short hair-style worn by the famous French actor Talma (1763–1826) for the role of Titus in *Brutus* and popular for its anti-Jacobin character.
4. *. . . in honour of the holy martyr Theodore Stratelates:* Theodore Stratelates (d. 319) is thought to have been a general (*stratelates*) in the army of Licinius, by whose order he was tortured and crucified at Heraclea in Thrace.
5. The Tilsit peace, concluded between Russia, France and Prussia in July 1807, led to a rift between Russia and Great Britain which doubtless meant, as Turgenev suggested in a letter of 1868 to

W. R. S. Ralston, that Ivan Petrovich was immediately obliged to leave London for Paris.

CHAPTER XI

1. *Symbols and Emblems:* This book, originally produced in Amsterdam on the orders of Peter the Great in 1705, was apparently known to Turgenev in its 1809 or 1811 edition. The book was in the library of his home at Spasskoye. In a letter of 1840 he describes how, at the age of 8 or 9, he broke into an old bookcase and came across a 'book of emblems':

For a whole day I thumbed through my marvellous book and went to sleep with my head full of a whole world of troubling shapes. I have forgotten many of them; I remember, for example: 'A roaring lion signifies great strength', 'A negro riding on a unicorn signifies craftiness' (why?) and so on. That night it was awful! Unicorns, negroes, tsars, suns, pyramids, swords, snakes all went whirling round in my poor head. I became an emblem myself, I 'signified' things – I shone like a sun, was reduced to mist, sat on a tree, lay in a pit, raced in the clouds, stood on a tower and with all my sitting, lying, racing and standing almost caught a fever.

2. The year 1825 is notable for the Decembrist Revolt, an attempt by army officers and other members of the gentry class (*dvoryanstvo*) to overthrow the autocracy. The failure of the revolt led to the hanging of five of the ringleaders and the despatch to Siberia of more than 100 other participants.

CHAPTER XII

1. *Mochalov:* Mochalov (1800–48), Russian actor, famous for his playing of Hamlet.

CHAPTER XV

1. Mademoiselle Mars (1779–1847), leading actress of the Comédie Française; Mademoiselle Rachel (1821–58), famous French tragic actress; Odry (1781–1853), famous for his roles in French farces; Madame Dorval (1798–1849), celebrated for her romantic acting in works by Hugo, de Vigny, etc.

CHAPTER XVI

1. ... *your poet Pushkin:* A. S. Pushkin (1799–1837), greatest of Russian poets. The words are taken from Zemfira's song in *The Gipsies* (1824), set to music by A. Verstovsky.

CHAPTER XVII

1. Ivan IV of Moscow reigned from 1547 to 1584. He acquired his title as a result of the death and destruction he visited on his wretched subjects; nevertheless, he made a practice of praying for the souls of his victims, whose names were specially listed for this purpose. In such a list, Turgenev suggests, three Pestovs were named.

CHAPTER XIX

1. Catherine II, Empress of Russia, reigned from 1762 to 1796. Her 'times' were noted for French and neo-classical influences.

CHAPTER XXI

1. *'Fridolin':* Schiller's ballad of 1797 was entitled *'Der Gang nach dem Eisenhammer'*.

CHAPTER XXII

1. ... *surely this Fridolin ... became her lover, didn't he?*; Fridolin, a young page in the service of a countess, is falsely accused of being the lady's lover. The jealous count despatches him to an iron foundry where two workmen have been instructed to throw him in the molten metal. Fridolin goes first to the countess, who asks him to attend Mass and pray for her. He does this and is saved from the death planned for him by the count who, persuaded of Fridolin's innocence, personally leads him to the unsuspecting countess.

CHAPTER XXVIII

1. *'de populariser l'idée du cadastre':* The idea of assessing the value, extent and ownership of land for purposes of taxation.

2. *Obermann:* A novel in letters (1804) by E. P. de Senancour (1770–1846), which became extremely popular in the 1830s.

CHAPTER XXXIII

1. *Lermontov:* Mikhail Yurievich Lermontov (1814–41) composed *Duma* (*The Thought*) in 1838. It was a poem which indicted the passivity of Lermontov's generation.
2. *Khomakyov:* A. S. Khomyakov (1804–60) was a leading exponent of Slavophilism.

CHAPTER XXXIX

1. *Jouvin gloves:* "Les Gants-Jouvin", the leading firm of glove-makers at Grenoble. I am indebted for this translation to Patrick Waddington's excellent ed. of *Dvoryanskoye gnezdo*, Pergamon Press, 1969, 291.
2. *Victoria Essence:* Turgenev's text has 'Victoria's Essence' in English, but this is most probably an incorrect translation of the French 'Essence de Victoria'. See Patrick Waddington, op. cit., 292.
3. *Herz:* Henri Herz (1806–88), popular French pianist and teacher of music.
4. *Fra poco:* The aria from Donizetti's opera *Lucia di Lammermoor*, 1835.

CHAPTER XL

1. *Metternich:* Prince von Metternich (1773–1859) was Austrian chancellor and foreign minister, and ardent champion of the Holy Alliance.
2. *'Son geloso'*, duet from Bellini's opera *La Sonnambula*, 1831; *'La ci darem'*, duet from Mozart's *Don Giovanni*, 1787; *'Mira la bianca luna'*, duet from Rossini's *Soirées musicales*, 1835.
3. *Thalberg:* Sigismond Thalberg (1812–71), virtuoso pianist and composer.
4. *George Sand:* Turgenev has permitted certain anachronisms to arise in Varvara Pavlovna's reading. In 1842 she would have known the works of the famous French novelists George Sand (1804–76) and Balzac (1799–1850), the French dramatist A. Scribe (1791–1861) and the very popular romantic novelist Paul de Kock (1793–1871). She might have known E. Sue (1804–57), whose work did not

become really popular until after *Les mystères de Paris* of 1842. It is unlikely that she would have known the work of either Dumas *père* (1803–70), whose *The Three Musketeers* and *The Count of Monte Cristo* did not appear until 1844 and 1845, or P. Féval (1817–87), whose first popular work, *Les mystères de Londres* (1844), was published under the pseudonym of Sir Francis Trolopp.

EPILOGUE

1. *to be Madame Doche:* Madame Doche (1821–1900), French actress, initially popular for comedy roles; she later became famous for her playing in *La Dame aux camélias* by A. Dumas. Since this work was not staged until 1852, in strict chronological terms Varvara Pavlovna could not have seen Madame Doche in this role (which was no doubt what Turgenev had in mind) in 1850.